Wood's Revenge

Steven Becker

* * *

Join my mailing list
and get a free copy of Wood's Ledge
http://mactravisbooks.com

Chapter 1

Protected by the roof over the large walk-around deck, Mac watched the wind-blown waves from the living quarters, and smiled, thankful for the relief from the heat brought by the rain. The house, built on concrete piers, provided safety against storm surges, possibly the most dangerous element, of the hurricanes common to the Florida Keys. This storm was not one of the dreaded cyclones that would force him to evacuate to the mainland, rather it was a large squall, accompanied by a perigean, or king tide. Having it blow through at high tide left the island vulnerable. Only a half dozen feet above sea level at its highest point, his home could easily be flooded from a storm like this.

Mel sat on the couch reading a book, ignoring Mac's anxiety as the water started to invade the clearing where the house was built. Mac had just put the finishing touches on the house that Wood, Mel's father, had originally built twenty years ago. He had been laboring on and off for almost a year to rebuild the structure damaged in a turf war with a rogue CIA agent. Several times he'd run out of money, but a recent adventure had netted enough to finally finish the job.

"Water's past the mangroves," he said, raising his voice

1

slightly to counter the staccato sound of the rain pelting the metal roof.

"We're ten feet up. Shouldn't be a big deal," Mel said without looking up. She had grown up here and understood storms and tides well enough to know when to freak out and when not to. Fairly infrequent, king tides occurred during a supermoon when the earth was at its closest point to the sun. The tides were predictable and the height known ahead of time. The only wild card was what a storm could add to it—and this was a strong one.

"I'm going to check the boats," he said, opening the screen door.

"Whatever makes you happy," she replied.

He grabbed the bright yellow slicker from a hook outside the door, put it on, and headed down the steps, eschewing his flip-flops, which would be worthless in the muck. Barefoot, he started along the worn path toward the trail leading to the small beach where the boats were kept.

He thought about Mel's mood as he walked. Lately she had been melancholy. The house was done, but it wasn't her dream as much as his. He knew she could only take so much of the Key's lifestyle before craving the activity of the mainland. Over the years he had learned when she needed something to sink her teeth into—and it was getting to be that time. At first it had been hard to let her go, often blaming it on himself and his inability to make her happy. Now, he knew it was just the way things were.

She was a lawyer, well connected in both the political and civil rights arenas, having prosecuted for the ACLU and Davies and Associates for years. He knew she missed the work.

The trail degraded fifty feet from the house, turning to ankle-deep muck as he hit the tide line. Slowly he waded into the water, careful to slide his feet and not step on one of the myriad of dangers brought in by the storm. It took almost five minutes to traverse the hundred-yard path. With every step the water became deeper and the muck thicker, sometimes sucking him almost thigh-deep into the ooze.

Finally, waist-deep in water, he reached what used to be the high-water line. The boats were still drifting together, tied to a single line reaching into the water attached to a lone pile, its top barely breaking the surface in the lull between waves. He had prepared as best he could for the freakishly high tide, but not the sudden squall. The twenty-one-foot center console was rafted to the forty-two-foot lobster boat with large red fenders placed between them to mitigate the effects of the waves. Off the stern of the trawler was an anchor line he had run out yesterday, using all the scope he had, to prevent the boats from swinging.

Assured that they were safe, he looked up at the sky, hoping the storm would ease up soon. It stared back at him like a woman, not giving any clues. Backing away from the tidal pull of the open water, he retreated to the tree line. The water was only calf-deep there, and he stood, watching the scene in front of him.

The mainland, usually a blurry line on the southern horizon, was hidden by the heavy rain. He'd heard some parts of the West referred to as Big Sky Country; this was what he called big water country. The small atoll surrounded by shallow flats lay five miles from Marathon on the Gulf side of the Keys. From the backside of the island he could see several other small islands and, on a clear day, the tip of Big Pine Key. From where he stood, he could see three hundred degrees of uninterrupted water—a view you could only get from an island in the middle of nowhere.

Marathon was shielded by a large squall, and out to the north he could see smaller scattered storms. Burdened with heavy rain, their dark clouds touched the water. They were fewer and farther between and he noticed the sky lightened beyond them. He estimated that high tide was right about now and breathed a sigh of relief that the worst was over.

* * *

Trufante and Pamela sat at the bar on the second floor of the two-story tiki hut next to Key's Fisheries, watching the storm approach. The bar looked out over the Gulf, allowing an unobstructed view of the weather. Fat drops of rain blew into the opening behind the counter and the bartenders hurried to drop the clear canvas curtain to protect them from the brunt of the rain.

Storms were just another excuse to party in the Keys. The boats were all in their slips with extra lines added, and the bored captains and mates were in the bar drinking tomorrow's tip money. The atmosphere became more boisterous as the alcohol flowed.

"We need to go dance," Pamela said, swaying to the Jimmy

Buffett song playing on the house speakers. "You promised we could go to a real dance club in Key West."

"Shoot, girl, it's not but three in the afternoon," he said in his heavy Cajun drawl and baring his thousand-dollar smile. "Them bars don't get hot till double-digit time." He looked around the room. "I'd be needing a bump if we gonna party that long."

"You know I would put it on the credit card if I could," she said, sucking her mojito through a straw.

"Yeah, babe, just beer till the first, I get it. Need the weather to break and I'll find some cash work," he said, draining his beer. It was still a mystery to him where she got her money from, but the first of the month was always a party, however as the days wore on, more and more went on the credit card. Making matters worse, the weather had been bad for almost two weeks now, first blowing from the north with a late season cold front and now this damn tide thing. They said it only happened every few years, but the timing sucked.

"No worries, babe. We'll get down there next month," she said, sliding her empty glass toward the bartender.

Trufante was feeling awkward these days. The story going around was that he was living off her, and that made him uncomfortable. His view was that he did what he did, and if she wanted to kick in and bring the party to the next level, that was cool—but not required. Living in her comfortable house and drinking imported beer were nice perks, but he'd been up and down enough to know it didn't really matter, and nothing lasted forever.

"These are on Jeff," the bartender said, placing fresh drinks in front of them.

Trufante looked down the bar, saw the bright orange hair, and nodded his head in thanks. He knew he'd have to go talk to him, but for now he'd enjoy the drink and avoid the man that bought it. Keys fishermen fell into two classes, with a large gray area between them. The first group played by the rules and usually survived, but were always near the edge. The second group were a different lot, often relying on smuggling or poaching, either from laziness or just a general disregard for the law. In the Keys when things got bad the ranks of the second group swelled. The fisheries, divided by the chain of islands into the Gulf and Atlantic zones had different regulations. Add in the federal and state demarcation lines and you often didn't know where you were or what the rules were. Both locals and tourists played this to their advantage. Mac could have written the book on the first group. That guy had more integrity than you could shake a gator tail at. Jeff was the opposite—trouble.

"Got to get this over with," he said to Pamela, who was bopping to some song only she heard.

Trufante walked through the crowded bar, the air stale and humid. The storm curtains might have kept the water out, but they cut off the breeze at the same time. It was raining hard now, and the crowd shifted slightly to avoid the drops coming through the palm frond roof. He slid through the group, fist-bumping some, and avoiding the looks of others, until he stood face-to-face with Jeff.

There wasn't much Trufante liked about him, except for the few instances he had scored a big payday for the Cajun. His shoulder-length frizzy hair was supposed to look sun bleached, but the word was it was permed and highlighted. His teeth were too white and the diamonds he wore in both ears were too big to be real.

"Trufante," he started. "That babe's still putting up with your sorry ass?" He looked down and tipped his drink in Pamela's direction.

Fortunately she was lost in her own head and missed it. "What you got goin' on?" Trufante asked, wanting to cut to the quick and get this over with. One round was not going to buy Jeff much time.

"Word is you could use some cash. Lookin' like the back end of the month is hard times for you and the little woman," he said, eying Pamela. "How the hell did a hillbilly like you land a babe like that?"

Trufante asked himself that question every day. "Just the old Cajun charm," he said, showing his grin that looked like the front end of a Cadillac. "Now what you got?"

"Look here." Jeff moved close. "This tide's bringing some fish down from the north. Some would say it's an easy catch. What do you say we go drag some nets out on the Gulf side when the wind quiets down some? Should be a good payday."

Trufante stared him down. "Those are red tide fish. That shit ain't good, dude."

"No, no, no," Jeff said, sipping his drink through the small straw. "These is just easy, if you know what I mean. The tide's going to pop those floodgates up in Miami like a cheerleader's cherry. The fish are just gonna take the ride."

7

"That's not exactly a quality catch," Trufante said. High tides and storms often brought trouble from up north. Once the floodgates holding the contaminated water from the sugar plantations opened, the fish would be pushed south. Usually the flood and fish kills ended well before the Keys, but this tide and the storm winds from the north were likely to push them farther south and west.

"Dude, this shit's gonna happen so fast they're still gonna be good," Jeff said. "You in or not?"

Trufante looked down the bar at Pamela. Bringing in a pile of cash for a day or two's work would surely make her happy and hold them over until the first of the month. It might also stop some of the rumors that she was supporting him. "Two days is all."

Jeff stuck out his hand to shake on the deal. Trufante ignored it and moved down the bar to Pamela. Two more fresh drinks awaited, and he knew he had struck a deal with the devil.

Chapter 2

Trufante looked out over the calm Gulf waters. It was a marked change from yesterday. The strong current was all that remained of the storms that had passed through. To hold their position, Jeff had to constantly gun the engine of the twenty-four-foot open-deck lobster boat to counter the tide.

Dropping back to neutral, the cloud of black smoke from the old diesel cleared, revealing the latest haul of fish flapping on the deck among the empty beer cans the two men had drunk. Both men quickly used shovels to scoop the fish into baskets where they would ice them down. Grabbing another beer, Trufante took his position in the patch of shade cast by the small wheelhouse. But the effort was mostly futile. The commercial fishing boat was all deck, with just the small wheelhouse forward.

"Ready for another run at 'em?" Jeff asked.

"Hell yeah," Trufante said, counting the money rolling in. Reluctantly, he left the shade, tossed a large buoy overboard, and started feeding the weighted net over the side of the boat. Soon a line of Styrofoam buoys floated behind them. Jeff idled across the current until the last buoy was thrown over, then turned and went back to the beginning of the line.

"Think we ought to drink a beer and give it a few minutes," Trufante said.

Jeff looked at the sun, sinking toward the horizon. "I guess. We only got 'bout two more hours of daylight. We need to make the run in at sunset with the rest of the tourists."

Trufante knew he was right. He looked around, seeing the reflection off a distant boat's windshield. They were about twenty miles off the backside of Marathon in thirty feet of water and had kept a lazy lookout all day. Continuing to keep an eye on the area, he knew if the boat came any closer, they would have ample time to ditch the nets and pick up the rods sitting in their holders for just such an occasion.

There were no other boats this far out, and only a half dozen private planes landing and taking off from Marathon's small airport could possibly have seen them. Still, the reflection made him wary.

Florida Fish and Game was who they needed to avoid, and running in at night they would be visible from miles away. Even the most dim-witted enforcement officer would know with this kind of boat, this time of year, there was no way they were on the level. Lobster and stone crab were out of season, and most commercial fishermen were after the schools of dolphin fish riding the Gulf Stream current on the Atlantic side. The water was too warm for grouper or snapper, and, in short, there was no reason for them to be here.

"Right on," Trufante said, pulling the first buoy in. He forgot about the reflection, knowing immediately from the weight that the net was loaded. It took both men to bring the captured fish aboard, and, after the last buoy was in, they sat on the deck toasting a fresh beer.

"We move fast, we can get one more run. This is too rich to pass up," Jeff said.

Trufante had his doubts they could sell what was already aboard. He moved upwind, away from the rotten stench of the fish drifting toward him on the breeze. Normally fish would stay fresh for almost a week if properly iced down. These were only hours out of the water and putrid. No buyer would purchase them whole—the easy way to sell them. Instead, they would have to filet every one of them, then run the meat through a bleach water solution. Maybe if they froze them they could pull it off, but fresh, there was no way they would pass the sniff test of a good or a moral buyer.

The cause was known to most of the local fishermen. The heavier-than-normal rains had caused Lake Okeechobee to swell, forcing the South Florida Water Management District bureaucrats to open the floodgates. The downstream effect from the high levels of pollutants and fertilizer in the water was deadly, causing red tides and fishing closures along the southwest coast of Florida. These were the same fish, swept out of the closure areas by the tide.

"You got someone lined up to take these?" Trufante asked, rising and shaking out the net.

"Think I would have come all this way with your sorry Cajun ass for company if I didn't have a buyer?" Jeff spat overboard. "I got this covered."

Thinking about Pamela's reaction when he walked into the house with a stack of hundreds was all the motivation he needed. Trufante tossed the first buoy over. He was skeptical, but it would only take another half hour. There was still enough daylight and plenty of beer left to make the trip back. The full length of the net was overboard and Jeff had turned to retrieve it when he saw half the string of buoys disappear.

"Snagged something," Trufante called out. It was not uncommon for floating debris or even a turtle to drag part of a net underwater. Just as the words were out of his mouth, the rest of the buoys were sucked under the surface. "Something big," he added, waiting for the floats to rise again.

Jeff circled back. A rip was visible on the surface, showing where the submerged net line still disturbed the current. Trufante leaned over the side, trying to see what was going on, but the water was cloudy from the storm. "We got enough fish, we can ditch it," Trufante said.

"You want it out of your share, we can ditch it. That's almost a grand in net, floats, and lead. I ain't leaving it," Jeff spat back.

Trufante was always one for the big picture. They had close to five grand in fish aboard, even at the discounted rate they would have to sell them at. Nets were expenses, and he was ready to move on.

"Why don't you take your sorry ass for a swim?" Jeff said.

Trufante looked at the water, watching the rip disappear as whatever had a hold of the net pulled it to the bottom. "Not today."

He didn't think he would see anything without a mask, and with the current smoking past the boat, he didn't trust Jeff either. "Why don't we sell this load and come back in the morning when the tide's slack. Visibility should be better, and I'll grab some gear from Mac."

"Works for me, but I'm holding out some from your share," Jeff said. He pointed the bow south toward the empty horizon and pushed the throttle forward.

"Get the numbers." Trufante grabbed a fresh beer from the cooler and took a long drag. When he finished, he tossed the can and removed the raw water sprayer to hose the deck and the baskets of fish, hoping it would take some of the smell with it. Once the deck was clear, he opened a large hatch and started digging into the hold packed with ice. He shoveled out large scoops, which he placed liberally on the baskets. Even after washing and icing down everything, the fish still smelled. He grabbed two fresh beers, handed one to Jeff, and went to the small space forward of the wheelhouse to get some fresh air.

The sixty-five-foot arc in the Seven Mile Bridge was the first thing to break the glassy surface of the water. The span was the tallest object for miles. Jeff was headed on a course that would intersect with Moser Channel, which ran underneath it. *Better than coming through Boot Key Harbor*, Trufante thought. If there was going to be any law around, they would be sitting in the crowded harbor, not worrying about traffic running near the center of the bridge, miles from land. They fell in behind several other boats, blending in with the Keys' rush hour.

Half an hour later, they passed underneath the bridge and turned east, staying well clear of the harbor entrance. Running parallel with the shore, but giving enough clearance to avoid the shallow flats, Jeff followed the coastline for a few miles before turning to port and entering Sisters Creek. The small inlet seldom had law enforcement and offered a backdoor route into the commercial harbor. Jeff pulled back on the throttle just after passing the second marker and steered to the west of the line of red marked pilings.

"Might wanna watch your wake," Trufante called over the engine noise.

"Ain't nobody around," Jeff said.

Trufante looked around at the houses on the right. The million dollar homes each had a dock extending into the channel, most with a large boat tied to it. "Only take one of those well-dressed cats to take a picture with their phone and report you." He knew from experience that reports were followed through, especially with commercial boats. "That pelican over there could read the registration numbers," he said, pointing to a lone bird in the mangroves on the left. Even he was not interested in their catch.

"I got that shit covered. Check it out when we stop. The four's a nine and the one's a four. They'll never track me down," Jeff said proudly.

"Except for that carrot top you got. Ain't no other around here that got a head of hair like that," Trufante said, moving behind the wheelhouse to use it for cover in case someone did snap a picture. At a half dozen inches over six foot, with his ponytail and grin, he was not exactly invisible.

Jeff slowed and followed the mangrove-lined canal to the left. After steering around a few bends, they entered Boot Key Harbor. They cut across the mooring field to the opposite side and entered one of the canals. Lobster and crab traps lined the concrete seawalls of the commercial fisheries they passed. Toward the end, the channel became tighter with mangroves encroaching from both sides. A large clearing with a few run-down buildings came into view, and they pulled up to a rickety wooden dock on the left.

As soon as he saw where they were headed, the stump of his finger started itching. "You're selling to Monster?" Trufante asked. The shack off to the left was where he had lost part of his finger to the chum machine.

"They'll pay," Jeff said, easing the bow of the boat to the dock.

Trufante knew what to do without being asked and was already forward with a line tied to the cleat. It was difficult, especially after the beers they had drunk, with the wind blowing them forward and pushing the boat past the dock. While Jeff manipulated the throttles, he jumped across the void and put a bight around the rusted cleat on the dock, then used the leverage to pull the boat in before tying it off. Jeff reversed the engine and swung the stern toward the dock, where Trufante was ready with another line.

"Hand 'em up and let's get this over with," Trufante said, extending his arms to take the first basket from Jeff. With the dozen baskets on the dock, Trufante went to look for a dolly, staying clear of the chum shack, while Jeff looked for the owner.

Fifteen painful minutes later, they were back on board. Trufante released the bow line, kicked the hull away from the old dock, and scratched his stump again. Jeff let the wind spin the boat around before Trufante released the stern line and jumped aboard. They headed back into the harbor. It wasn't until they were tied around the back side of Burdines gas dock that he relaxed. "We gonna split it here or what?" he asked as he sprayed down the deck.

"Too many eyes around. We should go back to your place," Jeff said.

Trufante suspected that he just wanted to get a look at Pamela, hopefully with not a lot of clothes on. "Truck works for me."

Jeff gave him the stink eye. "Pass me another beer then."

Trufante finished cleaning the deck and climbed onto the dock. Together the men walked across the crushed coral parking lot to Jeff's rundown truck. "Gotta drive you home anyway. That girl of yours is gonna be awful proud when she sees this payday."

"Whatever, man," Trufante said, giving in. He just wanted the cash and to be rid of Jeff. Tomorrow he would go get the net himself. Climbing in the truck, he kicked aside some empty beer cans on the floorboard. "You shouldn't be drivin' with this shit inside."

"And you're one to be giving advice?" Jeff asked. He started the truck, drained his beer, crushed the can, and tossed it at Trufante."

Five minutes later they pulled into Pamela's driveway. "Let's just do this here," Trufante said.

Jeff pulled a wad of cash from the cargo pocket of his shorts.

"How's this look?" He counted out twenty hundreds and handed them to Trufante.

"That ain't half," Trufante said, eyeing the stack of bills.

"Got expenses, and it was my idea. That's mate's pay," Jeff said.

"Yeah, if you want a mate that'll be telling everyone what we did. You took me 'cause I can keep a secret."

"Well, point taken," he said, peeling off another ten bills. "Get the net back, and there's another handful."

Trufante took the money and climbed out of the truck, his trademark smile not anywhere near breaking through his clenched jaw. "We'll see."

Chapter 3

Mac looked at the piles of debris stacked on the beach. It had taken all day to clean up the mess from the king tide and storms. The only useful material they had collected was a large pile of driftwood. Next to it was a stack of roots and organic material that would burn. Closer to the waterline, a colorful assortment of plastic, ranging from flip-flops to water bottles, sat waiting to be hauled to shore. There was no garbage collection out here.

Mac and Mel looked at each other through the cloud of flies swarming around them.

"Shouldn't be seatrout and snook this time of year," he said, looking at the pile of dead fish.

"They look bad," Mel said.

He poked the pile with a stick, releasing the bloated gasses from the distended stomach of a large snook. "The local fish look pretty healthy," he said, moving the stick to a bonefish, a species plentiful on the neighboring flats.

"It seems reasonable that the tide brought the fish down, but they shouldn't be rotten. These look like they have some kind of disease."

Mac had an idea what it was, but wasn't sure this was the time to voice his opinion. Over the last few years, he had increasingly found floaters like these when he was pulling traps or fishing the deeper Gulf waters. He'd asked around and done some research, finding out that red tides and fish kills up the coast were moving slowly south, the result of pollution released from the floodgates controlling the Everglades. Big Sugar was the culprit, and there were all kinds of activist groups protesting. Just the thing that would suck Mel in.

Her past as an ACLU lawyer had brought her to the pinnacle of activism. It was a huge relief when she had left that world after becoming an unwilling pawn in the corruption and financial agendas involved. But a cause like this might light the fire he knew still burned in her.

"Strong tide, who knows—" He was interrupted by the whine of an outboard engine heading toward the island.

They didn't get many visitors here. His only neighbor was a retired marine, Jesse McDermitt, and he was several miles away in the Content Keys. They stood side-by-side at the waterline watching the small boat cruise toward them. Both grew anxious in their own way, as they could see the thousand-dollar grin on the driver from a quarter mile away. Trufante guided the boat into the unmarked channel, dropped his speed when he made the turn, and coasted to a stop. When the bow of the aluminum skiff hit the beach, he killed the engine and quickly tilted it out of the water before the propeller fouled.

"Look here, if it ain't the happy couple," he called, ignoring the scowl on Mel's face.

Mac was not as concerned. The Cajun sometimes brought trouble, but was generally entertaining and a good mate. "What's up, Tru," he called back.

His long legs had him out of the boat and on dry land in two steps. At the bow, he easily pulled the lightweight boat onto the beach.

"Planning on staying?" Mel asked, her tone clearly uninviting.

"Shoot, girl, good to see you too," he said with a smile, her mood clearly not affecting him.

Trufante had been around since Katrina had barreled through the bayou a little over ten years ago. Like many of the Keys' residents, he was on the run from something, and Mac had gotten enough tidbits out of him over the years to piece together his story. The Cajun had been a concrete contractor outside of New Orleans and had somehow been awarded some government contracts to reinforce the levies holding back the Mississippi River. When the storm surge from the hurricane caused the work to fail, he hightailed it out of town on a small sailboat. Hopping from port to port along the Gulf Coast, he had finally found a home in Marathon. It was said the crazies were in Key West, or Key Weird, as the locals called it, but that was only by degrees. The further down the chain of islands you traveled, the crazier the people got. Mac figured Trufante had landed in about the right spot—halfway down.

"Y'all got anything goin' on?" Trufante asked.

Mac knew there was a reason he was here and looked over at the pile of trash. "Gonna dump this lot," he said.

"Man, forget that. Me and you ought to take a ride. I need a little help," Trufante said.

"Figures," Mel said and walked off.

"Help me out and I'll haul the load back for you," Trufante said quickly, before Mel was out of earshot. He needed to garner any favor he could from her.

"What do you need?" Mac asked. Given the choice between hauling a load of trash to Marathon or hanging out with Trufante for a couple of hours, he would generally choose the later. If there was any sign of trouble, Mac could back out. "I'm guessing you need a boat."

"And some dive gear," Trufante said. "Not too far out. Maybe ten miles from here we lost a net yesterday. That bastard Jeff's holding a bunch out of my pay to get it."

Mac was curious now. Maybe he could get some information on the fish kill. "Right. Let me go talk to Mel and grab some gear," he said and started walking toward the trail. Trufante started to follow and Mac turned around. "Better you stay here. You know how she gets." He walked away without looking back.

Mac started pulling gear out of the shed, thankful that it had remained above the flood line. He thought again that he should raise it a few feet. He piled the scuba gear into a wheelbarrow and looked up at the house. Reluctantly, he left the equipment and climbed the stairs.

Mel was at the table, writing furiously on a legal pad. "I'm going to take a ride with the boy wonder. He says he'll dump the trash if I go with him."

She didn't look up for a long minute. "Guess there's no use trying to warn you to stay away from him."

"We're taking the center-console. If he's up to anything stupid, I'll turn around. Sounds pretty harmless," Mac said.

"Usually does with that one, until the other foot drops," Mel said. "I want to go to shore when you get back and get some Internet time."

If that was all it was going to take to avoid a fight, he would gladly comply. "Sure thing," he said. "Be back in a couple of hours."

Mac breathed deeply as he walked down the steps, double-checked the contents of the wheelbarrow, and started pushing it down the path. Trufante was already aboard when he stopped at the waterline and started off-loading the gear. Wading to the boat, he handed the tank first, then came back for the buoyancy compensator, regulator, fins, and mask.

Trufante was at the helm, squinting at his phone when he came aboard. "Can you see this?"

Mac grabbed the phone and looked at the GPS numbers. He quickly entered them into the boat's unit and started the engine. Trufante released the line from the lone pile and they headed toward open water. Mac couldn't help but smile as the boat came up on plane and skipped over the small waves. It was a feeling of freedom that never got old, and he was brought back to reality faster than he would have liked by the GPS alarm. Trufante, who had drifted deep in the bucket seat, woke with a start.

"Get the buoy ready," Mac said, spinning the wheel and circling the waypoint. He switched the display to a split screen, showing their location on the left and a sonar shot of the bottom on the right. The line ran flat, not unusual for this area. Only a few small irregularities broke the solid line. From the orange color, Mac guessed they were over soft bottom, mostly turtle grass that usually had no structure and wondered why Trufante had been out here.

Suddenly, something broke the screen. "Drop!" Mac yelled as soon as he saw the line jump. Still focused on the screen, he idled over the image, seeing what looked to be the shape of a small boat below them. "That a wreck?"

Trufante returned a vacant look. "We was just netting. Don't know about no wreck. Must be what snagged the net."

Mac circled the buoy and studied the screen, then looked up to determine the best trajectory to anchor. Slowly he motored into the waves until he was about a hundred feet from the buoy. "Drop!" he called to Trufante, who was on the bow with the anchor in his hand. He released the rode and let the line slide through his hands as Mac backed the boat to set the hook. A few minutes later they were sitting next to the buoy and Trufante was gearing up to dive.

"What're you doing?" Mac asked.

"Goin' to get my five hundred back," Trufante said, pulling the BC straps tight.

"You know the deal. Not on my boat," Mac said. They'd been

through this before. It didn't matter how experienced a diver the Cajun was. Until he got certified, he was not diving off Mac's boats. "I'll lose my license. You want to free dive it, go ahead."

Trufante dropped the gear. "Shoot, I can't hold my breath for that long."

Mac was tempted to free dive just to show him, but decided it would be safer and quicker to don the scuba gear. If there was any work to be done to retrieve the net, he would need the bottled air. Mac took the gear from Trufante, lifted the tank onto his back, and swung the mask around to the front of his face. Sitting on the gunwale, he eased the straps of the BC out to fit him and buckled them. He swept his right arm around his back to retrieve the regulator and stuck it in his mouth. After confirming the air was on, he nodded to Trufante and rolled over the side.

The water was colder than he expected, probably from the extreme current coming from the north. Shivering, he released the air from the BC and drifted to the bottom. The water was green and still murky, reducing visibility to about ten feet, but he instantly saw the top of the wreck. Finning alongside it, he was surprised the canvas was still attached to the T-top and there was no growth at all. Not even the slime coat that seemed to form instantly.

He swam around the hull, estimating it to be about twenty-four feet. The twin outboards half buried in the sand would probably be useless, but there was some salvage value here. Finishing his survey, he started pulling the net off the structure and ascended with the leading edge. On the surface, he handed the buoy to Trufante and went back down to feed him the next. It was tedious work trying to recover the gear without destroying it, and it took almost half an hour before he handed the last buoy to the Cajun.

There was still a five-hundred PSI showing on his air gauge, enough to at least get another quick look at the wreck. He held his left arm over his head to discharge the air from the BC and was just about to drop below the surface when he heard an engine coming toward them. Trufante yelled for him to get aboard.

"Come on. It's the law," Trufante called.

"Get the anchor. I'll take care of myself," Mac yelled back. The approaching boat was still a ways off, but the chances it was going anywhere else were slim. He kicked back to the swim platform and pulled himself aboard, shedding the tank and BC as soon as he was on deck. The boat was still coming at them, the lights on its tower clearly indicating its authority.

Trufante pulled the anchor onto the roller and placed the safety lanyard on the chain, then ran back to the helm. The one-hundred-fifty horsepower engine started and he slammed the throttle down. Spinning the wheel, the boat plowed a semicircle and started a course back to shore. Mac turned the controls over to Trufante, slid the gear to the side and started pushing the net into the built-in fish box. He had the bulk of it in, with just a few buoys sticking out, when he felt the engine slow. When he looked up, flashing lights greeted him.

Chapter 4

Mac took over the helm and dropped the engine back to an idle, just enough power to maintain position. It was impossible to mistake the boat moving toward them. With the flashing lights on the tower and Sheriff displayed in large bold lettering on the white hull, he knew Trufante had led him into trouble again. When the boats were close to touching, the deputy dropped two fenders over the side and tossed a line to Trufante.

"What are you two doing out this way?" the deputy asked.

Mac breathed deeply, trying to remain calm. His relationship with the uniformed man was tenuous at best—at least from his perspective. He hadn't been arrested for anything, but he always seemed to be skirting trouble. Standing at the wheel, he felt helpless as the deputy scanned the deck of his boat. "Just out checking some new numbers," he said.

"What's with the buoys?" the deputy asked.

Mac knew he was skeptical and needed to explain. He took off his ball cap and rubbed the stubble on his head. "It's still all churned up on the ocean side. Thought we'd check out some lobster holes for next season. Ran across a string of abandoned traps. Busted them up and pulled this off," he said, wanting to keep the lie to a minimum.

"Sure you ain't up to anything I should know about?" he asked, clearly looking at Trufante.

The Cajun had his head down. "No, just took him along to run the boat while I was under," Mac answered. "It's a long way out for you, too."

"Looking for a missing boat," the deputy said.

"Not much of a search with just you," Mac said. Search and rescue operations tended to be larger than life, giving the competing agencies a chance to showcase their new toys.

"Just a report from one of the marinas up in Key Largo that a boat was missing. No missing persons reports, so, not worth the big search if it's just a wreck."

"What kind of boat was it?" Mac asked, already guessing at the answer.

"They said it was a twenty-four-foot center-console."

Mac nodded and put his cap back on. The deputy was right about the search. Without a missing persons report, the only ones interested in finding the boat would be the insurance company, placing this squarely in his wheelhouse. "Nothing floating around that we've seen," Mac said, careful with his choice of words.

"All right. If you see anything, let me know," the deputy said, catching the line as Trufante wasted no time tossing it to him. Seconds later, he spun the wheel and was gone.

"Got lucky there," Trufante said. "If you weren't here, he'd be hauling my ass to jail."

"You're probably right," Mac said, pushing the throttle forward. He waited until the boat was a good half mile away before accelerating. He wanted to be rid of the Cajun and whatever trouble he was in. If there was one boat out searching, there could be more, and if they ran into a Fish and Game officer, things might not be so easy trying to explain what they were doing with a gill net aboard. There were no fish, but he'd already had another boat confiscated when Trufante had gotten suckered into a lobster poaching scam. The similarities were too hard to ignore.

There was no feeling of elation or smile on his face this time when the boat got up on plane. He adjusted the rpms for a smooth ride, and a half hour later he was grateful when Wood's Island came into sight. Slowing, he turned into the channel and coasted to a stop at the piling. "If I were you, I'd get the net and be gone before Mel comes down," Mac said, letting Trufante out of his deal to take the trash. Better just to be rid of him. He helped Trufante load the net into the skiff and pushed him off, watching as he sped toward Marathon.

"Thanks for not asking him to dinner," Mel said, startling him.

Mac laughed. "Figured you didn't want to see him."

"Trash is still there," she said.

"You want to go to town. I'll take it in then," Mac said, turning toward the pile.

Thunder boomed somewhere nearby, and they both looked for the storm. This time of year, large anvil-shaped clouds could form almost instantaneously, bringing lightning, wind, and heavy rain.

They turned toward the direction of the noise, and though the brush blocked their view of the water, the dark cloud above indicated a large storm cell was approaching.

"Maybe I better take a raincheck on that," Mel said, already moving down the trail toward the house.

Mac followed, reaching the stairs just as another loud clap rocked the wooden structure. Large raindrops smacked him in the head as he climbed the stairs.

* * *

Mac was ready at dawn. Raising the wrecked boat would be more than he could do alone. It had taken some prodding, and an as yet undisclosed favor, but Mel had agreed to go with him. That's what he got for trying to negotiate with a lawyer, he thought, and went downstairs. From the shed, he started pulling out all the line and webbing he could find. Adding two fresh scuba tanks to the pile, he carted it down to the beach.

He would use the trawler for the recovery. The forty-two footer, ostensibly a lobster boat, had been painstakingly converted to meet his particular needs. It still served its original purpose, but the steel-hulled vessel had been customized for salvage work and diving as well. Among other improvements, the winch was rated for many times the load of the lobster and crab pots he pulled. Today it would fulfill its potential. Mel wandered down just as everything was loaded, carrying two mugs of coffee and a bag slung over her shoulder.

They left the island just as the sun broke the horizon, dappling the water with an orange glow. As beautiful as it was, he would be cautious; the color of the sky portended storms again this afternoon. Mac knew this was an everyday occurrence until late September, and the earlier they got back, the better chance they would have of dodging the inevitable. He had already untied the center-console from the trawler, securing it to the piling with enough line to swing when the tide changed. At the helm, he took a sip of coffee, started the engine, released the stern line, and hit the windlass switch. The boat had not been moved since the storm, and the anchor was still off the stern. With a couple of hundred feet of line out, he chose to use the mechanical advantage provided by the windlass. Slowly the line came in, dragging the boat toward the anchor and into deeper water. Once the anchor was stowed and secured, Mac negotiated the channel and steered toward the coordinates he had taken off the center-console's GPS.

The trawler ran most efficiently at eight knots, making it a slower run than yesterday. Mac didn't mind. He sat at the helm, the sea spreading out in front of him a glassy calm, allowing him to sip the hot coffee without spilling it. Mel sat beside him, a contented look on her face, something he had seen less frequently lately. With a challenge on the horizon, he was a happy man.

They pulled up to the coordinates and anchored by the marker buoy he and Trufante had left yesterday. Looking around them, he could see several storms brewing, but they were far enough away not to be an immediate concern. He took his time organizing the deck, checking the distant storms out of habit whenever he rose. Even with

Mel's help, it was a lot for two people to pull off the recovery, and he wanted everything in place before they made the attempt. Finally satisfied, he pulled on his dive gear and, with a hand on his mask, took a giant stride off the large dive platform.

Mac was always amazed at how alive the ocean was, changing from day to day. As soon as he hit the water, he could see the boat resting on the bottom. The visibility was so good, he could see sunlight reflect off the still-clean stainless steel on the bow. He ignored the small schools of baitfish that had already found the new structure, the first step in the process of becoming a reef. Circling the wreck, he wondered if it was worth the effort to remove the engines to lighten the load and decided to leave them in place. Even if they were scrap, he was at least removing contaminants from the water— if he could get them started it would be an added bonus.

After a brief survey, Mac kicked toward the surface, checking his air and bottom time as he ascended. The depth was thirty-five feet, just past the point where divers had to start thinking about bottom time and decompression. Although he would be working on the wreck while sitting several feet above the bottom, it was still close enough to worry about, and he knew he would be doing multiple descents, making the safety margin narrower.

He broke the surface by the transom and looked up at Mel. "Looks good. Toss over the straps," he called up to her. A minute later, he swam the yellow webbing to the wreck. There were two straps, one which he threaded through the small stainless steel eye used for hooking the boat to a trailer, located just below the bow, and the other he looped under the bracket between the engines. The straps would take most of the weight, but he would need to add tag lines to keep the boat upright as he pulled it from the water. Dropping the ends of the straps, he ascended again and returned to the wreck with two heavy lines. Placing these through the loops in the straps, he again ascended. After rigging the lighter tag lines to the midship cleats, he took a break on the swim platform and drank a bottle of water.

After a few minutes' rest, he took the pressure washer wand from Mel and finned back to the bottom. The pristine visibility quickly turned into a sandy quagmire as the pressure of the spray dislodged the sand surrounding the hull. In theory, this step would reduce the surface area connecting the hull to the bottom, decreasing the suction and making the initial lift easier.

Satisfied, he ascended through the silty water and climbed aboard. After removing his gear and drinking another bottle of water, he went to the winch. "Ready? One line at a time—nice and easy."

Mel nodded and went to the controls. Mac took a gloved hand and reached out for the line attached to the strap on the bow. He gave a thumbs-up signal, and the sound of the motor broke the silence. The line came taut in his hand, and the entire port side of the trawler dipped toward the water. The whine of the motor increased as the tension built, but the wreck had not budged. He looked back at Mel and shook his head. This was going to be harder than he thought.

"I'm going back down and see if I can slide a bumper under her," he said, reaching for one of the large red balls by the transom.

Ignoring Mel's inquisitive stare, he pulled the plug and released the air. It collapsed like a balloon and he held it up. "If I can get this under the hull and inflate it, the suction might break."

Back in the water, he worked the wand of the pressure washer under the bow, creating a space deep in the sand. Taking the deflated buoy, he shoved it into the opening, having to dig sand out several times before he had it where he wanted it. After tying it off, he ascended and grabbed the air hose from Mel. Back at the buoy, he pushed the inflator onto the valve and patiently watched the ball fill.

It was past noon by the time he had finished and they had repositioned the trawler so the winch was directly above the bow. He nodded to Mel. The winch motor whined again and he felt the trawler move under his feet, but this time the steel cable kept coming and finally he saw the yellow strap. With a smile on his face, Mac reached for the strap, tied a sheet bend with a large dock line to it, which he then tied to a large cleat. When the strap was released from the winch, the dock line took the pressure. The same procedure was repeated on the stern, and soon the wreck was visible just below them. He scratched his head, trying to figure out what to do next.

The buoy he had placed under the bow answered his question. Inflated at two atmospheres of pressure, the over-inflated buoy looked like it was ready to explode, but the additional buoyancy pulled the bow toward the surface, With the aid of the buoy, Mac and Mel worked each line, bringing the wreck closer to daylight with each effort. Finally, as the sun dipped toward the horizon, the gunwales broke the surface.

Mac was ready and swam a pump to the floating boat. Tossing it over the gunwale, he removed all but the strap on the bow. After climbing aboard, he signaled to Mel to start the trawler and gave her the thumbs-up to idle forward. It was a similar feeling to getting up on water skis as the bow rose with the forward momentum. Another thumbs-up and Mel increased speed slightly. Water poured out of the hull as it was pulled higher in the water. Holding on to the wheel, Mac waited until the front cooler was exposed. When he saw the lid, he went forward and placed the pump on the flat surface, then set the intake hose toward the stern and the outflow hose over the gunwale. Between the momentum of the tow and the flow from the pump, within a few minutes the water level had receded enough for the boat to ride easily behind the trawler.

Chapter 5

Mac tossed and turned all night thinking about the wreck. Its short time in the water left questions that would need to be answered. The reefs and shoals of the Keys were littered with wrecks dating back to the Mayans. Values varied, some having pure historical, others actual treasure, and some both. In his time here, Mac and Wood had found several wrecks and recovered a bit of treasure, enough to keep him hungry to find more, but not enough to finance a Mel Fisher style operation. Nor did he have any interest in an operation like that. He lived for fishing, diving, and lobstering. It brought in enough to support his lifestyle, especially now that he was living at Wood's. If he wanted excitement, he only needed to seek out the Cajun.

Since before dawn, he had been working on the wreck. Once it was light enough for the flames not to cause an alarm if they were seen from shore, he had set a fire with the driftwood. When it was hot, he started tossing the rotten fish on. This was the only way to insure they did not contaminate anything else. He heard the brush moving behind him and looked up to see Mel coming down the path.

He was on alert. Mac had developed a certain kind of radar

when she was upset. They had reached the point in their relationship where they didn't need to talk to communicate. He could tell by her restlessness over the past few weeks that they were getting out of alignment again. They had been close for years, back to when he had hitchhiked from Texas to the Keys in the early nineties. She had been in high school then and their age difference had kept them apart. Their relationship hadn't become romantic until a few years ago. And since then, it had been an on-and-off affair. There was definitely something between them, but they both had their own agendas and they didn't always line up.

"Hey," he called to her from a small clearing in the mangroves behind the beach where Wood had mounted a large winch to pull his boat out of sight. Mac stood behind the concrete block holding the winch, slowly turning the handle and hoping the rusty cable held as it pulled the wreck onto the beach.

"Hey back," she said, coming toward him. "Smells like a fish fry. How long have you been down here?"

He had decided to beach the wreck in order to work on it without having to climb in and out of the water. "A little before sunrise. Couldn't sleep," he said, walking back to the boat and lifting the battery he had brought from the shed on to the transom.

"That's my Mac. Got a mystery and you've got to figure it out," she said, looking at the boat. "There's no registration numbers."

"I saw that. Figure it's a documented vessel," Mac said, climbing aboard, he opened the lid to the battery compartment.

"Small for that. If I remember my maritime law, it has to be twenty-six feet or five tons. Might be close in length, but there's no way it meets the displacement tonnage," Mel recited.

Always the lawyer, Mac thought. "Might be government," he said, climbing back aboard. "There should be numbers on the interior. Let me just swap out this battery and I'll have a look." Reaching into the hold, he disconnected the terminals, pulled the waterlogged battery from the compartment and replaced it. He went to the helm, turned the key and was surprised to hear the port engine turn over when he pushed the start button. He knew better than to force it and shut it off. An engine that had been submerged needed special care. He could work on it later. Turning the key to the off position, he went to the door of the compartment in the console and pulled the handle, but it was stuck. "Locked. Can you grab me a flat-head screwdriver?"

Mel went to the toolbox sitting in the sand next to the boat, grabbed the tool and handed it up to him. Mac took it and went to work on the lock. Sticking the tip in the key slot, he slammed his palm against the butt of the screwdriver and tried to turn it. It took another two tries before the cylinder let go, and he stepped back as seawater poured from the compartment.

Mac had his back turned to the console when Mel called out.

"It's a body!"

Mac spun and faced the slumped-over figure. Moving to it, he gently pulled it back, as if it might be still alive. Then he saw the pale face of a man, eyes bulging out, staring back at him. "Shit."

"Is it dead?" Mel asked.

"Very," Mac said.

"Better call the sheriff," Mel said, pulling her phone from the back pocket of her shorts.

"Wait a minute. Let's think this through," Mac said. He pulled the body down, laid it on the deck and dragged it to the bow. Moving back to the console he slowly stuck his head into the dark space.

"Is that it?" she called up.

"Let me have your phone for a minute. I think I see something," Mac said, pulling his head out and taking several breaths of fresh air. The corpse had just started to decompose. Preserved by the surrounding water, he suspected it had been there less than a week.

She handed him the phone and he pressed the flashlight app— one of the few things he found worthwhile about the smartphone, With the phone extended in front of him, he moved back to the dark cavity and shined the light inside. The space was small, barely enough room for two. Inside were the various Coast Guard required safety items: life preservers, air horn, and flares, all still in their original packages. There was no sign of a fight and he didn't have to be a detective to know the man had been taken by surprise, or knew his murderers. Pushed to the back in a corner was a small case. He reached for it, turned, and set it on the deck. After another look, he saw nothing else of importance.

"What about the documentation numbers?" she asked. "If we know who the boat belongs to, maybe we can figure out who this is."

Mac looked again. He didn't see the required three-inch

numbers, but did see the metal manufacturer's tag. Using the camera's phone, he snapped a picture, adding another item on his list of pros for the device. "Here," he said, handing her the phone and climbing over the side.

They stood together on the beach staring at the boat. "We need to call the sheriff," Mel said again.

"Can we think about this for a minute? He's not getting any deader," Mac said, rubbing his head.

"This has Trufante's fingerprints all over it," Mel said. "We need to call it in and wash our hands of it."

He knew she was right, but he was curious. The freshness of the wreck, the lack of registration, and now the body. The deputy had been clear that he was just looking for a missing boat. That could make the man aboard the thief, but then who locked him in the cabin?

"Mac?" she said when he didn't respond, and brought the phone to her ear.

"Wait, Mel. Just a minute." He went back to the boat and grabbed the case. "Something weird's going on here. First the fish kill, then the body, and here." He handed her the case. "I'm not even sure whose jurisdiction this is in. The wreck was in federal waters." In truth, the last thing he wanted was the sheriff out here. He and the new man had gotten off to a bad start, and he doubted a personal visit would go well.

She sat on a stump with the case on her lap. "It's a cell phone," she said, opening the cover of the waterproof case.

"No way it works after being in the water," he said.

"This is a pretty rugged setup," she said, pressing the power button.

The phone gave him an idea. "I'm going to see if I can start the electronics. See if there is a track on the GPS that shows where the boat has been." She didn't look up.

Her head was still down, fingers flying over the keyboard. A swarm of black flies greeted him when he moved to the console. He and Mel were not the only ones to discover the body. The smell soon reached him and he stepped back. "We have to do something with the body."

"We?" Mel asked. "I'm calling someone right now. It's a murder, Mac."

"It'll be the same body if it's just floating around, and we can still call it in. This is bigger than one dead man. If we turn it over to the sheriff, it'll end there," Mac said.

Mel stared at the screen for a minute. "Don't you watch CSI— crime scene?" She paused. "This is interesting."

"Is that good interesting or bad interesting?" Mac asked.

"I'm not sure, but I think whoever this is worked for the National Science Foundation," she said.

"Who would kill a scientist?" Mac asked, but he already knew the answer.

"What did you say about a fish kill?"

"Trufante and one of his no-good buddies were out there netting. Apparently that king tide and storm pushed the leading edge of the red tide fish down here. They thought it would be easy pickings," Mac explained.

"That idiot's selling diseased fish now?" Mel looked up.

Mac just shrugged. The breeze kicked up, pushing the smell toward them. "We need to make a decision."

Mel was quiet, but Mac could tell from the look on her face that her brain was working in overdrive. "You're right. If we give the crime scene to the sheriff, he'll do everything he can to bury it. The last thing his campaign needs is an ecological disaster in his backyard." She paused. "We'll tell him we were out fishing and saw if floating."

"And then?" Mac asked.

"Then we figure this out. If someone or something wants a scientist dead, I'm interested," Mel said. "Could be the Feds are already involved, and in a bad way."

Mac saw the light in her eyes that had been missing for the last few weeks. She had been looking for a cause, and now it seemed she had found one. "Let me use your phone. I'll make the call."

She handed him the phone and watched while he started to dial. "Wait. We need to get out where we 'found' the body. If they have any kind of technology, they can track the call to here."

"I'll get a tarp, and we probably need to wear gloves, too," Mac said, leaving the beach.

"I'm going to hang onto this," she said, sticking the dead man's phone in her pocket.

They changed into clothes that they would later burn and grabbed lobstering gloves, as they were the only ones available. Back on the beach, Mac looked at the two boats bobbing in the light chop and chose the center-console. There was no way he was going to endanger the trawler if this went badly.

Taking an old painter's tarp, he spread it on the deck and rolled the body onto it. Mel came aboard, and they tucked the ends in, making what looked like a large burrito. It took both of them to get the dead weight over the side of the beached boat and onto the center-console. Once it was loaded, they hopped off, stripped, and tossed their clothes onto the smoldering fire. After changing again, they pushed the boat back into the water.

"Where are we going?" Mel yelled over the engine.

"Coconut Key," Mac said. "I'll go in the backside. We'll tell them we were drifting the channel by East Bahia Honda and saw something in the water."

Mel grabbed the stainless steel tower as Mac brought the boat up on plane. They were silent; the roar of the engine and their own thoughts about what they were about to do kept conversation to a minimum. Ten minutes later, Mac slowed and idled toward the mangrove-covered key. He checked the current and adjusted their position so the drift would put the boat where he wanted it. They both went forward to the body.

"Is this the right thing to do?" Mel asked.

"Too late now. We've already messed up whatever crime scene there was," Mac said, grabbing one end of the burrito. Mel grabbed the other and they rolled the body overboard, each holding the end of the tarp. Mac said a silent prayer, stowed the drop cloth, and went to the VHF radio. After the dispatcher told them to stay put, he idled about a hundred feet away from the body and dropped anchor.

What felt like an hour was probably only twenty minutes. Finally, they heard an outboard coming toward them. The sheriff's boat, lights flashing, came down off plane and idled over. Mac immediately grimaced.

"Afternoon, Travis," the deputy said. "Interesting seeing you out here."

Mac tried to keep a stone face. "We were just fishing," he said.

"Between you and Trufante, it's always something. Gotta tell you, it's a bit suspicious, after seeing you yesterday, that you come across a floater today."

Mac shrugged. "You want us to stick around or what?"

"At least till the coroner gets here. Can I trust you to come by and make a statement, or do I have to haul you in?" His attitude changed when he saw Mel come around the console.

"We'll be by later today," Mel said. "I'll make sure of it."

"All right, Ms. Woodson. I'd trust your word."

Two other boats approached and the deputy went for his radio, giving instructions. Within minutes Mac and Mel were all but forgotten as everyone watched the coroner wade out and check the body. He finished his initial exam and called for a backboard. The body was quickly loaded onto the deputy's boat.

"Today, Travis," the deputy yelled across as he pressed down on the throttle and followed the two other boats toward Marathon.

Chapter 6

"First we see what's on the cell phone. Then we decide how and when we give a statement," Mel said.

There was no point in fighting her once her lawyer brain kicked in, not that he had any plans of facing the sheriff right away. And there was always the concept of "Keys time" he could fall back on. Things rarely stayed on schedule here. "I'd like to have another look at the boat too," Mac said, spinning the wheel to starboard. The weather had settled, and the southeast wind was back. The swells brought in from the Atlantic were blocked by the mainland, leaving the Gulf-side waters calm. He focused on the islands in the distance and adjusted course slightly to port. As the boat skipped easily over the light chop, he thought about what they had found. The recovered boat was in good condition, the engines would take some work, and the electronics were probably ruined, but there was no major damage he had found on his initial look. This led him to the obvious question of how the boat sank, and then who killed the man they had found. His initial thought was that the murderer shoved the body in the console and pulled the drain plug.

The insurance company would pay for the boat as is, but a few days' work, especially if he could get the engines started, would more than double the payday. He also wanted the boat out of sight if the deputy got impatient and came for a visit. The western side of the island would be the best place to stash the boat. It was less accessible and visited only occasionally by flats fishermen seeking bonefish or permit in the skinny water. Mel could help him move the boat, but to repair the engines he would need help, and he wondered what she would say if Trufante showed up. The Cajun was trouble. But good help, especially mechanics, were hard to find here. Mac chose the devil he knew over the one he didn't—especially when it came to having strangers to the island.

"Salvage on that boat's going to be high, especially if I can get the engines running," he said over the whine of the motor, hoping to break the ice. He glanced over at her, knowing the look on her face, and dropped it. She was either off in her own thoughts, or knew where he was going with this. Having a lawyer for a girlfriend had its perks, but also its pitfalls.

The island came into view and he steered toward the unmarked channel leading to the beach. In typical backcountry Keys style, Wood had placed a single pile near the beach, short enough to be almost underwater at high tide, and a small stick marking a rock pile just on the outside of the channel. Both were clearly visible in the current low tide, but there were no shapes or colors showing which side was safe and which would ground you. The Keys were littered with these kinds of markers, which often caused more trouble than they prevented when tourists misread them and grounded. Only insider knowledge or a very careful study, in the right light, would show where the channel was. He slowed and then stopped, letting the wind push the smaller boat against the port side of the trawler.

Mel helped secure the boats and headed back to the house. Thankfully, it had been sunny today, allowing the solar system to fully charge the battery bank that powered the island. As long as the power lasted, she would be content working on the cell phone and her laptop. He waded to the beach and started inspecting the boat, noticing things he had not seen in his quick survey earlier.

Starting at the bow, he went slowly over each section of the hull. The low tide, although not as radical as it had been a few days ago, was still lower than normal, and the boat was high and dry, allowing him to see well below the waterline. The gelcoat was largely pristine, indicating that the boat was either new, or the operator was skilled. The highly polished outer layer of fiberglass often held clues, but in this case there were only a few scratches just below the rub rail, which were pretty common and probably came from brushing against a dock. He moved around the hull, rubbing his hands over it as if it would tell its story. There were no registration numbers, no name or hailing port on the boat. Mel had mentioned the man worked for the National Science Foundation, and so far, that fit what he saw. Finally he reached the transom and saw the drain plug missing confirming what he had guessed.

Next he climbed aboard and, starting at the bow, carefully checked every compartment. The anchor and ground tackle were more than adequate for the size of the boat and appeared to be well used. The other forward compartments were empty, their hasps all open, allowing whatever had been in them to be taken by the sea. He moved back to the helm and checked the electronics, doubting they would work. The small rubber cover that protected the slot where a memory card could be inserted was still in place and, to his surprise when he opened it, a card was there. Whoever had killed the man and scuttled the boat was not very thorough. He pushed it with his index finger and it popped out enough for him to retrieve it. Secure in his pocket, he continued.

Behind the bench seat was a live well. The top was open and the drain plug in place, indicating that it had possibly been in use at the time of the accident. Glancing under the gunwales, there were no fishing rods, but they could have floated out when the boat sank. Finally, after studying the deck and gunwales, it was the lack of blood stains that told him it had not been used for its intended purpose as a fishing boat. Even the most meticulous owners had a hard time removing all traces of fish blood.

There were two built-in fish boxes in the rear deck—both closed. On his knees, he opened the port side one. It was empty, and he moved to the starboard. Two fish floated on the surface of the water trapped inside the insulated compartment. One a redfish, the other a snook, both unusual in these waters this time of year.

A quick examination of the fish found nothing overtly wrong with them. Setting them aside, he continued to check the storage compartment built into the transom. They held nothing but dock lines and a quart of oil.

Back in the console, he checked again for any numbers indicating registration and, after moving the life jackets, saw only the same tag as before.

There was nothing else inside. He grabbed the two fish, slung his leg over the side and headed toward the house. After carefully wrapping the fish in a double plastic bag, he set them in the chest freezer by the shed and went upstairs.

Mel looked up from the computer screen when he entered, a perplexed look on her face. He ignored her and went to the kitchen, where he grabbed a beer.

"I'm working on the registration. A real internet connection would help," she said. "I'm stuck using the god-awful reception on my cell phone for a hot spot. I could do better with a tin hat."

He didn't take the bait—he liked it that way.

* * *

Philip Dusharde sat in a comfortable chair on the painted deck, staring at the gingerbread detailing made to look like it was holding up the wrapped beams supporting the roof. The deck was on the second story of a house built above drained swampland, now landscaped to look like a golf course. The house always made him happy, unfortunately, the location was far from optimal. Twin fans installed in the beadboard ceiling cooled him, as did the drink in his hand. He ignored the condensation dripping from the glass onto his pressed chinos and waited for the stuttering, accented voice of the man on the phone to finish.

"Your funds have been wired," he said, taking a sip of the old-fashioned. "In fact, I added a small bonus."

"That is not why I am calling," the man said.

"Then what, pray tell, is this call for?" Dusharde asked, starting to get annoyed. The Cuban was leaving a bad taste in his mouth, ruining the comfortable feeling the house gave him and reminding him where he was—Clewiston—the agricultural hub of the sugar industry, located on the south shore of Lake Okeechobee. Forced by both his business and political interests to maintain residence in Hendry County, he had built his forty-acre compound to transport him to where he would have rather been—anywhere with "beach" after the name. But business dictated he would live here and the eighty-foot yacht he kept in Miami would have to do when he needed to escape.

The man paused, as if scared to speak.

"Go on," Philip urged.

"The scientist and his boat are gone," he stuttered.

"Yes, I am aware of that," Philip said. The man had messaged him with pictures of both the dead scientist and then the sinking boat. He had an urge to check them again, but they were deleted from his phone.

"When I was leaving, I saw a boat pull up in the area," the man said.

"Did they see you?" Philip sat up straighter and put his drink down on a coaster to protect the table.

"I can't be sure. I ran far enough to be out of sight and turned on the radar. From what I saw, they stayed in the area for a couple of hours."

"Maybe they're just fishermen. That is what those people do down there."

The man seemed more relaxed talking about his home. "There's no reason to go that far. And sitting there for that long, it doesn't make sense. It's seagrass, not good bottom for fishing."

"I think you're worrying over nothing," Dusharde said to set the man at ease, but not really knowing what he was talking about. "I do appreciate you bringing your concerns to my attention." Philip dismissed him with these words. He had been angry that the man had called, but he had done the right thing—at least for Dusharde Sugar.

Philip picked up his drink and slowly drained it as he looked at the phone on the table. The first thing he did was delete the man's contact information, then checked the photo app and text messages for any trail. Tomorrow he would have the phone destroyed and get a new one. He had been warned about the cloud, and although he didn't understand it, he had people to take care of anything that went there.

He set the glass back down and dialed a number from memory. A woman answered on the second ring. "We have a problem," he told her, and went on to describe the conversation he had just had.

"I'll handle it," said a voice that sounded like fingernails on a chalkboard. The Southern accent was the only thing that made her tone remotely bearable.

He smiled, knowing that he had in his employ one of the most ruthless, calculating, and vengeful people he had ever met. She was perfect. "Very well, then. We have the town hall meeting with that state representative coming up this week?" he asked.

"Yes. Vernon Wade will be in town this weekend. I will have the appropriate supporters on hand as usual," she said.

"We may need something stronger than that. He's going off the reservation on us."

Without a goodbye, he hung up, dreading another political visit. If it were only as easy to take out a representative as it had been to take out a scientist, there would be no legislature left. He got up and went through the French doors to his study, where the ingredients to make his drink were laid out on the wet bar. Pulling down a fresh glass from the shelf, he used an eyedropper to pull a small amount of bitters from a cork stoppered decanter and carefully dripped eleven drops of the dark substance into the glass, he then added a slice of orange grown on his property and genetically modified just for this purpose. From another glass container he took a cube of sugar and held it to the light, examining the crystals. This was his sugar. The thousands of acres surrounding the compound where the cane was raised were his empire, and he would continue to do everything in his power to keep his legacy intact. With a smile, he gently dumped the cube in the glass and with a stone pestle started muddling the ingredients together, careful to not allow any pulp from the orange into the drink. Adding a single large ice cube, he covered the concoction with a private label bourbon and swirled the glass in his hands.

He brought the drink to his lips and tasted the bitter sweetness—it was the sugar that made it just right—Dusharde Sugar.

Chapter 7

Mac left Mel, still busy at her laptop, and went downstairs. He wanted to check out the fish from the boat, and there was nothing to be gained from hovering over her except another speech about joining the twenty-first century. He was content to stay in the twentieth.

Removing the bag with the fish from the chest freezer, he brought it to the fish cleaning table mounted to the back of the shed. On a hook extending from the building was a kerosene lamp, which he lit, both for light and to keep the bugs away. He started with the snook. The fish looked washed out, its color and lateral line were faded. Mac couldn't be sure if it had been placed in the fish box while still alive, not that it would matter. It had been trapped in the compartment for several days. Before slicing the belly, he checked the mouth. He looked for any sign of a hook having penetrated or torn the membrane and found none. Snook were wary and he guessed it had either been brought aboard dead or netted in a semiconscious state.

Slowly he worked the nine-inch fillet knife across the stone, then, satisfied it was sharp, he sliced the belly, using just enough force to penetrate the skin. Setting the knife down, he removed the stomach and gently peeled away the protective membrane. The stench was overpowering, causing Mac to take a step back. Taking a deep breath, he went back to the table to examine the fodder. A pile of partially digested shrimp was massed together along with several small baitfish. It was the shrimp that caught his attention and with the knife he separated one from the pile.

The bugs were getting braver, smelling the offal on the table, and started flying sorties around Mac. Using one hand he swatted them away and with the tip of the knife examined the shrimp. It was clearly infected by something. Even in its decomposed state it was off-color, and the smell was a sure indicator. With the flat part of the blade, he scooped up the fish, stomach, and its contents. He placed them in a baggie, sealed it, and put it back in the freezer. A marine biologist would be needed to confirm what he thought—that the fish was infected with red tide.

The algae bloom was a plague to many of the towns on the west coast of Florida, resulting in large fish kills. Beaches were shut down, causing all the tourist-related businesses to suffer from the plague as well. How it originated he didn't know, only its effect. While he hosed the table down he thought about what he had just seen. Never had he heard of any red tide incident this close, and the pieces of the puzzle started coming together in his head. Extinguishing the lamp, he went back upstairs.

Mel was still at the table. "Hey, I found some interesting stuff here," she said, sliding the computer screen toward him.

He backed away, not from disinterest, but needing a shower to wash the smell off. "Hold that. I'll be right back," he said, walking into the bedroom and out the back door to the deck. The outside shower was shielded by a lattice screen reaching about head high, not that there was a need for privacy. To be seen here would take an FBI-style surveillance unit. He waited for the hot water, generated by the new solar tubing on the roof, and boosted by an on-demand heater. He was fine with the eighty-degree water that came straight from the tap, but Mel insisted on the boost. Grateful, at least today, for her insistence on the addition of the heater, it still took two rounds of scrubbing and rinsing before he felt free of the stench. Turning off the water, he toweled himself dry and headed back inside. Dressed in his standard T-shirt and cargo shorts, he went into the living room.

"Okay, let's have a look," he said, moving toward her.

The phone they had found lay next to her laptop, connected by a cable she had used to transfer its contents to the larger screen. He pulled the computer closer. "Any luck on the owner?" Mac asked, studying the table in front of him.

"Not directly, but the contact list is interesting. I'm sure this guy was a scientist," she said, leaning back in her chair and rubbing her eyes. "He appears to have worked for Florida Coastal Everglades, which is a division of the National Science Foundation. Most of the other stuff here is over my pay grade."

"That's where I am too. We need to get someone to look at the fish," he said, sitting down and pulling the computer closer. A grid of rows and columns filled the screen. He knew the basics of spreadsheets, at least enough to navigate around one. Before GPS and memory chips, he had stored his Loran numbers in one. Using the touch pad, he scrolled around the cells trying to make sense of the data. Across the top were listed several species of fish: snook, redfish, sea trout, snapper, barracuda, bonefish, and cobia. Down the side, in the first column were dates. It was certainly a compilation of the quantity of a species of fish on a specific day, but he didn't know what it represented.

"Can you show me how to move the screen?" he asked.

She laughed and came to his side, reaching over and using two fingers to slide the data to the left.

"Stop," he said. They were in the current month and he saw the numbers jump. "That's the two days of the king tide when the fish washed up here." The numbers showed a huge increase in all species. Where the entries had been in the low single digits, often with zeros for many days, double digits were entered during the high tide.

Mel leaned in and scrolled lower, but the screen was blank. "It stops three days ago."

Mac thought for a second, looking at the blank cells and putting together the timeline in his head. "Trufante was out there the day before yesterday. So it looks like the boat went down in the storm."

"From everything we've seen, it wasn't the storm," Mel said.

* * *

Jane sipped from her water bottle, took a deep breath, and checked her heart rate. It had taken longer than she wanted for it to drop, and she shook her head, angry with herself for slipping. With a determined look she set down the bottle and went back to her workout. After going through several martial arts forms, she did three violent sets of pull ups, pushups, and squats, then collapsed on the floor. It took a minute to catch her breath, and after checking the monitor on her watch again, she smiled.

She lay down and stretched for a few minutes, working through the muscles she had just taxed. With her workout complete, she grabbed her water bottle and towel and went back into the house. At her desk, she checked her email. There was no message from the men she had hired—not that she thought they would complete the task so quickly. It was not her first experience subcontracting work in the Keys, and all had the same result—slower and sloppier than she would have liked. The only way to get this done right was to get down there and handle it herself.

After showering, she changed into yoga pants and a formfitting top—both in black. She brewed a pot of coffee, ate an energy bar, and moved to a closed door that looked like a closet. The difference between this door and a standard closet door was evident after she placed her eye close to a woman's eye in a picture just down the hall, and it swung open on four heavy-duty hinges. Faced with wood to match the rest of the house, the door was actually solid steel. An electromagnetic lock triggered by a retinal scanner, concealed in the eye in the photograph, insured she was the only one to gain entry. Once inside, she turned on the lights and smiled as she surveyed her weapons collection. Passing by the antique swords, she removed an

AK-47 and a twelve-gauge shotgun from their clips on the wall and placed them in a long black bag. After loading the ammunition, she scanned the handguns, settling on a pair of Glock 43 9m and two extra six-round magazines. Placing the handguns in a smaller bag, she moved to a workbench. Homeland Security would have been on high alert if they could see the contents of the bins and cases stored under the bench. Pulling out a steel case, she opened it and removed several small containers marked C4, which she set on the counter. Next to them she placed several cell phone detonators, and, picking one up, pressed the two detonator barbs into the clay-like explosive. She place the rigged charge in a small insulated cooler and the rest of the material in the smaller bag with the pistol. After loading several boxes of ammunition, she took one last look at her collection, locked the room, and left the house.

She loaded the trunk of her black Audi R8 with an overnight bag, the long satchel filled with her weapons of choice, and the small cooler with the detonators. Taking her coffee, she settled into the luxurious interior and pushed the garage door opener. The roar of the ten-cylinder, six-hundred horsepower engine put a smile on her face. There were no regrets spending the extra money on upgrading from the standard engine. Her life was all about power. Always vigilant of reporters stalking her for a story about Dusharde Sugar, the quick acceleration and extra speed had paid off more than once. Checking her mirrors before pulling out, she backed into the street and pressed hard on the gas pedal, smiling when the engine responded to her demand.

There were a lot of drawbacks about her main residence in Clewiston. Mainly the lack of a life, social or otherwise, but this was her weekday residence. Although most of her job could be done electronically, Philip insisted she be close by. The weekends were another matter, and the R8 made short work of the hour-and-a-half drive to her condo on South Beach in Miami.

At close to a hundred miles per hour, the broken yellow line looked almost solid as she accelerated onto Highway 27. The headlights of the R8 illuminated the road, penetrating the blackness surrounding her. Once in a while another pair of lights appeared in the distance. If they were red, she made it a contest to see how quickly she could overtake the vehicle. If they were white and coming head-on, they would quickly turn into a blur and disappear. Pressing lightly on the brakes, the hundred-and-fifty-thousand-dollar car slowed, hovering near eighty. Unfortunately, this was as fast as she would let it go, with the contents in the trunk likely to be a problem if she was pulled over by the Highway Patrol.

Several times before, she had been stopped at close to a hundred, but her charms quickly pacified the officers. But the last had been a woman, not so easily swayed by her talents, and that ticket clung to her record like a dirty sock to a clean towel. Around her the Everglades passed silently, their enveloping darkness soon broken by the lights of Fort Lauderdale in the distance. The highway was more crowded now, forcing her to slow as the road, a barrier between the Everglades on her right and development on her left, approached civilization. Traffic slowed even more as she approached

Miami, where rush hour often extended into the night. The road turned toward the east and now the lights of the city surrounded her. She merged onto the Florida Turnpike, still heading south. She flashed a tight grin when she continued straight instead of turning onto Highway 836, which would take her to her condo—what lay ahead could prove to be more fun than anything South Beach had to offer.

* * *

Trufante sat at the bar with his last twenty on the worn counter. Pamela was next to him, singing along with some lame Jimmy Buffet song the guy in the corner was playing on an acoustic guitar. His patience was thin, and he was ready for sleep. The party, spanning twenty-four nonstop hours, had been an exhausting jaunt from Marathon to Key West and back. But for whatever it had cost, Pamela was back to normal, and he knew this would settle her for a while, though the thought had crossed his mind that he was getting too old for this.

He nursed his beer trying to hold his head straight while waiting for Jeff to show up with his five hundred dollars for the net. It might have been a better idea to go home and get some rest rather than meet him tonight, but the pile of hundreds hadn't lasted long, and he needed to hold onto this payoff and not stuff it up his already sore and swollen nose.

"Come on, babe. Let's blow this place," he said, leaning toward Pamela.

"I like this song," she said, resuming the lyrics to another stupid sailor song.

"It's last call for this dude," he said. "We gotta hit it after this." He drank the last of the beer, continuing to stare at the door and hoping the song would be over soon. This was way out of character for the guy legendary for his ability to rock it for days, not just a single night. "Maybe I'm coming down with something."

The song ended and he was about to snatch the lone bill on the bar when he felt a hand on his shoulder. Immediately he knew it was not Pamela.

"Buy you and the lady a drink, mate?" a voice behind him said with a fake British accent that did nothing to conceal his Cuban heritage.

Trufante turned to see a cartoonish character looking back at him. The man was a rail thin five foot four, with a large head and oily dark hair capped with an old captain's hat. Beneath the brim, ink-black eyes looked about twice the size they should be. "Hector, what do you want?" Trufante asked.

"Let's take a walk, mate," he said.

"What's with the stupid accent and the hat?" Trufante asked, suspicious of why he was here. Hector and his brother Edgar, who had cut the tip off his finger in a bait grinder several years ago, were the dregs of Monster Bait.

"It's a disguise, you idiot. The boss wants a word," he said.

"What for?" Trufante asked, trying to figure out what had gone wrong now.

"Seems your mate ratted you out," he said. "Now, let's go."

Trufante winced as he felt the tip of a knife in his side. "This doesn't affect the lady. I'll go, but she stays."

"He said nothing about a broad."

Now he was trying to sound like Bogart. Trufante leaned over to Pamela. "Go find Mac. Tell him I'm at Monster Bait." He felt the knife jab him again. "Please."

Edgar was waiting outside smoking a cigarette. The exact opposite of his brother—short, fat, and round, he reeked of something Trufante couldn't put his finger on, but it wasn't good. "Come on, loser," he said.

Trufante stood between the two brothers. Towering close to a foot above them, he looked around for anything he could do to change the situation. Hector prodded him with the blade again, removing any chance for running. They stuffed him in the jump seat in back of their worn-out Mitsubishi pickup, rusted through from neglect and the harsh climate. He tried to turn sideways to get his knees out of his chest, but most of the seat was already taken by the large gill net. Even in the low light, it looked like the net he and Jeff had used the other day.

The brothers got in. The engine coughed several times before starting, and Trufante gagged on the exhaust seeping through the floorboard. Both front windows were rolled down, but they provided little relief in the backseat. The ride was short and bumpy, and as soon as they pulled off the main road into the driveway for Monster Bait, he was jarred by the neglected gravel surface. His head smacked the low interior several times as Edgar plowed through the rain-filled potholes. Thankfully, they stopped in a large parking area surrounded by piles of lobster and crab traps.

"Come on, mate," Hector said, brandishing the knife in plain sight now. He motioned toward the small shack.

Trufante winced, his stub burning as he walked toward the building where Edgar had mangled him. He could still remember that night, when a deal on a square grouper had gone south. Thankfully, they walked past the shack, continuing toward a larger structure.

"In there, matey," Hector said, pushing him forward.

"You sorry ass Cajun. Landed in a whole new mess of shit now," Edgar said, tossing the cigarette butt toward Trufante and opening the door. The smell of rotten fish wafted into the night. "Come on in, Cajun," he said, motioning with a pistol he had withdrawn from his waistband.

There was no chance of escape now, and Trufante walked in front of Edgar, who he swore was giggling behind him as they entered the building. A half dozen bare incandescent bulbs hung from the ceiling casting just enough light to so he could see the large white bins filled with fish and ice. He recognized their haul from the other day.

"Look at this shit. I don't think even Manuel could sell this," Edgar said, pointing the gun at one of the bins.

"It was Jeff's deal. I'm just the help," Trufante said, choking on the stench. Quality fish were often iced for up to a week before sale. These were only two days old and clearly rotten.

"The boss wants a refund and this shit disposed of," Hector said.

"But Jeff . . ."

"Over there, Cajun," he said, waving the gun across the room at a figure tied up in the corner.

He saw the shadows behind him, but Trufante was too slow to act. Hector and Edgar were on him, quickly tying his hands and feet. They pushed him into the corner with Jeff.

"I know you two white trash pieces of crap burnt through all your money already, so tomorrow morning you are going fishing. Except you are going to put the fish back and make this like it never happened."

Chapter 8

Once again, sleep eluded Mac, and he was up before dawn. There were too many coincidences for this not to bring trouble, and he wanted the salvaged boat on the other side of the island. It would be less visible there, and he planned on leaving it in a way that if it were found, he could claim ignorance. Working alone, he used the center-console to pull the boat off the beach. Without power to the hydraulic lift motors, he had to leave the heavy engines down, causing the boat to draw close to three feet of water. This forced him into a circuitous route that took far longer than the quarter mile around the island.

Leaving the navigation lights off, to avoid being seen by the handful of fishermen already running out to the Gulf, he worked a large circle into deeper water, cutting back in when he passed the shallowest flat. A few minutes later, he dropped anchor, released the tow line and pushed the salvage boat toward the beach. Fortunately, it was close to the bottom of the tide, making it easier to lodge the lower units and propellers in the sandy bottom. A standard anchor in this type of bottom would require an eight-to-one scope, or, in this case, with three feet of water and another three-foot rise to the bow, almost fifty feet of line in the water. Wanting to keep the boat close to the beach and out of sight, that amount of line would create a hundred-foot swing when the tide changed.

Instead, he chose a pole system. Mounted on the transom, the pole dropped straight down into the bottom, securing the boat exactly where the fisherman wanted it. In some cases they used two poles in tandem to eliminate the swing of the boat. His choice was a much simpler length of PVC pipe left over from the remodel of the house. Taking the ten-foot-long, two-inch diameter pipe, he used a small sledgehammer to drive it deep into the sandy bottom directly between the twin outboards where it would be hard to see. He was covered in sweat when he finished, but the pipe was only two feet above the water level. At high tide, only a few inches would show. With a piece of line he tied the boat off, grabbed the anchor as a decoy, and slid over the side. He dropped it about twenty feet from the bow and continued to wade back to his center-console. Looking back at his work, he was satisfied—unless someone boarded the boat, they would never see the ruse.

When he returned, Mel was waiting on the small beach with a determined look on her face and a messenger bag slung over her shoulder. It was a look he hadn't seen in a long time, and he wasn't sure if this was a good or a bad thing. They had decided to take the trawler to Marathon. There was no guarantee this would be a quick trip, and he wanted to be prepared.

After packing the snook he had examined earlier in a cooler, he stashed it aboard and started the engines. Nudging the starboard throttle just enough to push the boat forward to the pile, he waited for Mel to pull the line off. Once they were free, he used both controls—port in reverse and starboard forward to spin the boat—and then he pushed them both together, steering a heading out the channel and toward Marathon. It was a beautiful morning, the start of a day he would rather be out fishing. His mind churned as he steered, his hand worked the wheel, knowing the course and how to avoid the sandbars.

"I'm going to take her around and tie up at the Anchor." Rusty's place had plenty of room in the turning basin, and if the old man was around he could likely borrow a car. Half an hour later, the smell of Rufus's fish sandwiches had his mouth watering as they turned into the canal leading to the dock. There were two sailboats in residence, leaving plenty of room to tie off.

Rusty appeared just as Mac positioned the boat. He went back and grabbed the stern line, tossing it across to Rusty to help stop the forward momentum of the boat. The tide was coming in fast now, and Mac waited for Rusty to secure the line before he backed the stern to the dock. Mel hopped over the gunwale and tied the bow line to a cleat.

"Might want to put a spring on her too," Rusty said, his eyes looking at the sailboat in front of the trawler.

"I got it, old man," Mac joked. Rusty was a retired marine and diver who had probably forgotten more than most men would ever learn. He might have put on a few pounds over the years, but underneath lay dormant the Marine he had been. "Maybe you could tell Rufus we'd love a few sandwiches."

"Come on up to the bar when you get squared away," he said, looking over at Mel, who was already on the dock with her messenger bag. "If you're thinking of staying, there's a power hookup on the piling there."

"Thanks. We might take you up on that," Mac said, hopping onto the dock with the cooler in hand. Together the three of them made their way to the bar. "I'm serious about the sandwiches."

"Thought you brought your own," Rusty said, gesturing to the cooler, and walked over to the outdoor kitchen. Mac looked over and waved to the old Rastafarian cook.

Inside, the bar was quiet. The Rusty Anchor was a locals' spot, a little off the beaten path for the tourists cruising US 1 looking for action. If the wind were up, there would be several fishermen hanging around, and later the locals would fill the place. This early on a pristine day, the bar was empty.

"Okay to use the Wi-Fi?" Mel asked.

"You'd know better than me. Julie set it up the last time she was through here," he said.

Mel and Rusty's daughter had grown up together. "How is she?"

"All classified, but her and Deuce seem to be getting on real well," he said. "Y'all want a beer or something with those sandwiches?" Rufus had just walked in with two plates and set them on the bar.

They shook their heads at the same time and asked for water.

Mel had the laptop open and her fingers were flying across the keyboard. Every few minutes, she stopped and took a bite of her sandwich.

"What'cha got cookin' over there?" Rusty asked.

Mac knew Mel was too engrossed in what she was doing to answer. "Hey. You know any marine biologist types around? Maybe someone who could look at something and keep it quiet?" Mac asked.

Rusty looked at the cooler and then over at Mac. "I'd expect Trufante to be walking in here any minute, as secretive as you two are."

Mac thought about bringing him into the loop, but decided against it. The authorities already knew about one murder and the sinking of the boat. There was no reason to involve Rusty. "Just caught something I'm not real sure of."

Rusty gave him a look that clearly said he knew better, but let it go. "There's a group from that Turtle Hospital that comes in here some nights. Good folk, mainly. Maybe ask over there." He rubbed his chin. "Girl named Jen. Doesn't drink much, looks pretty responsible."

Mac thought about bringing an unknown into the equation. He decided to trust a bartender's personality assessment, and they needed someone to look at the fish. Alicia's boyfriend, TJ, ran a dive shop up in Key Largo. He had some kind of marine science background too, but that was sixty miles away, and on a day like this he would be out on charters.

"Turtle Hospital it is. What do we owe you?" Mac asked.

"I'll start you up a tab. Sounds like you two are up to something that'll keep you in town for a few days."

Mac walked over to Mel and looked over her shoulder at the screen. "Can you break away for a few minutes so we can get these fish checked out?"

She didn't look up. "Sure. Just emailing Alicia to see if she can help with this phone. There are some password protected apps on it."

"Funny, I was just thinking about them. Figure they're going to be out all day," Mac said, looking out at the water, wishing he would be as well.

"Take your car?" Mac asked.

Rusty reached below the bar and tossed him a set of keys. "Just don't wreck it," he said.

* * *

Trufante had slept despite the surroundings, mainly due to his after-binge hangover. He woke, fidgeting with his ties. With every movement, the barnacle-covered trapline that the brothers had tied him with cut into his skin.

"This is your fault."

Trufante turned to the voice. "What are you talking about? It was your idea."

"If I didn't have to meet you to get that net back . . . "

Light shot into their eyes, blinding them momentarily when the door opened.

"You boys have some explaining to do," a woman's voice called out.

Trufante squinted into the light, trying to see who she was.

"Bring them over here," she said.

Hector and Edgar each grabbed one arm, pulling Trufante out of the building and dropping him on the crushed coral outside. He didn't resist, grateful for the fresh air and to be away from the fish. A minute later, Jeff was deposited next to him.

"These the guys that brought in the fish?" she asked.

"Yes, ma'am," Hector said, losing the British accent from last night. "This is them. Got the net back too."

"Good. Now boys," the woman said, pulling the bands back on a speargun. Trufante saw the barbed end point toward him and felt another old injury twitch. "You set this deal up?"

"We both came up with it," Trufante said. Despite his loathing for Jeff, he was a stand-up guy and not going to throw him under the point of the spear. Maybe together they could get out of this.

She pointed the spear at Jeff. "No. It was him. He made me take my boat and net these fish. I knew it was bad," Jeff whined.

Trufante turned and looked at him, amazed he had the balls to outright lie. Before he could come up with a denial, he saw the glint of metal as the spear flashed by and winced. It was not meant for him. The three barbs entered Jeff's thigh, taking him to the ground. He squirmed, writhing in pain with both hands on the shaft, trying to pull it out. The woman calmly walked up to him and placed her shoe against his leg. Trufante thought she might show mercy and remove the spear. Instead, she pressed down and twisted the barbed tip deeper. Jeff screamed in pain.

"That's what you get for lying," she said. "You two," she called to Hector and Edgar. "Get him on the boat and load the fish."

"What are you going to do with me?" Jeff whimpered.

"Take the fish out and dump the load somewhere they won't be found," she said to both men.

Hector and Edgar stood to the side giggling, like two high school girls sharing a secret.

"But what about this?" Jeff grabbed the shaft.

She shook her head dismissively, reached over and yanked the spear out. Jeff screamed again and crumpled on the gravel, unconscious.

Trufante watched as the two men hauled Jeff toward the dock and loaded him on his boat. They came back down the path, each one giving Trufante the evil eye, before entering the storage building. A forklift emerged a few minutes later with the crates and moved slowly toward the dock. It stopped and the two men grunted and grumbled as they loaded the bins of fish onto the boat. The last one loaded, Hector returned the forklift and came toward them.

"Might as well get going," she said to Trufante. "In the trunk of the car is a cooler." She pointed the bloody tip of the spear at the Audi. "Put it on the boat."

Awkwardly, he gained his feet and shuffled to the car. The trunk was open, and he reached in, both hands still bound together, to grab the handles of a soft-sided cooler, which he carried to the dock.

"Ahoy, matey. What's in the bag?" Hector asked.

"Lady said to put it on the boat," Trufante said, extending his long frame across the gap between the boat and the dock.

"Cheers, mate," Hector said, jumping off and releasing the lines. "Maybe she bought you some beer for the ride back."

Somehow he didn't think so, but with Edgar's gun trained on them, he had no choice but to set it under the seat.

Jeff was still crumpled on the deck. Trufante went to the helm and turned the key. The old diesel started with a throaty cough and he pulled away from the dock, wanting to be rid of the woman and the two brothers. He turned before they left the channel and saw the brothers and the woman staring at him. Nothing good ever happened to him at Monster Bait.

Chapter 9

Mac and Mel left the Anchor and turned left onto US 1. After about a mile, Mac saw the sign for the Turtle Hospital in the distance and slowed.

"It's all the way up there. What are you doing?" Mel asked.

"Look. That's Pamela, Tru's girlfriend," Mac said, pulling over to the side. "Something's not right."

"I'll say. The fact that you're pulling over to help the loser's girlfriend. Come on, Mac. We have stuff to do."

"It'll only take a minute. Looks like something's wrong," he said, getting out of the car and walking to the bench.

The walking and bike trail was a dozen feet off the highway, protected by a barrier of grass and trees. Mac walked up to the prone figure on the bench and shook her shoulder.

"Hey, Pamela, you okay?" he asked.

She moved slightly and turned toward him, squinting into the sunlight. It must have been a rough night. Her hair was a mess, and mascara had run and dried in black lines down her face. "Huh?"

"Pamela, it's Mac. Tru's friend," he said, waiting for her to get her bearings.

"Mac Travis. Look here. Tru said to find you. I been walking all night," she said.

"It's okay. I'm here. But what about Tru?" Mac asked.

"These creepers came into the bar and took him last night."

"Do you know who they were?"

"No, but the guy was talking in a strange accent. Kept calling Tru matey, and he called me a broad," Pamela said, running her fingers through her hair. "Can we get some water or food or something? It's been a long strange trip."

"Yeah. Sorry, come on," Mac said, leading her to the car.

"Look what the cat dragged in," Mel said.

"Come on. She needs help and Tru's in trouble," Mac said, helping Pamela into the back seat.

He went back around to the driver's side and got back in. Mel's look tore through him. "What?"

"Mac Travis. Picking up strays and trying to save the world," she said.

He could see the old Mel coming out. She had a plan, and anything that interfered with it got brushed to the side, including himself at times. "It's got to be connected. Let me get her a bottle of water and some food. She can wait in the car," he said, starting the engine and pulling into traffic. A few blocks ahead he saw a gas station. After stopping in front of the pump, he gave Mel a "play nice" look and went in, coming back a with a large bottle of water and a bag of chips. Handing them through the open window, Pamela took them greedily. He decided to top off the gas to make sure Rusty got the car back better than he'd taken it and pumped a few gallons into the tank.

Leaving the gas station, he drove another few blocks and turned right into the Turtle Hospital. The lot was almost full, and he parked next to their orange and white "turtle ambulance." The facility had grown over the years rescuing, rehabilitating, and releasing thousands of turtles. You could still tell it was built from the bones an old motel, but they had been successful and were able to expand.

"We'll be right back," Mac said to Pamela. There was no response, and he looked back at her. She looked like a feral cat, eating greedily, and constantly scanning their surroundings for danger. Stuffing her face with chips and alternately washing them down with large gulps from the almost-empty water bottle, she looked like she hadn't slept in days—which was probably the case, he thought, thinking back on Trufante's history.

Together they walked into the office. It looked like a tour was getting started, and it took a few minutes for the woman behind the counter to acknowledge them.

"We're looking for someone named Jen," Mac said.

The woman gave him a protective look. "She expecting you?"

"No. We got kind of referred to her about a marine biology question," Mel said, shoving Mac aside. "My dad was Bill Woodson. I think he knew the guy that founded this place. Just take a minute."

Now she smiled. "Hold on then. Let me see if she's free," she said, getting up from the stool and walking out the back door. A minute later, she was back with another woman.

"This is Jen," she said.

"What can I help you with?" the woman asked.

"We found some fish washed up on the beach. Something's not right with them, and we were looking to get an opinion," Mel said.

"I have a few minutes. Why don't you bring them around back," she said.

"I'll get the cooler," Mac said, going toward the door. He left the air conditioned building and walked across the parking lot. The car was empty. The empty water bottle and bag of chips were all that remained of Pamela. Shaking his head, he went to the trunk, opened it, and removed the cooler. It was probably a good thing it had been locked in the trunk, he thought. As ravenous as Pamela was, she might have had eaten some bad sashimi.

He took the cooler back to the office and went in. Jen led them through a side door and they entered the medical part of the facility. Mac glanced around, surprised that it looked like any hospital he had been in. Walking past a large room that looked like it was set up for surgery, Jen took them into an exam room.

"Okay. Let's see what you have," she said.

Mac set the cooler on the table and stepped away. Jen opened the lid and removed the gutted snook and its stomach contents from the baggie. She set them aside and took out the redfish. Under a strong light, she examined the fish. "These from down here?"

He shook his head. "Strange this time of year. I'm thinking that king tide and storm brought them down," he said.

She nodded her head. "We got a lot of turtle activity the last few days too," she said, taking a scalpel from a drawer and slicing the stomach open. Mac winced, but the fish were still frozen. A minute later, she laid the stomach contents on a stainless steel pan.

After examining them she looked up. "I worked up at the Mote Marine Lab in Sarasota during a red tide. This looks just like what I saw from those fish."

"I've never heard of red tide reaching this far south," Mac said.

"Ever hear of Friends of the Everglades?" she asked.

Mel answered, "Big Sugar."

"What do these fish have to do with sugar?" Mac asked.

Before she could answer, they heard a crash and ran for the door. Outside, a group of people were gathered around one of the ambulances that had slammed into the large concrete base of a power pole and crashed at the base of the sign.

"It's Pamela," Mel said.

But Mac had already taken off. He ran toward the scene, pushing through the people gathered around. When he reached the driver's side it was empty. Stepping back, he looked for Pamela.

Mel joined Mac. "We gotta go before the police get here," she said, tugging him away from the ambulance. "That deputy still wants to talk to us about the body, and this reeks of Trufante."

They slid through the crowd, making their way to the car. There was no getting through the parking lot with the crowd of people surrounding the wrecked ambulance. He backed up instead, hoping the rain-soaked grass would support the car. Slowly, he spun the wheel and started forward. The tires spun, kicking a stream of mud behind them, but the car inched forward enough for the treads to grab something solid and propel them onto the bike path. Several people yelled at him for cutting them off, and in the background he heard the first siren. Spinning the wheel toward the road, he jumped the curb and pulled onto the pavement. A quick glance in the rearview mirror showed several first responders behind him.

He accelerated, heading toward the Seven Mile Bridge. The road was clear ahead, but across the way traffic was already starting to back up as rubberneckers slowed to check out the accident. Just as he started to relax, thinking that topping off the gas tank was not going to be enough payback, he heard a voice from the back seat.

"*Steal your face right off your head*, Mac Travis. That was some escape," Pamela said, leaning forward between them.

He didn't have to look across to Mel to see her eyes boring into him.

* * *

Trufante took one last look at the dock. They were gone, and he breathed deeply. He turned the corner and headed for the channel.

"So, that's a fine automobile," Trufante said to Jeff.

"What the hell, Trufante. I got a hole in my leg, and you're talking about cars?" Jeff grumbled.

"Sure would like to take a ride in her," Trufante said, revealing his thousand-dollar grin. "All we got to do is dump the fish and we're good. What's with the negativity?"

"They got gators smarter than your dumb ass," Jeff said, crawling toward the helm. He pulled himself up and tried to put weight on the leg. Wincing in pain, he fell back on the seat.

"Before you get comfortable, think you could cut me loose?" Trufante asked, holding out his bound hands.

Jeff slid over and took the wheel from him. "Help yourself."

Trufante moved to the gunwale, where a rusty fillet knife was set in a rod holder. He took the knife and in few seconds was free. Rubbing the abrasions on his wrists, he returned to the helm. "Where we takin' 'em?"

"Thought over to the bridge rubble. We can load the nets and sink them. Let 'em rot down there," Jeff said.

"Sounds like a plan," Trufante said. "How 'bout one of those beers now?"

"That's the first smart thing you've said this week," Jeff said, turning the wheel hard to port after clearing the last marker. He accelerated toward open water.

Trufante reached into the cabin and pulled out the cooler. Placing it on the seat, he pulled the zipper and opened the lid. "Ain't no beer in here, man."

Jeff looked over. "Shit."

Trufante knew what he was looking at. "I guess we're supposed to go down with the fishes."

"Toss that shit overboard," Jeff yelled.

"Wait a minute. She ain't gonna blow it yet. Gotta be cool here—too close in. She'd want us in the deep water past the reef." Trufante poked a finger in the wiring. "Just gotta figure what triggers her."

"What the hell. You're going to blow us up," Jeff screamed.

"Exactly," Trufante said. "We gotta be dead to live."

Jeff looked at him. It took a minute for him to figure out what Trufante was talking about. "Not as dumb as you look." He slowed the boat as they approached the reef. "How's she going to know when to call it."

"Those two nimrods probably told her it would take us about forty-five minutes to get past the reef. I'd bet she waits an hour, just in case," Trufante said, looking back at the net in the corner by the transom. "How deep are we?"

"Just passing a hundred," Jeff said.

"A little deeper. We don't want anyone looking for a wreck and not finding anything," he said, reaching for the net. He laid it out on the deck and placed the cooler in the center. He wound the netting around the cooler, cinching it with the buoy line.

"Two hundred fifty," Jeff called out the sounding.

"Slow down," Trufante said, grabbing a dock line and attaching one end to the bundle. He tossed it over and tied off the line when it was twenty feet back.

"Ain't much of a safety margin," Jeff said.

"Let me know when we get to four hundred. Ain't nobody diving that deep for us losers," he said.

A minute later, Jeff nodded to him and he released the line. "Best run a wide circle around her. I'll start getting rid of the fish."

"No. We can still salvage something out of this and sell them," Jeff said.

"Haven't you had enough of this?" Trufante said.

"Got a guy in Key West that'll take them. No point coming back to Marathon. We're dead—remember."

Just as the words were out of his mouth, the bomb blew.

Chapter 10

Jane looked at the plume of smoke to the south, then at the two brothers, laughing and slapping each other on the back. She would have been happy to be speeding north on US 1 and pulling into South Beach in time for a cocktail—but there were still loose ends.

"Clean up this mess. Get rid of any trace of those fish and those two idiots," she scolded them. "Then forget you ever saw me."

They moved away quickly, which did nothing to calm her down, almost preferring one of them to mouth off and give her an excuse to expel some of her pent-up anger. Murder at a distance was distasteful. In this case it was the best way, but that didn't mean she liked it. She looked at Edgar, wondering how much satisfaction she could get from poking a hole through his fat stomach. The thinner one would be more challenging. Maybe a simple garrote. He talked too much anyway. She smiled thinking of the irony. Still, she was not satisfied.

"Is there a boat here I can use?" she asked.

"Couple of old ones and that hot rod over there," Hector said, pointing past two run-down fishing boats.

The reflection of the sun on the polished chrome was the first thing that caught her eye. She surveyed the twenty-foot boat, knowing it would be fast. "Whose is it?"

"Owner of the place, Manuel," Edgar said. "He's particular about who even touches it."

"Never mind him. Where are the keys?" Her adrenaline was flowing just looking at it.

"You sure? He can be a mean hombre," Hector said.

She stared him down. Yes, she was sure, needing it to verify that those two idiots had died properly and that the fish and the boat were gone. He came back a few minutes later with a key ring.

"If anyone asks, tell them the Audi's there for collateral," she said, taking the keys and walking toward the boat.

"You need any help? One of us to go with you?" Edgar asked.

She really wanted to poke him, but restrained herself. "No, thanks. I got this." She had to sit on the dock to climb down into the boat because of its low freeboard. Once aboard, she settled into the bucket seat. Checking the gauges and controls, she couldn't wait to get going and put the key in the ignition. At first it didn't start and she saw the brothers coming toward her. Too proud to ask for help, especially from these two, she racked her brain for what could be wrong. The answer came and she looked back at the transom and saw the chrome plated carburetor cover. She went back toward the engine, lifted an access cover, and primed the fuel line. Back at the helm, she smiled at Hector and Edgar and turned the key. The roar of the engine and the vibration of the hull beneath her were like foreplay. She couldn't wait to get out on the open water.

Leaving the engine idling, she released the lines and expertly dealt with the wind and current, letting them assist her in pushing the boat away from the dock. Once clear, she pressed the throttle forward and the boat moved into the canal. She knew boats, but not this area, and took her time navigating out of the harbor. Once clear of the markers, she turned toward the plume of smoke and accelerated.

Dancing across the small waves, the boat flew up on plane. Grinning, she looked down, scanning the gauges. The tachometer was still well below the redline. Slowly she increased power, watching the speedometer climb to fifty knots. At this speed, she needed to steer each wave as the lightweight hull bounced on the crests. If she misjudged one, it could flip the boat. Several times the propellor came out of the water as the boat became airborne, but that only made her smile. The bad taste she had in her mouth from watching the explosion from afar was fading as the boat quickly crossed the reef line.

The smoke from the explosion had long dissipated, and she had only a vague idea of where the explosion had occurred and could find no sign of it now. The wave action distracted her momentarily as she had to slow for the rollers, increasing in size when she passed the reef line. There were two other boats nearby, circling around an invisible spot, and she guessed they had been fishing the reef and responded when they saw the explosion.

It took her only seconds to reach them. "Hey, guys," she yelled over the throaty idle of the engine to one of the boats as she approached. "What happened?"

"Don't know. We were fishing off the light and saw something blow. Can't see any sign of it now," one of the men responded. "We called the Coast Guard. They should be here any minute. Maybe they can figure it out."

"Thanks," she said, smiling at him. She cast an eye toward shore, looking for any other boats heading their way. The last thing she needed was to be seen by law enforcement. A second later, she heard one of the men on the other boat yell that he had found something and she idled toward him.

"What do you got?" she asked.

He held up a life preserver and a piece of wood. Something was not making sense here. Neither had any sign of fire or damage—they were too clean. She wanted a closer look, but a quick glance showed several larger boats heading their way.

"See you around, boys. Looks like the cavalry's here," she said, cutting the wheel to starboard and spinning away from them. She accelerated, steering a wide loop to avoid being seen by the approaching responders. When she felt she was a safe distance away, she stopped and watched the scene. Bobbing on the waves, she didn't expect the low profile of the boat to catch the attention of the sheriff and Coast Guard vessels now on site. They appeared to be asking the other boats questions and then started working a search pattern. A few minutes later she heard the thump thump of a helicopter approaching and knew it was time to go.

Running back, she tempered her speed. As much as she wanted to open up the throttle, she knew it would only attract attention. Deep in thought, she almost missed the first marker for the harbor. Finding only the two pieces of debris was troubling, and she expected that something was not right. Thinking about the old lobster boat, and feeling the power beneath her feet, gave her an idea.

She slowed and pulled out her phone. She could easily outrun the old boat if it was still floating. "Hector?" she yelled into the phone. The engine was too loud to hear, forcing her to slow to an idle, where it was barely audible. "Where would they have gone, if the boat didn't blow?"

"What do you mean? We saw it," he said.

She was not going to debate him. "Tell me," she ordered.

There was silence on the line for a minute and then he answered.

* * *

Trufante yelled over the roar of the engine. "Wait a minute!"

Jeff slowed. They were just past the opening in the middle of the Seven Mile Bridge, several miles from where the bomb exploded. "What?"

"Just thinkin'," Trufante said.

"That's never good."

Trufante ignored the barb. He looked back at the site of the explosion and saw several boats on their way. It looked like two were already in the area. "Look there." He pointed his long arm at a silver flash in the distance. It was moving at twice the speed of the other boats. "I know that boat."

"Not too many hot rods out here," Jeff said.

"Too much of a coincidence. You got binoculars?" Trufante asked.

Jeff shrugged and reached into the compartment below the wheel. "Use them for spotting birds when the dolphins running," he said, handing them to him.

Trufante cleaned the dirty lenses with his shirt and put them to his head. "Damn if that ain't the lady. She's got Manuel's boat."

"What's that to us? We're dead, remember?" Jeff asked.

"You're not getting the gravity of the situation. Just tossing a few life preservers and a couple of pieces of wood ain't gonna satisfy anyone with half a brain," Trufante said. "Especially right after it blew. Another few hours, they would have wrote it off to the seas spreading the debris, but not this soon."

"It was your idea," Jeff said.

Trufante scratched his forehead and ran a hand through his long, stringy hair. "Wasn't expecting the she monster to come looking herself. Coast Guard or sheriff would take it as if the boat sank, but she planted the bomb. She'd know there was not enough damage."

"Well, what do you expect we should do?" Jeff asked, taking the binoculars back and focusing on the site.

"If there was a beer, I'd drink it, but seeing there's not, we gotta get outta here. And another boat's probably a good idea if she's looking for us."

"Got that right. And I can barely put any weight on my leg,"

Jeff said, putting the binoculars back and taking out a bottle. "This might help with the pain, though." He took a deep swig of the amber liquid.

"Maybe that's not a bad idea," Trufante said, taking the bottle from him. "We need to hole up somewhere and figure this out. Maybe we should take a run by Wood's old place."

"Mac don't like me. And Wood's daughter—she won't even look at me," Jeff said, taking the bottle back.

"I heard that. There's a bunch of islands up in there. We just need to hang out there till dark."

Jeff took another swig and spun the wheel toward the bridge. He pushed down the throttle, causing the engine to stutter and blow a cloud of black smoke before it stubbornly accelerated. They passed under the bridge and headed toward the mangrove-covered islands in the distance. Trufante watched both ahead and behind, not trusting Jeff. He barely trusted him sober, now, after he had taken at least a half dozen more swigs from the bottle, he trusted him less.

* * *

Pamela's head stuck over the front seat between Mac and Mel. "I've got a bad feeling about this," she said.

"Me too, but it's not about that," Mel said, moving toward the window and away from her.

The smoke plume was dissipating and Mac automatically looked around for a few landmarks to triangulate the spot. They were sitting in the parking lot by the Pigeon Key Bridge, the last turnoff before committing to a fourteen-mile drive—both directions of the Seven Mile. The apex of the roof of the tiki bar across US 1 lined up nicely, and he looked for a second reference point, but from where they sat, there was just water.

"What do you mean?" he asked Pamela.

"Tru's out there. I just know it," she said with a detectable quiver in her voice.

"And how do you know this?" Mel questioned her.

Mac stayed quiet for a few minutes, hoping the two women would sort this out without him getting involved.

"Those guys that took him from the bar. They work over at the bait place."

Mac turned to her. "You remember them now?" he asked, hoping she had sobered up enough to be some help.

"Well, we were in the bar, and those two guys come in and grab him. He told me to find you, and here I am," she said proudly.

Mac was getting frustrated.

"Do you know who they were?" Mel asked, questioning her like a witness.

"From the bait place. Smell. One's skinny, the other's gordo," she giggled.

"Come on. What else did they say?"

"They didn't. Just marched him out of the bar, leaving me there to pay the bill." She started to cry. "I can feel it. Whatever that was," she looked to the water, "Tru's in trouble."

"It's okay," Mac said, trying to figure out a way to placate her.

He turned to Mel. "Maybe we should run out there if she's so sure."

"The only thing she's sure about is her next drink," Mel said. "You want to go chase around out there, drop me at Rusty's so I can do some real work."

Mac pulled out of the space and into the parking lot. The smoke was gone now, but he thought he knew where the explosion was. It was only a question of how far out. He pulled onto US 1, turning left and headed back to the Rusty Anchor.

They pulled into the lot. "This won't take long. If Hector and Edgar are involved, it might have been him out there," Mac said, getting out of the car and heading to the basin. Mel nodded and walked toward the bar.

Pamela followed him, but was little help once they were aboard. He started the engines and tossed the lines. Within a few minutes they were out of the canal and heading southwest on a course that would put Sombrero Light to their port side. Mac could already see the reflection of several boats hovering around the area. Unless there was a hot dolphin bite, that was the spot. He pushed the boat up on plane and cruised toward the scene, surprised when a small speedboat crossed his path.

"Mac. He was here!" Pamela clung to him when they reached the site. "I know it, but he's alive. He's okay!"

He was about to ask how she knew, but decided to hold that question for when he had a big glass of scotch in front of him, not two sheriffs' boats and a Coast Guard cutter. He steered to deeper water to allow the investigation to continue and picked up the microphone. On channel sixteen he hailed the Coast Guard, asking if he could aid in the search and was interrupted by a voice he didn't want to hear.

"Travis, what are you doing out here?"

It was the deputy. "Just aiding in the search if I can," he answered.

"Maybe you and I ought to have that conversation, sooner rather than later."

Chapter 11

Mac looked across the water at the deputy reluctantly catching the line he tossed over. He set two fenders over the gunwales to protect the hulls and secured the boats together.

"What about Tru?" Pamela asked. *"You don't need a weatherman to know which way the wind blows."*

"Hopefully, this will just take a minute," Mac said. "Stay here." The last thing he needed was her quoting Dylan lyrics to the deputy. Giving her the best reassuring look he had in his arsenal, which wasn't worth much, he straddled the gunwales and climbed onto the sheriff's boat.

"Okay, Travis," the deputy started, pulling his notepad and a pen from the myriad of pockets woven into his pants. "You seem to be in all the wrong places these days. Want to explain?" He waited, poised to take notes.

Mac removed his cap and rubbed his head. "It's a small town."

"You're going to have to do better than that. First the floater in the backcountry, and now showing up, minutes after an explosion, out here. And wasn't it you and your buddy Trufante that I saw the other day with those buoys? Suspicious activity, if you ask me."

Mac thought for a minute before answering. The deputy was tying things together faster than he would have liked. "You're just all over, aren't you? Sheriff's office must be running thin to have you working so hard," Mac said, trying to buy some time.

He didn't take the bait. "Too may coincidences, Travis. Maybe I ought to take you in for questioning."

"No need for that." Mac needed to give him some reassurance. "You know I'm on the water about every day and Trufante works as my mate. The other day, we were checking on some stuff after the storm. Every fisherman does that. The body, I don't know. I run that course a couple times a week between Wood's place and town. It was just there."

"Gonna be harder to explain being out here with her," he said.

"She found me at the Anchor, all worked up and worried about Trufante being out here. He was supposed to be fishing the reef today and she saw the explosion. Kind of freaked her out. The only way I could calm her down was to run her out here."

"He's out there," Pamela called out, pointing toward the Seven Mile Bridge. "*There must be some kind a way outta here*, Mac Travis, *said the joker to the thief*," she said, loud enough to be heard on the other boat.

"She's not all there, is she?" the deputy whispered sympathetically.

Mac just nodded, confirming his look. The police radio clipped to his belt went off. He listened to the dispatcher and spoke softly into the microphone clipped to his lapel. "Well, Travis, good luck with that one," he said. "Got a stolen boat to find. Guess I can at least eliminate you from that one," he said, putting the notebook and pen back in his pockets.

"So, we're good?" Mac asked.

"Good for now, anyway. I know where to find you if I need you."

Mac wasn't going to stick around for him to change his mind. He climbed over the gunwales to the trawler and within seconds had the lines off and was floating freely. Back in the wheelhouse, he started the engine and idled away. "Well, where to?"

* * *

Trufante was getting worried about Jeff's condition. "Maybe you ought to let me take her," he yelled over the sound of the engine. They were through the main span of the Seven Mile Bridge moving toward the backcountry, an area riddled with hidden obstacles.

"Why not," he said. "Give me some more time to drink."

Jeff moved away from the helm a second before Trufante was ready to take it. The boat fishtailed on a wave, causing Trufante to lose his balance and sending Jeff crashing into the gunwale. Trufante grabbed for the wheel and quickly had the boat under control. It was Jeff he was worried about now. Looking back to check if anyone, especially that speedboat, was after them, he saw Jeff slide across the deck and grab the bottle. He leaned against the gunwale and took another swig, finishing what was left before tossing it overboard.

Trufante watched the bottle hit the water and looked up. A

flash had caught his eye. The reflection of the sun on a windshield. Reaching into the compartment below the wheel, he removed the binoculars. The wave action made it difficult to focus and he had to slow down to get a better look. Putting aside the glasses, he cursed in Creole under his breath—it was Manuel's hot rod.

His only hope was that if the woman didn't know these waters, the coral heads and shoals could be an equalizing factor between the two boats. Several small islands were ahead, but steering directly toward the shallow water surrounding them would be too obvious. He needed a hidden obstacle. Steering straight ahead, he tried to calculate how long it would take the speedboat to reach them. It would be close, and that could be to his advantage.

"What are you doing?" Jeff staggered toward him. "That's Elbow Bank your runnin' at."

"Yeah, and our girlfriend is right behind us," Trufante said, cutting the wheel slightly. He had to rely on the speed of the boat chasing them, hoping the woman would blindly follow, not thinking about anything except catching them. "Watch this action."

He skirted the hidden obstacle and looked behind to place the shoal directly between the two boats. She followed and he unleashed his thousand-dollar grin, but it was premature. Bullets flew past his head, causing him to duck and inadvertently spin the wheel. Staying low to avoid the gunfire, he tried to correct course. It was too late; they were both past the bank and she was gaining on them.

Given another few miles, he could have lost her in the maze of islands spread out in front of them. He looked down at the chart plotter, thankfully something that Jeff had spent money on. The GPS device overlaid the boat's position on a nautical chart, a critical instrument for fishermen. They were running through the channel between Horseshoe and West Bahia Honda Key. Wood's Island had just become visible on the horizon. Looking back, he saw her, only a hundred yards behind now and gaining. His only chance to avoid her was to steer wide of the shoals guarding the entrance to Spanish Channel, making it look like he was circling back and hope that she cut the corner.

He cut the wheel hard to port, spinning the boat almost a hundred and eighty degrees. Trusting the electronics more than his memory, he stared at the chart plotter and depth finder, staying to four feet of water as he rounded the bend and entered the channel. Turning back again, he watched her, his grin showing every bit of the Cadillac grill he was famous for. She took the bait, steering too close to the shallows. Even above the engine noise of the lobster boat, he heard the speedboat's lower unit ground, spouting a huge stream of water into the air as the angle of the propeller shifted skyward.

"Got her!" Jeff slammed him on the back.

Trufante was not as confident as he slowed and looked back at her. The two boats were close enough that he could see her glare at him, one hand holding her phone to her ear, the other pointing the gun at them. He could see her close one eye and the flash of the barrel as a burst of gunfire tore apart the space his head had just occupied. Shards of fiberglass rained down on him.

Grabbing the wheel, he pulled himself level with the gunwales and heard the gun fire again. Another round of bullets struck around him. From this position, able to see over the windshield, he pushed down the throttle. The boat accelerated and he nudged the wheel to avoid a large brown spot ahead. The chart plotter was too high to see from here—he would have to rely on his memory and the old mariners rhyme: *"Brown, brown, run aground. White, white, and you might. Green, green, nice and clean. Blue, blue, sail on through."* Slowly he cut the wheel and watched the water color ahead. A little farther and they would be out of range.

Finally he felt secure enough to stand and look back. The speedboat was visible in the distance, but there was a mile between them now. Wood's Island was dead ahead, and he smiled seeing the trawler was gone. The only problem was they were directly in her line of sight.

Jeff slammed him on the back. "We made it!"

"Not so fast. She can still see us. Gonna have to go around to the back side," Trufante said.

"Whatever, man. Mac keep any beer out there?"

"We need to get out of here as quick as a snapper goes for a shrimp. I seen her on the phone. I'd be expecting those two nimrods anytime. Just hope they don't bring Manuel into this." He passed the small channel leading to the lone pile with the center-console drifting from a line looped around it, and he cut the wheel to avoid the flats ahead. Steering a wide circle, he rounded the northern side of the island, wondering what their next step was. Ditching Jeff and taking the center-console might solve his problems. Mac would understand, and it seemed like the only way out until he rounded the point and saw the boat anchored off the beach.

Slowly he idled the lobster boat over the white sand flats. When he felt the first tug of the bottom on the bow, he stopped before the propeller hit. The old twenty-foot boat had an inboard diesel engine, setting the propeller higher than the bow. "Wait here and sleep it off," he said to Jeff, who was already snoozing in the shade of the overhang.

He slid over the gunwale, unable to gauge the depth of the gin-clear water. Hip deep, he waded toward the empty boat, scanning the shore for any sign of its occupants. Nothing moved except a pair of bonefish he spooked. Using the anchor line, he pulled himself toward the boat and was surprised when he reached it to see the PVC pipe. Curious now, he climbed the dive ladder and went to the cockpit. Shaking his head, he saw water pooled in the bottom of the gauges and wondered what was up. The question was, could he make it run.

The key was still in the ignition. He turned it and pressed the start buttons for each engine. Not expecting anything, he was surprised to hear the motors turn over, but they did not start. This was interesting, he thought, and went to the transom, where he removed the cowling from the port engine. It had definitely been underwater. Under normal circumstances, the oil should be drained and replaced from both the lower unit and engine itself, then the fuel lines would be purged of water, but he heard the throaty roar of the speedboat and knew these were not normal times.

Pulling the fuel line from the engine, he depressed the ball and tasted the gas. It appeared good and he reconnected the line. A few squeezes and the ball tightened, indicating the line was primed, and he went to the helm. With his fingers crossed he pressed the start button for the port engine and held his breath as it turned over. The starter ground against the flywheel and finally the engine sputtered to life. He left it running hoping it would even out while he replaced the cowling and removed the line from the PVC pipe. Back at the helm, he pushed the throttle forward, retrieved the anchor, and idled to Jeff's boat.

"Come on, dude," he yelled to Jeff. "Wake your ass up before the she-devil finds us."

Jeff's head rose over the gunwale and he suddenly came to life. "What the fuck?" He stared at the boat.

"Hop in. We can hightail it outta here in this," Trufante said.

Jeff climbed over the gunwale, looking back at the fish rotting in the white bins. "We should take this and sell it," he said, starting back to the lobster boat.

"Screw that. It's rotten. Even Billy Bones ain't buying that shit," Trufante said, pushing down on the throttle and sending Jeff reeling backward toward the transom. He crashed against the gunwale and collapsed on the deck.

The longer the engine ran, the more it evened out. He left the wheel for a second and kicked Jeff. "Get up, dude. You gotta drive."

Finally Jeff rose and went to the wheel.

"Ain't got no electronics, just the compass. I'm going to work on the starboard engine," Trufante said, setting one leg over the transom into the motor well.

"Where are we going?" Jeff asked.

"Key West, dude—where else?"

Chapter 12

Mel leaned back in the chair and rubbed her eyes.

"Still alive?" Rusty asked from across the bar.

She got up to stretch and looked around. The previously deserted bar was now close to full. She went toward him. "Do you know anything about Big Sugar?"

"Just enough to enjoy a little in my coffee," he laughed. "And enough to know it's dirty politics in this state."

What she had just found out amazed her. "How come no one outside of Florida knows about this?" All those years working federal cases and living in Virginia and she had never heard of the travesty that a handful of companies were committing to the Everglades.

"Everglades have been buggered up since Ponce de Leon first laid eyes on them," Rusty said.

"Those fish Mac had are just the tip of a big iceberg. I'm surprised there has been no other fallout here." From what she had read, Fort Myers had been especially hard hit, and that was only a couple of hours away. The sugar industry had caused a multitude of problems, and it had been going on far longer than most people thought.

Rusty walked away to serve someone, then came back over, handed her a soda water and looked over her shoulder at the screen.

Mel recited from her notes. "Back in the 1920s, the first diversion ditches were dug to create more agricultural land for the sugar companies. After the 1928 hurricane flooded low-lying settlements along Lake Okeechobee, the Army Corp of Engineers came in and started shoring up the south shore. The Herbert Hoover Dike was begun and the earthen berm continued to rise, blocking not only the flooding, but also the natural drainage from the Kissimmee Basin and the lake through the Everglades and into Florida Bay.

"In the thirties, developers turned their sights on southeast Florida. Seeking more land from Palm Beach to Miami, they looked west to the Everglades. Canals were dug and huge swaths of the ecosystem were lost forever. Now the whole shooting match is controlled by bureaucrats."

"Big Sugar and real estate tycoons." Rusty shook his head. "That's the history of Florida right there." He went to help a couple that had just come in.

"Don't forget the South Florida Water Management District," a woman at the next table said.

Mel looked over at her. It was the marine biologist from the Turtle Hospital. "Jen, right?" she asked.

"A whole bunch of us are part of Friends of the Everglades. Check out the website." She slid her chair over and reached for the keyboard.

Mel watched as the site appeared, and she started reading.

"Those fish that you guys brought in today, where did you get them?" Jen asked.

"Mac found them out in the Gulf." She looked at the younger woman, wondering how much she could trust her. Deciding they at least shared a common concern for the environment, she leaned in so no one could overhear. "Out by Sprigger Bank." She started pecking on the keyboard, opened the spreadsheet from the dead man's phone and slid the computer back to Jen.

Jen looked at the numbers, scrolling back and forth. "Fish kills. The supermoon and that storm must have pushed the edge of the red tide down. Where'd you get this?"

Mel hesitated. She liked the young woman, but hadn't known her long enough to trust her. "The Internet. I've been through so many sites, I'm not sure which one." At least that much was true.

"Hey, any chance of getting a water sample where he found the fish?" Jen asked.

Mel felt alive with a cause now. "Sure," she said, wondering where Mac was.

* * *

Mac stared at the catatonic woman sitting next to him in the wheelhouse. Pamela had gone into a trance, trying to channel her inner Trufante. He looked out at the water and wondered whether he should dump her off and head back to the Anchor. Mel would be wondering where he was by now, and bringing Pamela with him was a recipe for trouble. But he agreed with her that Trufante was involved in the explosion and he felt like he had an obligation to his friend.

She interrupted his inner turmoil.

"New boat," she said.

Great, Mac thought. She was as whacked-out as her mentor. Cheqea and he had known each other since his first days here in the early nineties. Trufante had mentioned that Pamela had been hanging out with the old chief. Whether the Indian actually had any powers or got her followers so stoned on her mixture of fermented seaweed and homegrown weed that they thought she did, he had no idea. But Pamela had obviously bought in. "What about a new boat?"

"Shush, I'm getting something."

He gripped the throttle, wanting to start up, but in her present state he was wary of her going over the edge. "Listen, we should go back and get Mel."

She ignored him and started rocking back and forth. Mac started the engine, not caring now. The sooner he got her off the boat, the better. He spun the wheel and pushed down the throttle, steering a heading toward the Rusty Anchor.

"Where are we going, Mac Travis?" she asked, snapping out of her trance.

"Back to Mel. She's at the Anchor. We'll figure out what to do about Tru when we get there." Mac pushed down the throttle to preempt any further conversation. They pulled into the canal several minutes later and docked in the vacant spot they had left. "Maybe you should wait here. See if you can channel him again, or whatever it is you got going," Mac said.

"True that, Mac Travis. *You go your way and I'll go mine.*"

Mac hoped that would indeed be the case, but suspected she was not going anywhere. From the time he had met her, he had been suspect. The woman was an enigma: a hippy with a credit card, and that usually meant trust fund. The type of person he had no time for. He tied off the lines, adding an extra spring line astern, as Rusty had advised, and walked toward the bar.

It was busier now as the locals were getting off work. Mel sat in the corner at a table, talking to another woman whom he recognized as the marine biologist from the turtle place. As he got closer, he saw the look on Mel's face and knew he was in trouble. Dodging the mystic on the boat and the advocate sitting in front of him, he moved to the bar.

"Looks like you could use a cold one," Rusty said, sliding a beer down toward Mac.

"Women with a cause," Mac lamented, taking a sip.

* * *

Jane slammed her hands on the wheel and tried the throttle one more time, even though she knew she was only digging the boat in deeper. She had no idea the water was this shallow this far out. At least around Miami, everything was properly marked. It was not her lack of knowledge that upset her, but rather that those two idiots had outwitted her twice now—in one afternoon.

She shut off the engine and called Hector, who said he would be out in twenty minutes. After yelling at him to make it ten and leave his brother behind, she sat down and planned her next move. Coming down here might have been a mistake. It was not her element, and it showed. The only way out was to erase any evidence that she had been here.

Her phone rang, bringing her back from her tantrum, and she looked at the screen. It showed Philip's name. Taking a deep breath, she tried to collect herself and answered. He was not the kind of man you sent to voicemail.

"Yes," she answered.

"Have you seen the news?" he asked.

"No. I've been a little busy putting things in order here."

"There was a report about a dead body found floating near Marathon yesterday. All the networks are picking it up. They made an ID, and it's the scientist," he said calmly.

Despite his apparent demeanor, she knew he was angry. "I'll handle it." She looked back at Marathon, wondering where Hector was.

"Just remember we are under a deadline. The congressman will be here this weekend for the rally. Everything needs to be in order by then."

The line went dead and she stared at the phone. This kind of conversation was typical for him, nothing to worry about on that account. But with the spectacle he was about to unleash, there was no room for error. Although business rivals, the major players in sugar allied in their fight for survival. Often one group would support

Democrats and the other Republicans just to further rig the game and have everyone in their pockets. It had worked. Even public initiatives like the land buyback, where the state was empowered by the voters to purchase agricultural lands, allowing them to become overgrown, mosquito-infested swamps again, were squashed by the political clout of the alliance.

The environmental groups wanted the natural water flow restored, and he would be happy to accommodate them. They didn't like the way Alligator Alley and Highway 41 cut across the state blocking the historical flow. Well, he could fix that too, but not in the multiyear, billion-dollar plans they had that would take away his land and penalize him financially. He was going to do it the easy way.

It was a win-win. Give the activists what they wanted and claim more land for sugar.

The sound of an outboard distracted her from her thoughts and she looked toward the bridge. A jet ski was heading in her direction, and she thought about picking the gnat off the water with one of the few remaining bullets she had left when she saw it was Hector. A minute later, he pulled next to the grounded boat.

"Give you a hand?" he asked.

"You can cut that smug bullshit right now," she said, thankful that he had left his obnoxious brother back at the bait house. "Couldn't you find anything bigger?"

"Manuel is in a rage. If it weren't for claiming your car as collateral, he'd be out here himself. As it is, I had to run across the street and rent this."

At least he had a little ingenuity. "Well, what now?"

"It's no big deal. The tide is coming up. I'll pull you off." He slid the jet ski onto the sandbar and lifted the seat. Removing a tow rope used to pull water skiers, he hooked one end on the bow cleat of the hot rod and the other end to the jet ski. "Which end do you want?"

The jet ski scared her. Preferring the power and comfort of bigger, more luxurious vessels, she had never been on one; her only experience with the craft was their obnoxious sound ruining the solitude of her retreats. She climbed over the low gunwale of the hot rod and went to the helm.

Hector came behind the boat and pushed against the transom— the boat didn't budge.

She would have shot him then if she didn't need him, but she needed to get the two fishermen. They were going to pay for this. Her attention turned back to the jet ski. Hector started the engine and moved forward, slowly taking the slack out of the line. As it tightened he increased speed and, with a snap, the rope was taut. He gunned the engine, sending a plume of water back.

"Goddamn bastard," she yelled over the roar of the jet ski's engine straining against the larger craft. "You and all those other sorry fuckers will pay for this." Water continued to rain down on her as Hector continued to try and pull the boat off.

She was about to throttle him but stopped herself and breathed deeply—in for four counts, hold for two, out for four, and another hold. Box breathing, one of her gurus had told her. It worked, and she felt her blood pressure drop below the red line. Whatever it took, she needed him to navigate these waters and find the fishermen. A flash from the windshield of a passing boat caught her eye. It was too far away to see much detail, but she could clearly see the smile of the driver.

Soaking wet, she climbed out of the grounded hot rod and motioned for Hector. He circled back, a wary look in his eyes, which she disarmed with a fake smile. "Can that thing take both of us?"

Without waiting for an answer, she climbed on the back. Pulling the gun from her designer bag, she shoved it in the front of her shorts, gunslinger style, and pushed the bag over her shoulder. Fortunately, she had dressed for the Keys and not South Beach.

Chapter 13

Trufante struggled with the starboard engine while the boat plowed through the water. Rigged for twin engines, it was not designed to run on one, making it impossible to get up on plane.

"Why we goin' this way? Back way's faster," Jeff said. "We gotta pass right by her again to get under the bridge."

"Got no electronics. You want to find that backdoor passage without eyes?" Trufante went back to work. It was indescribably harder to work on a boat while underway, and the engine was giving him trouble.

"Right. See your point there."

Trufante turned his attention back to the engine, wishing he had a beer to remove the taste of fuel in his mouth from clearing the line.

"Try her now," he yelled.

The flywheel spun, but the motor would not catch.

"Hey. Some fool with a jet ski is trying to pull your ladyfriend off the sandbar."

Trufante lifted his head up just in time to see the plume of water drench the woman at the wheel of the speedboat. He stopped for a minute and went to the helm. Both men watched the show as the jet ski tried to pull the other boat off the sandbar. "She's gonna be pissed now," Trufante said, exposing his big grin.

He went back to the engine. Disconnecting the fuel line, he put his index finger over the opening to stop the flow. Instead of feeling gas pushing through the line he felt a suction. The other engine had created a vacuum. They would have to stop to start both engines. After replacing the line and cowling, he returned to the helm.

"We're gonna have to stop," he said, looking back at the action on the flats. The speedboat was still there with a jet ski alongside it, and he could see the woman yelling at a man that looked like Hector. She climbed on behind him. The jet ski took off toward Marathon, made a tight turn and then headed directly for them. The gap was closing quickly.

"Holy crap. They're coming after us," Jeff said, ducking as a bullet grazed the fiberglass ceiling above him.

Trufante had to act fast. There was no way they could stop and prime the fuel line to get the other engine running. Without it, the jet ski would easily overtake them. Another bullet flew past, but he ignored it, trying to figure a way out. Jeff was heading for the bridge and he looked back. They would be on them in minutes.

"We can ditch them round the back of Molasses Key," Jeff said.

Trufante shook his head, looking back at the jet ski approaching them. It was skipping off the waves, fishtailing when it lost control. He had some experience with the craft from a gig he had taken at a tourist rental in Key West during a slow fishing season.

Working as a helper on a parasail boat hadn't been his thing, but he had been around jet skis and tried to remember their quirks.

Brake and steer, he remembered the two things the personal watercraft couldn't do. There was no reverse, no rudder or propeller in the water to slow the forward progress; they stopped when they ran out of inertia. And without power there was no way to steer.

"We've got to let them catch up," Trufante said, trying to visualize his idea. "Let 'em come alongside."

"And what about the gun?" Jeff asked.

"She's gonna shoot at our sorry asses one way or another. I'm hoping if we look like we're giving up—" Another round of gunfire slammed into the boat, sending both men to the deck.

"She stopped shooting," Trufante said, rising above the gunwale and looking back at the jet ski.

"But we're hit," Jeff said, pointing back to the fuel line spurting gas onto the deck. "We gotta get back."

The engine was starting to miss now, probably from air entering the fuel line. "Can you make Pigeon Key?"

Jeff turned the wheel and headed toward the small island at the end of the old span of the bridge. The boat sputtered again and Trufante looked back at the jet ski. They had turned to follow. The island was getting closer. The small key, situated two miles from Marathon and still connected by a section of the old Seven Mile Bridge, was still inhabited. He'd met a few of the college-age students in a bar talking about some kind of research they were doing there.

"See the dock?" he yelled at Jeff, pointing to the small pier sticking out into the Gulf side.

"What about her?" he asked, looking back at the jet ski.

"We'll just have to take out chances."

The engine sputtered again. It was getting worse and sounded like it was about to stall. Trufante ran back to the transom and pumped the primer ball. Gas squirted over the deck from a nick in the line. One of the bullets must have grazed it. Placing his free hand over the gash, he squeezed the ball and felt the rpms rise. The jet ski was still following, but cautiously. Something had spooked the woman, or she was out of ammunition.

* * *

Jane yelled over the whine of the jet ski, "Can you keep this thing straight?" She hit the release and the empty magazine dropped. He hit another wave and she dropped it into the water. With one arm still tight around Hector, she slung her purse in front of her, fished out another magazine, and tried to slam it into the receiver. The jet ski bounced again, spinning to the side when it lost contact with the water and she almost lost her grip on the gun. "I have to reload. Can you help me out here?" she screamed.

She felt him ease off the throttle slightly, and, instead of careening off the tops of the waves, the reduced speed allowed them to ride them. She saw the island ahead. "Run them into it," she said, pointing over Hector's shoulder. She took a deep breath, willed the magazine into the gun, and when it clicked into place, pulled back the slide to chamber a round.

Hector started to make his move to the outside. She took aim and fired twice. Both shots struck the boat, and she saw the driver and the tall Cajun duck. But they held their course. "Get closer," she yelled to Hector, firing again. She was being conservative with her shots, not wanting to have to reload on the water again. Looking around, she saw another problem and slid the gun back into her shorts. The bridge traffic had come to a crawl, and she could see the passengers watching them. Now she had to worry about eyewitnesses calling the police.

"What should I do?" Hector called back to her.

She was getting angrier by the second. Losing to two rednecks was not in her DNA. "You know where those two live?" she asked. Putting her ego away was hard, but she needed to get a handle on the big picture. Going to jail for shooting two rednecks would ruin Dusharde's plan. There were other ways of handling this. She would just have to forsake the gratification of doing it herself.

"Yeah."

She was about to order Hector back to land when she saw the boat turn toward them.

* * *

Mac resigned himself to deal with the three women. Fortunately, Pamela was still in a trance. He looked over at her body jerking every few seconds, like someone was shooting at her. Mel and Jen boarded the boat and he released the lines. The trawler moved slowly out of the canal and he turned left toward Vaca Cut, the closer pass to the Gulf side, hoping to reach the site before it got dark.

"What's with her?" Mel asked.

"Been hanging out with Cheqea. Tru told me she was all into that Indian mystic crap."

Mel looked at her and shook her head. "How are you going to find the spot?"

"Do you still have the SD card from the wreck's GPS?" Mac asked.

She dug around in her bag and handed it to him. Key Colony Beach was just ahead now, and he turned into the channel. The pass was narrow but well marked. They skirted the charter dock on their port side, went under a small bridge and were looking at the open water of the Gulf. Mac pushed the throttles down and fumbled with the memory card, finally getting it in the slot of his GPS.

Navigating from screen to screen, he loaded the data from the card onto the unit and watched as it plotted the waypoints on the chart. In addition to the points, he clicked the button marked *Tracks* and dotted lines appeared, showing the path the boat had followed.

"That looks like the area," Mac said, pointing to a waypoint.

"It's the furthest west. Maybe that means something," Mel said.

Jen leaned in and looked at the screen. "It means the contaminated area is getting closer. I bet if we go into the log and compare the waypoints with the dates they were entered there will be a pattern."

Mac hit *GoTo* and adjusted his course to the bearing from the GPS. Once the boat settled onto the new heading, he studied the tracks. Most were in-and-out shots from the same point in Islamorada. "That's a long way for from here."

"It's clearly moving fast toward Marathon. I need to get water samples and then somewhere to run the data on the waypoints and see if we can figure out how much time we have. The filters at the hospital can't deal with this kind of algae bloom. There are twenty turtles in our tanks now. They could all die."

She was working herself into a panic. "Calm down. We'll get the samples and get the data run. This was brought down by the king tide and storm. The ocean has its own magic and usually heals itself," Mac said.

"But. The turtles . . ."

"Mac, she might be right," Mel said, coming out of the cabin. She had her laptop under her arm and a chart in her hand. "I pulled the dates and waypoints from the data and plotted them on the chart." She spread the chart out on the seat. "It's moving by itself. The tide might have pushed it faster, but it was moving at about three miles a day on its own."

Mac did the math in his head, realizing that if she was right it would only be three days before it reached Wood's Island and one more for the Turtle Hospital. "I wonder why there haven't been any reports?"

Mel knew firsthand how tight-lipped the locals could be. "You know the guys that fish this far out on the back side. They're not going to do anything to bring in the authorities."

He knew the feeling the residents had about the myriad of agencies that had flooded the area, all trying to protect it. What they did was cost jobs and step on each other's feet. It took a lifetime of experience—not a classroom—to even begin to understand the ecosystem here. There were too many variables controlling the unique ecosystem where the Atlantic and Gulf of Mexico were separated by the thin strip of coral atolls. The massive Gulf Stream current, running just offshore, only added to the complexity.

"If it's moving by itself, it has to be coming from somewhere. If we can find the source, we can fix it."

"If it were only that simple. She's right, though. This should be modeled. We need to add in the major and minor currents as well as the tides and weather for the days between the waypoints."

"Alicia," they both said at the same time.

"I like her," Pamela said, coming back to life.

"Who?" Jen asked, ignoring the outburst.

"Alicia Phon, *she's so fine. She's so fine she blow my mind.*" Pamela started humming again.

"She's an ex-CIA analyst. Lives with a friend of Tru's in Key Largo named TJ," Mel started.

"Woman's a computer genius," Mac said and accelerated.

Chapter 14

Trufante looked around for a way out. Gas poured through his fingers still gripping the shredded line, but it was a no-win situation. When Jeff accelerated, the suction created by the fuel injectors pulled air into the line, causing the engine to sputter. If he released pressure, Trufante could control the flow, but the jet ski would easily catch them. The end result was the boat acted like it was out of gas, surging, then slowing to almost a stall. A wave caught Trufante, throwing him off balance. Gas spurted from the line and he looked down at his two hands, each holding a piece of the line.

"Turn it off quick," he yelled to Jeff. They were underneath the new span of the Seven Mile Bridge, only a few hundred feet from Pigeon Key. "I got gas all over. She fires at us again, we're gonna blow."

The engine surged again, and Trufante knew it was for the last time. They needed to get off the boat. Behind them, the jet ski seemed to sense their predicament and accelerated, quickly closing the gap. "Get ready to bail!" Trufante yelled. His long frame was coiled up like a cat, ready to fly over the gunwales. It'd been a long time since he'd run, but back in the day, he used to be fast, and he wondered if he could make the two-mile sprint across the old bridge to Marathon. If he could get off the bridge, he would be able to blend in somewhere.

He heard a woman scream and looked ahead at the crowd gathered around the concrete walled perimeter of the old saltwater pool. Fifty feet from land, the engine finally died and he wasted no time. Springing from the gunwale, he was in the water in seconds, stroking for the concrete seawall, separating the old pool from the ocean. Originally built in the fifties as a tourist attraction, the pool had fallen into disrepair and had been used as a small harbor for years. Recently, money had been raised by the Pigeon Key Foundation, and the pool had been repaired.

Without looking back, he stroked for the concrete wall, deciding that Jeff was on his own. A small group of tourists stood on a newly built dock, staring into the water. He heard the roar of the jet ski, but there was nothing he could do except claw at the water in an attempt to get away. The tourists scattered as he reached the wall and tried to haul himself over. He grabbed the new wood and pulled, using his feet to propel himself from the water. A girl shrieked and he smiled, trying to reassure her, but she ran to her parents with a frightened look on her face.

Behind him he heard the jet ski and looked back. Straddling the concrete seawall with one foot in the ocean and the other in the pool, he saw them. The tourists were gone now, and he could see why. The jet ski was out of control, in the air and flying toward him like a missile. The looks of terror on the faces of Hector and the woman froze in his mind. Jeff was trying to get out of the water, but it was too late. Once the watercraft was out of the water there was no way to control it. The only way to stop was naturally as the inertia died, or by hitting something, and Jeff was directly in its path.

Diving into the pool, Trufante took one last look and saw the nose of the jet ski hit Jeff in the back. His weight did nothing to slow the craft. In slow motion, it careened over the pool, and, with Jeff's body cushioning the blow, was stopped by the base of a tree. Treading water, he looked for a way to escape unnoticed when something brushed against his leg. Again, he had to leave Jeff to his own devices.

The rough skin tore at his thigh and he looked down at the six-foot bonnethead shark swimming between his legs. Without a thought about Jeff, Hector or the woman, he pulled himself from the pool and collapsed on the dock. Sharks were worse than guns, in his opinion, and he released his breath after the life-threatening experience, only to look up and see the barrel of a pistol pointed at his head.

"Look, the big man's afraid of the silly shark," he heard a young girl yell from across the pool. Her father pulled her quickly out of sight before he could rebut the comment. There was no such thing as a silly shark.

"Idiot," the woman yelled. "Go, find us a way off this island. And not in a boat," she ordered Hector and turned to Trufante. "You and your friend have caused enough trouble. Let's go." She motioned the barrel toward a steep curving ramp that led to the old section of the Seven Mile Bridge.

He started up the old exit ramp and reached the bridge, looking back at Jeff. Surrounded by a group of people, he couldn't tell if he was dead or alive, but expected the latter. Drunks bounce—they don't break. Facing ahead now he saw the stream of tourists walking to and from Marathon to the key. Trufante looked around for any way out. The water, fifty feet below, might look clear and inviting, but he knew the currents running through the bridge piers could kill him as easily as the gun pointed at his back. At least he had avoided the shark. The honk of a horn brought him back to reality, and he looked back to see Hector driving a golf cart toward them.

"How's this?" he asked.

The woman gave him a shut-up look and pushed Trufante into the back seat. She slid in next to him and Hector pressed the gas pedal. The cart gained speed, slowly covering the two-mile stretch of old pavement.

* * *

Mac had the trawler running at twelve knots. With its bow easily cutting through the small windblown waves, Sprigger Bank would be a two-hour trip. Once they were through Vaca Cut and in open water, he set the autopilot and sat back in the captain's chair. Mel and Jen were below, working on the dead man's phone, and Pamela sat across from him, mindlessly watching the water ahead, with a deep frown etched in her face. He thought about trying to talk to her, but after the past few hours of her company, he doubted he'd get a coherent answer. With both stone crab and lobster season closed, the run was easier without having to watch for the trap buoys, though he would have to pay attention for several shoals.

He let his mind drift to try and solve the mystery of the fish and the dead man while he watched the water. Back in the day, he and Wood had prospected the waters around Sprigger Bank. The fishing was good, but the lobster and crab were only mediocre, owing to the unbroken plains of seagrass in the area. The bank was a long run and because it lay just outside of the Everglades National Park boundary there were often Fish and Game officers in the area—not a good mix for commercial fishermen.

There were often research boats there as well, and he remembered what had been eluding him. He pulled out his cell phone. There were still three bars of service, and he scrolled through his contacts. Alicia's name came up and he started pecking into the small keyboard, something he was only fair at on land, but in the choppy waters he quickly became frustrated and hit the phone icon.

She answered and they chatted for a minute, but he quickly got to the point before the reception faded.

"Can you pull up anything you can find on Springer Bank?" he asked.

"Sure, what are you looking for?"

"Might be NOAA or maybe another of the alphabet agencies—something scientific," he said.

Mel must have heard him and came to his side with a questioning look on her face. He mouthed Alicia and put her on speakerphone. "National Science Agency," Mel said, handing him a slip of paper with coordinates written on it.

"Try this. Latitude 24.91 293492; Longitude 80.93 798347," he recited.

"Got it. Give me a minute," Alicia said. A few minutes later she was back on the line. He set the phone on the armrest so Mel and Jen could hear. "It's an FCE LTER site."

"A what?" Mel asked.

"Florida Coastal Everglades Long Term Ecological Research. TS/Ph11."

"PH what?" Mel asked.

Jen interrupted. "I read about this. It's the last water-testing station for the Taylor Slough drainage."

They looked blankly at her.

"There are two natural runoffs from the Everglades: Shark River, which is larger and exits the mainland around Ten Thousand Islands below Fort Myers, and Taylor Slough, which runs toward the east and empties into Florida Bay."

"So the contaminated fish has something to do with runoff from the Everglades," Mel said.

"It would appear so. If we can get the data from the station, we might be able to figure out what happened," Jen said.

"I can tell you what happened," Mac started. "The storm and tides brought agricultural chemicals all the way down here. They've been fighting this battle around Fort Myers and Port St. Lucie on the East Coast for years. That's where they have been pumping the floodwaters. Now, there is pressure to restore the natural flow, and here's the result."

"Give me a few minutes and I can get the data," Alicia interrupted.

"Thanks," Mel said and hung up.

"I still want to see the site. Data or not, there's nothing like hands-on, and I'm betting that station has something to do with the dead man," Mac said, turning the autopilot off and taking control of the boat. He checked the GPS and corrected course to avoid a small shoal directly in their path.

Mel and Jen went below. A minute later, Mel returned with the open laptop in her hands. "Look at this. I bet if we follow the trail of testing stations, we can find the source."

Mac had to shield his eyes from the setting sun to see the screen. Icons littered the display, but he was quickly able to sort them out and follow the trail of Taylor Slough stations. Number eleven, the one at Sprigger Bank, was the last in the string. Two more followed the coastline of the Keys, then they became more concentrated on the mainland. The path of test stations skirted the edge of the Everglades running adjacent to Homestead.

"So, just connect the dots and find the bad guys," Mac said.

"You're not thinking about doing this yourself?" Mel asked.

"You trust anyone else out there?"

She paused for a minute. "There's a few advocacy groups trying to stop Big Sugar and restore the Everglades. I can make some calls."

"And while you're doing that, I'll just take a cruise and see where this leads." He looked up and peered into the glare of the sun on the water. "That's the marker right up there," he said, pointing at a crooked pole in the distance.

"What do you expect to find?" Mel asked.

"Never know until you get there. I've seen a few of these sites over the years. Just a big grid on the bottom," he said, slowing to an idle and steering wide around the marker. Around them the sea was a darker brown, indicating shallow water.

"Any idea where the site is?" Mac asked Jen.

"Never been out here, but the GPS points extended to six places are usually dead-on."

Mac looked at the chart plotter. The waypoint was in the middle of the bank, too shallow for the four-foot draft of the trawler to attempt. "I'm going to anchor and have a look." He coasted up to the mudflat in front of the boat and dropped the anchor, then backed down to set it. Once he was sure it was buried in the mud, he watched the waves and the drift of the boat to make sure they wouldn't be pushed onto the flats. Satisfied, he went below and came back a few minutes later with a mask and fins.

"I'll just be a few," he said. Sitting on the dive platform off the transom, he spit in the mask, rinsed it with seawater and put it over his head. The fins were longer than normal, used for free diving, and he put them to the side, deciding against them. There was nothing to be gained by the added propulsion. The larger fins would only stir up the silt, and the bottom could easily damage the carbon tips. And in four feet of water, he could walk.

With the mask in place, he nodded to Mel and Jen and slid into the water.

Recalling their position in relation to the icon on the chart plotter, he swam toward the area. The GPS was accurate to thirty feet, but he could only see about ten feet around him. Slowly he scanned the bottom while he swam toward the invisible mark. The seagrass was still in the slack current, and he could see small mangrove snapper darting around him. Ahead, the bottom dipped to eight feet and he saw something man-made. He grabbed a quick breath and submerged to check it out. The white tape pinned to the seafloor clearly marked the border of the test area. He surfaced directly above it and took another breath. Something had not looked right.

He breathed up, enriching his lungs with oxygen, and descended. Running his hands along the bottom, he could see the area had been disturbed. It had the familiar look of bottom that had been dredged.

Chapter 15

Jane sat back as Hector pegged the accelerator, honking the horn at anyone in their way. The golf cart reached maximum speed, which was just faster than she could run. Reaching the end of the two-mile section of bridge, he steered around the bollards set to keep larger vehicles out. Heading for the parking lot just ahead, he jumped a curb and accelerated onto the road.

"How far's the bait place?" she yelled at Hector.

"It's about a mile on the right. We can cross up there." He pointed at an intersection ahead.

She gritted her teeth, willing the golf cart to go faster as he pulled onto US 1. Traffic stacked up behind them, and she sensed the drivers' impatience at the slow speed of the cart. Finally they reached the intersection and he turned off the main highway. Cutting through a neighborhood, she looked at the line of mobile homes and canals, not failing to notice that the boats behind them were worth more than the houses.

Hector turned into an unmarked alley, and she found herself in the gravel lot of Monster Bait.

"Take him to your brother. He was bragging how he made him

talk once. Let him have another shot at it," she said.

Hector laughed and headed toward the small shack where Trufante had lost the tip of his finger. They pulled up in front of the shack and she looked back at Trufante.

"There's no need for that. I'll tell you what you want," Trufante groveled.

Hector left and returned with Edgar. Both brothers were sporting big grins.

"Nothing like a little pain to get the truth," she said, nudging him forward with the barrel of her gun. She knew the information would probably be easy to get without the torture, but she was looking forward to seeing how he had lost part of his finger.

"Really. This about the fish? Got them out by Sprigger Bank. Anything you want to know, you just ask," Trufante said.

He hesitated outside the door, but she pushed him through. Edgar had already fired up the machine and stood in front of them with his bloodstained rubber apron and gloves. Trufante took a step back, but again she pushed him forward.

"Come on. Mac must have found the boat the net snagged. I don't know anything else."

"He found a boat?" Jane asked, signaling to Edgar to turn off the machine.

"That boat we had was out at Wood's place. Got her running and all, just one engine, though."

She signaled Edgar to start the grinder again and grabbed Trufante's hand. "What else do you know?" His fingers were within a few inches disappearing into the dark cavity, and she could see the razor-sharp tips of the spinning teeth used to pulverize fish into chum. He must have seen them too and started to fight, causing her to lose her grip.

"Come on. I'll take you out there if you want. Whatever, just turn that thing off."

She pulled her hand across her neck in a slicing motion, amused that the Cajun thought that she was calling for his death, then saw his relief when Edgar frowned and shut down the engine. "Get a fast boat," she ordered Hector. "Take your brother and make sure there is nothing going on out there."

"There was nothing left after we finished," Hector whined.

She glared at him and turned to Trufante. "Come on, lover boy, you're coming with me."

"What do we do if there's someone out there?" Hector asked.

"Tell them I have their friend."

A large check had placated Manuel and now, glad to be back in the Audi, she breathed deeply, then wrinkled her nose as Trufante's smell invaded her space. "Go find a hose and do something about your hygiene," she said. "And I'm watching you." She lowered the windows and got out of the car, watching the tall Cajun as he went behind one of the sheds. A minute later, she could see a stream of water flowing on the ground. In her trunk was a towel, which she handed to him, sacrificing it, mostly to save the leather seats.

He dried off and looked at her. "What do you need me for?"

"Because I like your company," she smirked and ordered him

into the car with the barrel of the gun. She waited until he was settled, then went to the driver's side and slid into the seat. With the gun under her thigh, she pressed the child safety button and placed the shifter in drive. Once past the potholed driveway, she turned right onto the road, then made another right onto US 1. Traffic was light and she shifted quickly, pulling around a semi and taking the left lane.

"Hot damn. This baby goes. What'cha got for horses under that hood?" Trufante asked, showing his grin.

"Just glad it's not a boat," she said, turning her attention back to the road. After passing numerous versions of the same strip center, filled with the typical tourist wares: T-shirts, sandals, shells, and restaurants with thatched roofs, she wondered why this was called paradise. Maybe Key West had something not present here, but you had to suffer over a hundred miles of crap to get there.

She closed the windows, hoping the stench of the overripe male next to her had dissipated, and turned on the air conditioner. Glancing over at Trufante, still smiling and enjoying the ride, she picked up her cell phone and hit several buttons. The call started on the car's speakers, but she quickly changed it to her phone. This was not going to be pleasant. The mess she had come down here to clean up was worse.

Dusharde answered immediately and asked her status in his businesslike manner. Murder and kidnapping were on par with signing a contract to him—and her. In that regard, they worked easily together. "I have some issues," she started.

* * *

Mac swam back to the trawler in the dark. The sun had set and the brief twilight had ended while he was checking the site. He climbed aboard and brushed aside the inquiring looks of Mel and Jen until he had the gear stowed.

"What's it supposed to look like down there?" he asked Jen.

"Same as the rest of the bottom, just marked off to make sure they test the same area."

"What are they looking for?" Mac asked.

"They take samples of the seagrass to test for algae and contaminants."

"What if there is none?"

"No what? They need plant life to test."

He moved to the side and peered into the dark water, trying to figure out what someone would gain from destroying the sampling area. There were three other testing sites in the bay, and he wondered if they had been dredged as well. "There's nothing else to be gained here," he said. "Might as well head back in."

Without waiting for an answer, he hit the windlass switch and slowly pulled forward, gauging the whine of the motor to tell him how fast the anchor was coming aboard. When the chain hit the roller, he went forward to secure the ground tackle.

"What about Tru?" Pamela asked.

Mac looked over at her. She looked like she was back in their world again.

"You promised we would find him. I can feel him," she said.

He had forgotten about the Cajun and now looked toward the lights of Marathon in the distance, wondering where he could be. While he thought, he stared out at the dark water. Far in the distance he saw the green and red lights of another boat coming toward them, and he wondered what anyone would be doing out here at night.

The other boat was too far away to worry about now, but he needed to keep an eye on it. He could tell from the configuration of its lights that it was not larger than forty feet, making it more maneuverable and probably faster than the trawler.

"What's that boat doing out here?" Mel asked. She knew these waters and who ran them.

"Not sure, but they're bearing down on us," Mac said. He suspected trouble. There were few reasons a boat this size would be out at night, and none were good. Sure, there was a chance it was a fisherman, but there was nothing special about these waters. During the day, you could run out here and get away from the crowds. At night, though, this area was dangerous. He also doubted it was a drug runner or smuggler. They generally ran farther out, in deeper water.

He thought about what weapons were available. "Can you get the shotgun from the hold under the V berth?" he asked Mel.

She returned a minute later with the weapon. From a small compartment by the wheel he pulled out a box of shells, mostly used for his bang stick in case a shark got too close while he was diving. The boat continued to close and he steered to starboard, giving leeway to the Bamboo Banks. The other boat seemed to match his course and he started to worry.

"Can you run the boat?" he asked Mel. She moved next to him

and took the wheel and he traced an invisible line on the chart plotter with his forefinger for her to steer. Moving past a scared-looking Jen, he wished he had never gotten her involved in this.

"Pamela," he nudged her. "We need you." She was an enigma to him, but they had been in several predicaments together when facing down a crooked antiquities dealer, and at least he knew she wouldn't panic.

"Mac Travis, time to rock 'n' roll?" she asked like she knew what was happening.

Not wanting to get into her head, he handed her the bang stick and found a long-handled gaff. "There's zip ties and duct tape in the cabin. Can you attach this to the end of the pole?" He waited for her to move, thankful that Jen followed her below. Scanning the water again, he loaded the shotgun and chambered the first round.

The boat was less than a quarter mile away, and still moving toward them. He could do nothing but wait. Pamela came back with the makeshift spear. With the addition of the gaff, the bang stick was almost ten feet long, and he tested it against the deck to make sure that it would fire without breaking the temporary bindings. The empty chamber clicked. He reversed the stick and placed a shell in the chamber.

Looking up again, he realized there was little chance this was going to end well. The boat was coming straight for them, and it was close enough to see the details of the twenty-foot center-console. Even with only a single outboard hanging on the transom, it was faster and drew less water than the trawler. Just as he was about to raise the shotgun to his shoulder to fire a warning round, something whizzed by him, taking a piece of the fiberglass bulkhead with it. He wasted no time and aimed at the approaching boat. Just as he fired, Mel veered off and his shot went wild. Another round hit the boat and he ordered Pamela and Jen into the cabin with directions to stay low.

"What do you want to do?" Mel yelled over the engine. "We can't outrun them."

She was right. The pursuing boat had a top speed of around forty knots, while his trawler could go twenty on a flat, calm day. He moved to her and studied the chart plotter. The only way to get away was to lead them onto a shoal. The Bamboo Banks, a string of shoals and corral heads in seven feet of water, lay alongside. If he could lead the other boat into them, then quickly change course, he might be able to run them aground. But just as he thought it, the other boat pulled alongside and he saw the two brothers leaning against the rocket launcher, both pointing guns at them.

They might not have been the shiniest lures in the tackle box, but they knew these waters. His plan was dead before it began.

"Put it down, Travis," Hector called out. "And cut the engine."

Mac did as he asked. They were underpowered and outgunned. "What do you want?" he yelled across the water.

"You and your boy Trufante have stuck your noses in the wrong hole this time," Hector said. "Poor Cajun's taking a joyride into the Everglades right now."

He saw a strange look come over Pamela at the mention of Trufante's name. She crawled on the deck, careful to stay below the gunwale and out of sight. Mac glanced down and saw what she was up to. He needed to buy some time.

"What's in the Glades that has them so interested?" he asked.

Hector ignored the question, but he could see from the look on Edgar's sadistic face that Trufante was in trouble.

"She's one mean woman," Edgar said, laughing.

The brothers had lost their focus, at least for a moment, and Mac knew this was their only chance. He dove for the deck, going for the shotgun. Reaching it, he placed the barrel on the gunwale and fired blindly. Two shots fired back, sending splinters flying. He motioned to Pamela to take the gun and mimicked a trigger squeeze with his forefinger. She nodded and took the weapon. Crawling on the deck, he reached the bang stick and grabbed the shaft. With a glance at Pamela, he held three fingers, then two, and finally one. On the silent count, he heard the blast of the gun and, using it for cover, rose enough to throw the stick at the engine.

Another blast came from the shotgun and he heard a scream from the other boat. He drew a deep breath and cocked his arm. With no time to aim, he threw the spear as hard as he could in the direction of the outboard. Seconds later, there was a loud explosion and debris rained down around them. He wasted no time and went for the helm. Pushing Mel aside, he started the engines and jammed the throttle forward. It was several seconds later that he allowed himself to look at the damage. The small boat was bow up, its transom and engine had already disappeared beneath the surface. He didn't wait to see if Hector or Edgar were alive.

Chapter 16

Trufante watched the landscape fly by. After following US 1 past several bays, they had entered the lonely stretch of road through the southern Everglades leading to Florida City. He started to get anxious once they lost sight of the water; the flatlands made him uncomfortable. So did the woman driving. She had been unresponsive to his queries, ignoring him in favor of her techno music. Surprised when she turned left at a sign for Everglades National Park, he started to make a map in his head, not of the roads and landmarks, but rather of the canals and waterways. Thanks to an inborn, or inbred, navigation gene found in Cajuns who grew up in the bayous of Louisiana, if there was water around, he was never lost. From what he could see in the moonlight, they were passing through an agricultural area. The fields soon gave way to nature, and suddenly she turned left and slowed to avoid a yellow barricade with a No Trespassing sign. In the dim moonlight, he could see they had entered some kind of industrial facility.

Canals ran parallel to the streets, some larger than others. If he could get a boat, he was sure he could find his way home. That thought was erased from his mind when the car stopped and she pulled the gun from under her thigh. It had been there the whole time. Even if he had been able to reach the gun, as fast as she had been driving, the move could have been deadly.

"Stay here, and no trouble," she said, exiting the car.

She went to a squat concrete building. Even in the narrow beam of the headlights, Trufante could see it was abandoned and in bad shape.

He tried to locate the ignition, and found a start button, which he pushed to no avail. Jammed in the passenger seat with the console between him and the controls, there was no way even his long legs could reach the pedals. His attention turned to the woman, who pulled some pipes and a rack from the room and threw them across the floor. A minute later she came toward the passenger door and opened the handle. The other hand, holding the gun, never moved from him.

"Out," she ordered.

He pulled his six-foot-plus frame out of the car and stood next to her.

"Let's go." She jammed the barrel of the gun in his back.

He started toward the building. She pulled his arm and directed him around the side into an open warehouse door.

They were interrupted by the shrill ring of her phone. She answered and he listened to the one-sided conversation. "What do you mean they sunk your boat and got away? I sent you to do a simple job and you fouled that up like everything else you idiots touch."

She listened to what must have been an explanation.

"Share your location and I'll send you some help," she said and hung up. A scowl crossed her face as she approached him.

"It seems your friends are causing me trouble," she said, handing him the phone. "You will tell them you are my guest."

Trufante took the phone and stared at the screen.

"Surely even a fool like you knows how to use it."

He dialed, waited for several seconds, then held the phone away from his ear and shrugged. Mac answering was a long shot, especially if he was on the water.

She understood the gesture and reached for the phone.

"We have your friend—the tall, dumb one. This is none of your business. He will be released in due time." She left the message and hung up.

"What now?" he asked. "Still could use a bite to eat. Maybe a beer, too."

She ignored the comment and led him to a small room that had probably at one time been a storeroom. From the light from her phone he could see the low ceiling. Heat pent up from the day blasted from the room when she opened the door, and something slithered past them. He was about to turn and ask for better accommodations when he felt a foot in the small of his back that sent him sprawling into the corner. The door slammed, leaving him in the dark.

* * *

Mel ran the boat while Mac worked the Navionics app on the screen of his phone. It would have been easier on the chart plotter, but at night, in these waters, he wanted her to have all the benefits of the real-time display. The app had considerably more detail than the NOAA chart loaded in the boat's plotter. He had set a course to the north in the general direction of Key Largo, hoping to get some help from Alicia and get Jen back to Marathon. The girl had already seen too much.

After first determining the course on his phone, he traced a wavy line on the screen, showing Mel where the channel ran. In the backcountry of the Keys there was no such thing as a straight line, especially as you moved north toward the Everglades. She nodded that she understood and he went back to his phone. Pinching the screen, he zoomed out to see the big picture on the chart, then panned toward the north. He vaguely remembered where the other test sites were and worked his way toward where Taylor Slough exited into Florida Bay. TS/Ph11, the site he had just seen for himself and the furthest from the source, was the end of the line. He suspected the other sites were compromised as well, and he intended to find the source.

The signal strengthened as they approached the southern tip of Florida, and he Googled the coordinates for the next site. TS/Ph10 was only slightly off their present course. With his phone in hand, he moved back to Mel and entered the coordinates in the GPS. She changed course slightly to the north and they covered the ten miles in silence.

After anchoring on the site, he geared up again. It was deeper here, but for his purposes, the free-diving gear would still be adequate, though this time he chose to use fins. Grabbing a dive light and a lobster bag, he slid off the swim platform and entered the murky water. The bright LED light reflected off the bottom, showing the same damage as the previous site. He swung the beam of light around until the bare sand yielded back to seagrass. It was out of the marked test area, but close enough for his purposes. He finned toward the limits of the dredged area and pulled several clumps of grass from the marl. Placing the samples in the lobster bag, he returned to the trawler and climbed aboard.

After stowing his gear, he looked at the contents of the bag. The grass looked normal under the lights from the boat, but that was no indication it didn't harbor the fish-killing algae. He needed a scientist's opinion.

"What do you think?" he asked Jen.

"I couldn't tell you anything without running some tests and evaluating it under a microscope. Having a similar, healthy sample would be good, too."

Her answer confirmed his decision to make a quick stop in Key Largo.

The night would have been perfect if it were not for the mood on the boat. There was no sound except the rumble of the engine as the boat sliced through the small moonlit-dappled waves. The silence was broken by a shrill ring from Mac's phone. He reached for it. The screen said *unknown number* and he set it back down, cursing the telemarketers who had invaded the cell phone space. A minute later it vibrated, showing the icon for a new voicemail.

Suddenly Pamela was alert as they huddled around the phone and he replayed the message through the speaker. The woman's voice finished and they looked at each other.

"There's a timeline for something," Mel said. "Play it again."

Mac hit the play button.

"They're going to kill him," Pamela wailed.

"Not right away. She is using him to stop us from doing whatever she thinks we're doing," Mel said. "She thinks we know more than we do." She was in full lawyer mode now and Mac let her go. "We must be getting close to something for them to take him," she said.

"We have to get back to land to get these samples analyzed," Mac said, moving to the wheel. He turned to the lights of Key Largo and pushed down the throttle.

"Forget the samples. What about Tru?" Pamela called over the roar of the engine.

"We'll get him back," Mac said.

Mel and Jen were focused on their phones for the remaining half hour it took to pass to the Atlantic side. Mac steered through the narrow cut and turned north. It took all his attention to find the unfamiliar entrance to the canal in the dark. Without landmarks, he steered by the chart plotter, found the opening in the mangroves, cut the wheel to port and entered the small lagoon. Using the big red and white flag from TJ's dive shop to guide him, they approached the dock. Mel had already alerted Alicia they were on their way, and the couple was waiting for them on the dock.

After introducing Jen, and a round of quick hugs, they rushed up the back stairs of the dive shop to the apartment. Back in the war room, a computer enclave that resembled the flight deck of the *Starship Enterprise*, they all stared at the big screen monitors mounted to the wall as Alicia started to populate the screens. She had worked quickly after they had called and already had several maps up.

One showed the historical path of the Everglades' drainage. The next showed the current discharge. Mac was shocked at the alterations from the natural water flow. On another screen was a detailed map from the South Florida Water Management District, the agency in charge of routing floodwater from Lake Okeechobee and the Kissimmee drainage through an intricate maze of canals and floodgates. Most of the water was routed to the west coast through the Caloosahatchee River. Mac suspected this accounted for the red tides and the large fish kills in that area.

Alicia started to talk now, explaining the history, but Mac stopped her, more concerned about the present. "We need to get the seagrass samples to a lab and then figure out what they're up to," he said.

"And Tru," Pamela said. "We have to help him."

"It's all tied together," Mel said. "And apparently they need him alive."

"But . . ." Pamela started.

"We'll get him, but first we need to figure out what they're up to," Mac said.

TJ sat in the captain's chair, the original fixture in the room, used to control his gaming empire. "Follow the flow, man."

They all turned to him. Moving his cursor along the map, he traced the flow of water.

He had their attention now. "Look at the data," he said, changing one of the screens to a complicated spreadsheet.

"What's that?" Mel asked.

"Florida Coastal Everglades collection results for the last fifteen years. These sites were started just after two thousand."

They studied the numbers on the screen.

He highlighted some numbers and summarized. "It seems that this last flood pushed farther south than anything before it. It wasn't the worst storm or the strongest tide we've had, but they must have compounded each other."

"How'd you get this?" Mel asked.

"Classified, babe," he kidded.

Chapter 17

Mac was the last to say goodbye and thanked Jen for her help after her friend arrived to pick her up. There was a sadness in her eyes that Mac understood. She wanted to finish the journey, but Mac couldn't put her in danger.

"You can stay here tonight if you want," Alicia offered.

Mac pursed his lips and shook his head. As much as he wanted a bed and a good night's sleep, the clock was ticking. "Thanks, but we need to head back out."

"We're here if you need us," TJ said. He looked at the trawler. "What's she draw?"

"A little over four feet," Mac said.

"Why don't you take the six-pack dive boat. It draws a hair over two feet, and you can tilt the engine if you get in trouble," TJ offered. "Just filled her too."

Mac knew he was right. Where they were headed was not like the more open backcountry near Marathon. Although the entire backside of the Keys was riddled with obstacles, it was much worse where they were headed.

"I can't put you out," Mac said.

"Those Big Sugar guys'll put me out of business if you don't figure this out. The tourists get word of the fish kills, they'll be no diving here."

"We appreciate it," Mel said, then she said goodbye to Mac. She would be heading to the Florida Coastal Everglades offices outside of Fort Lauderdale tomorrow to see what she could accomplish there.

Pamela stood on the deck of the trawler waiting. Mac went over and boarded. He told her about the change of plans and brought over some supplies, and the shotgun. He couldn't help but notice that her demeanor had changed, knowing their path would lead to Trufante. Mac gave Alicia a quick hug and hopped onboard the twenty-four-foot cuddy cabin. He started the engines and waited for Pamela. She said goodbye and joined him by the helm. They cast the lines and headed back out. Immediately he was grateful for the smaller boat.

"Can you follow the channel?" Mac asked Pamela. Keeping her busy would also keep her focused. "I'm going to enter the coordinates for the other sites." She nodded and took the wheel. Removing a piece of paper from the pocket of his cargo shorts, he laid it out on the console and started entering the numbers for the other test sites in the chart plotter. After turning the individual waypoints into a route, a line appeared connecting the dots and running up toward Homestead.

"That's where we're going?" Pamela asked.

"Yeah. Just follow the yellow brick road. Somewhere up this

trail, we'll find what we're looking for."

They stood together in silence as she steered southwest. The Marvin D Adams Waterway they had just used was a faster route, but far better approached from the south where they had come from. Heading north, Tavernier Creek was the safer route back to the bay side. They entered the winding waterway a half hour later and Mac sent Pamela forward with a spotlight. He called out where he expected markers to be and she panned the light across the dark water until the reflectors caught the light. The chart plotter was an aid only; its margin of error of thirty feet seemed minor, but that margin could easily ground them here.

Finally, after a tense passage, they emerged into Florida Bay. Mac remained vigilant, pointing out the numerous shoals and hazards. He was trusting someone else's electronics, something he was always wary of, though knowing it was used as a dive boat was reassuring. Most charters in Key Largo took their clients to John Pennekamp Park, and, although beautiful, the diving was a little pedestrian for TJ's clients. He and Alicia had built a reputation for more adventurous charters using custom nitrox mixes to increase bottom time in deeper water. Some of the sites they dove were like finding a needle in a haystack and required fine-tuned electronics to find them. Still, instead of cutting cross-country, he decided on the marked channel running parallel to Key Largo.

With Pamela's help locating the markers, he followed the channel through Tarpon Basin and back into the bay. It was slow, but safe, and when the sun finally broke the horizon, they found themselves staring at the tip of mainland Florida. Mac stopped the boat a quarter mile from the coast in Barnes Sound, to the northeast of US 1. In front of them was a river that was too symmetrical to be natural.

"Can you pull the canal system up on your phone?" The chart plotter clearly showed the man-made canal in front of them, but had no details. TJ had given them a list of web sites that could help once they were inland.

"C111. They call it the Aerojet Canal," she said, working the screen on her phone. "Looks like you could fit a jet in it."

He estimated the width to be over a hundred feet. "That's exactly what it was cut for. They brought the jet engines for the Saturn rockets through here on barges in the sixties. They were too wide for the highways, so they cut this canal through the Everglades."

"Tru's in there," she said.

Mac ignored her. He was more interested in the entrance to the canal. The markers stopped well short of it. "How far will this take us?"

She pinched and panned the screen of her phone. "If they're all connected, it goes all the way to Lake Okeechobee. But there are some blanks."

Mac wondered about the floodgates. He had heard about the mechanical controls to allow excess water through or hold back irrigation water depending on the season.

"There's very little detail, but this looks big."

Mac steered toward the inlet. The sun had risen enough by now to illustrate exactly what was happening, and it sickened him. A thin stream of brown water was flowing from the canal. He could only imagine what it would be like when the floodgates were open. The famous River of Grass would turn into the River of Death.

"Come on, Mac Travis. *We ain't got time to sit and wonder why, babe*," she said, humming the Dylan song.

"Let's do it." He pushed down on the throttle, stopping at a fast idle. The depth finder showed eighteen feet and steady, the dredged bottom starting well before the canal entrance. The bottom continued to hold and he accelerated slightly as they met the current from the canal. Pushing through the inlet, he saw several fishermen on the banks, their cars and trucks parked on what appeared to be an access road behind them.

"Look up there!" Pamela warned.

He'd lost focus for a second, watching one of the fishermen bring a fish to the bank. Ahead were a half dozen huge culvert pipes.

"What now?"

She went back to her phone. "They're eighty-four inches in diameter. What's that mean to us?"

Mac was thankful the cuddy cabin didn't have a tower. He pushed down on the throttles, wanting enough momentum to maintain steerage, expecting the current to be stiffer as the canal narrowed. As they got closer, he could see ripples on the surface as the water exited the restriction. Powering up again, he slid the boat into the pipe. It was an eerie feeling with only inches to spare on each side, but the culverts were only ten feet long, and he could see light ahead. Before he knew it, they were clear and the canal widened again.

The waterway stayed dead straight for a few miles, giving him a chance to look at the map on Pamela's phone. "There's another test station right up here."

* * *

Trufante woke in darkness, then remembered the room had no windows. He turned toward the only source of light, a thin band coming from under the door. He moved around, trying to stretch, and gaining his feet he used the wall to push himself up. Just as he rose, he slammed his head into the low ceiling and winced in pain. Ducking now, he went to the light, twice tripping on pipes before he reached it. With both hands he tried to turn the handle, but it was locked.

In the darkness it was impossible to see if there was another way out, and he started to worry. Sealed inside of a concrete building in the middle of the Everglades was not a good scenario. He went back to the door and froze when he heard something. There were voices outside, and he strained to hear what they were saying. It sounded like a large group, and out of desperation he started banging on the door. The voices were coming closer and he heard something on the other side.

"Do you think it's a trap?" someone asked.

"You know that team plays dirty. Must be one of their guys

trying to draw us into the open."

Trufante tried to figure out what this army talk was all about, and then it dawned on him. "Hey, guys, it ain't a trap. I'm stuck in here," he yelled, banging on the door again. He could hear them talking quietly.

"I'm telling you right now, if this is a trap, the game's over, and you'll lose for cheating," someone said.

"Right. No cheating. Really, I ain't got no idea what y'all are up to, but this she-devil of a woman stuck me in here last night."

He could hear activity outside the door, then he heard a crash and the door vibrated. It fell away from the rusted steel hinges and light entered the room. It took a minute for his eyes to adjust to the brightness, but when he did he saw a half dozen teenagers surrounding him, each with a weapon pointed at him. The first thing that came to mind were the gang shootings, but after a closer look the guns looked different, and he remembered the conversation.

"Y'all can put those down 'fore you hurt someone," he said.

The leader stepped forward and holstered his pistol. Trufante's eyes followed the weapon and he relaxed. In a small compartment to the side of the gun were several CO_2 cartridges. He looked around at the other weapons and saw the standard paintball paraphernalia.

"What are you doing here?" the leader asked.

"Same could be asked about you boys," he said, with an emphasis on boys.

"I asked you first," he said, boldly.

"Hey, Max, forget this dude. Ethan's team's gonna get the drop on us," one of the other guys said.

"Y'all need to post some guards. Tell you what," he said, thinking how he could play this to his advantage. "I help you take down this Ethan cat, and y'all get me back to civilization." He scanned the gutted building. Conduits and ductwork hung from the ceilings and walls. The electrical panel had been jimmied open and all the copper wire pulled.

"What do you know about tactics?" Max asked.

"First Bayou Brigade. Team leader," Trufante said proudly.

"Louisiana?"

"Goddamn Everglades got nothing on the ole bayou. Now do we have a deal?"

Max looked around at the others. "Sure," he said.

"I'll be needing a weapon then," Trufante said.

One of the boys handed him a rifle with a belt of cartridges and extra ammo. "All right, now where's this Ethan dude at?"

Just as he said it, an orange splatter appeared on the concrete wall above his head. There was no First Bayou Brigade, and this was the first Trufante had ever seen of paintball. He wasn't impressed. If it couldn't take down a gator, what was the point? "Spread out. Everyone at least twenty yards apart. You two, go around the perimeter and find them, then report back." He took control of the troops.

Another shot marked the wall behind him. Turning, he fired several rounds and heard someone cry out that they were hit. "Score one for us," he said to Max. If the circumstances were different, this could actually be fun. "We need to pin them down somewhere, you know, push them into an enclosed space."

"The rocket silo," Max said. "It's the building over there." He pointed to a large steel building.

"Rockets? For real?" Trufante muttered.

"Don't you know where we are?" Max asked.

"No, man. Told you that she-devil locked me up last night."

"This is the old Aerojet rocket plant."

Trufante gave him a queer look, smiling and showing his grin. He knew this was his best chance to get out of here. "Rally them troops and start moving them toward it." He leaned over and drew a quick map of his plan in the half inch of dirt on the concrete floor. "This is how we're gonna do it."

Chapter 18

Mel said goodbye and thanked Alicia for the ride to Miami International Airport. From here she would rent a car. The ex-CIA agent had offered to accompany her, but Mel had decided it wasn't worth the risk if identities were checked. It was better to be a private citizen, although she expected there were files on her in more than one government office. After fighting the ACLU's battles for years, her name was well known in some circles—not always for the right things. Her relationship with Bradley Davies and his law firm probably had a red flag on her as well. As she drove north on I-95, she wondered if her old boss was still locked up and where.

The town of Davie was just west of Fort Lauderdale and home to the US Department of the Interior's Everglades Restoration Initiative. Already she had discovered a conflict between the National Science Foundation and the DOI. From her experience with government, this would only be the first of many, and she planned to use one to leverage the information she wanted. She had made several calls to some old contacts to both garner information and to see if she could get an appointment. Exiting I-595 at South University Drive, she breathed deeply, wondering what kind of reception she was going to get. The calls she had made during the two-hour drive had yielded more information than she knew what to do with about the history and political intrigue surrounding Big Sugar.

It was a twisted relationship, with both people's health and the environment compromised. She already knew how it started from Alicia's history lesson last night, but she soon found everything had escalated in the sixties. It seemed the sugar industry paid Harvard scientists to publish a study blaming fat and cholesterol for coronary heart disease while largely exculpating sugar. This study, published in the prestigious *New England Journal of Medicine*, in 1967, helped set the agenda for decades of public health policy designed to steer Americans into low-fat foods, which increased carbohydrate consumption and exacerbated the obesity epidemic as well as selling truckloads of sugar. This revelation was one of the first instances where the Big Sugar companies had worked together to buy influence.

Leaving the health matters aside, she called another friend, who gave her the political background. She drove with her jaw dropped, almost rear-ending two other cars as she listened to how it had started in the 1800s. Back then, the cornerstone of federal sugar policy was not a dietary guideline but a tariff on sugar imports. The sugar companies again banded together forcing a law that made a distinction between refined and raw sugar. Again this was to their advantage.

The miles flew by as she listened, and it only got worse. In order to protect domestic refiners, then the largest manufacturing employer in Northern cities, the tariff distinguished between two kinds of sugar: "refined" and "raw." Refined sugar that was meant for direct consumption paid a much higher rate than did raw sugar crystals intended for further refining and whitening. But by the late 1870s, new industrial sugar factories in the Caribbean began to jeopardize this protectionist structure. Technologically sophisticated, these factories could produce sugar that, while raw by the government's standard, was consistently much closer to refined sugar than ever before. The American industry now faced potential competition from abroad.

The country's largest refiners mobilized on several fronts. They lobbied the United States Congress to adopt chemical instruments that could measure the percentage of sucrose in a sugar cargo, and to deem sugar "refined" only when its sucrose content was sufficiently high enough. Previously, customs officers had judged the purpose of a sugar cargo by its color, smell, taste, and texture, as people throughout the sugar trade had done for centuries. Now refiners argued that such sensory methods were ripe for abuse because they depended on a subjective appraisal. They demanded a scientific standard instead—one that would reveal some "raw" sugar to be nearly pure and thus subject to higher tariffs—and they prevailed. It was amazing to her that this wasn't publicized. It read like a thriller novel.

Their plea for scientific objectivity may have sounded sensible, but it masked nefarious aims. If refiners were to bribe a customs chemist to shade his results in their favor—as they were routinely accused of doing for decades, beginning in the 1870s—such corruption would be much harder for the government to detect than it had been when everyone could see and smell the same sugar.

All the while America's appetite for sugar grew. In the decades after the Civil War, Americans' per-capita consumption of sugar more than doubled, from thirty pounds in the late 1800s to eighty pounds only thirty years later. As a result, by 1880, sugar subsidies accounted for a sixth of the federal budget.

Then there were the bribes. Her last call was to a friend at the *Miami Herald*. He revealed that in the last twenty years the industry contributed almost sixty million dollars to influence Florida elections, and that was the publicly disclosed amounts. Meanwhile, and not surprisingly, state officials had resisted efforts to make sugar companies pay for their damage to the Everglades.

With a pile of money and some powerful lobbyists, which Mel was not surprised to hear that Davies was one of, Big Sugar succeeded in bringing control of the Everglades back to the state level, where they could more easily manipulate it. Several measures were passed, all watered down and penned by the sugar companies' attorneys. Cleanup costs were capped, and a proposed area of the middle Everglades was slated for restoration. That was during the Clinton years, and it was no different when the Republicans took control of Congress. Big Sugar didn't care who was in power. They funneled money in whatever direction they needed to keep their subsidies in place.

With her head spinning, Mel pulled in and parked. Even for her brain, often tried by the craftiest minds in the legal profession, this was convoluted. Wishing for a change of clothes, she got out of the car and entered the building. In the office of the Everglades Initiative, she looked at the disinterested woman sitting beneath the seal of the Department of the Interior.

She announced herself and sat down to wait, trying to think if there was any other industry that had their hand in the destruction of the environment and of people's health at the same time.

"Come on in, Ms. Woodson." The woman who opened the door greeted her with a handshake, then escorted her to an office with a generous view of the parking lot.

Mel was about to ask what was up with the frosty reception, but once the door closed, the woman embraced her.

"Just an act for anyone watching. The big bureaucrat can't be seen hugging the infamous Melanie Woodson." They both laughed.

"Damn, Janet, you had me going there for a minute. How's Jim?" Mel asked.

"Retired now. Only reason I still work is to get out of the house," she said, laughing. "And the insurance."

Mel thought that odd that a contemporary of hers, especially one in government service, could even think about retiring. After exchanging a few minutes of pleasantries, Janet pulled a legal pad in front of her and started taking notes. Mel explained what had happened since the storm.

"So there was no ID on the body you found?" Janet asked,

underlining something on her paper.

Mel dodged the question. "Mac's had some trouble with the local law enforcement from time to time. We've pretty much stayed away from the investigation."

"But you thought he was a scientist?"

"From what we pulled off his phone, yes," Mel answered, wondering why the questions were more centered around the dead body than the polluted water. Patiently, she answered Janet's questions, becoming more wary and vague as she went.

"What about the test sites? They were clearly tampered with," she said, checking her phone again, hoping for some confirmation from Jen about the test results.

"That's more the National Science Foundation's deal. They run the test sites," Janet said.

"I've done enough homework on the sugar industry and the travesties they've committed to both our health and the environment to know there's a ton of blame shifting going on. I thought maybe you could help me make a difference. Let the doctors straighten out the medical stuff, and I don't really care about the real estate, but the environment—"

Janet interrupted, "What is it that you want me to do?"

Mel wrung her hands in her lap, frustrated about how this was going. She had made a mistake trusting a friendship and coming in without a plan or expectations—she knew better, and had to watch how emotionally involved she was getting. She tried a different angle. "I have some property, from my dad, down there. If those fish kills reach the middle Keys, it'll be worthless."

"Honey, I feel your pain. There's some paperwork I can get you to fill out, it usually takes a while, but I can push it through. Let me see what I can do for you," Janet said, rising from her seat.

Mel was shocked she was being dismissed like this. Not only did she expect their friendship, dating back to their days at Virginia Law School, to carry weight, but Janet had a position of authority here and the means to help her. "Well, if that's all you can do." She got up and waited for the other woman to come around the desk. They embraced again, but this time Mel could tell it was not heartfelt.

"I can find my way out. You look busy," Mel said, opening the door. She wanted out of there fast.

Stopping in the bathroom off the lobby on the way out of the building, she washed her face and looked in the mirror. What looked back was not the impression she wanted to give. It was the look of worn-out desperation. She wondered if she should have stopped at a store and bought business clothes and some makeup before her meeting and decided that wasn't it. She had been routinely dismissed by an old friend and bureaucrat. It was hard to believe some of the claims about Big Sugar, but she was starting to get a taste of just how powerful they were. It looked like Mac was right, and the only way to fix it was to do an end run around the government.

She got back in the car, checked the rearview mirror and backed out of the space. A dark blue four-door sedan, barely identifiable from the other million just like it, pulled out from behind the building. It stopped and waited. She thought the driver wanted her parking space, but instead the car followed her out of the lot. She didn't think anything of it as the driver turned in the same direction as she did onto the road and quickly dropped several cars back.

As she drove, she replayed the meeting in her head, looking for clues or reasons why Janet had been patronizing, allowing her to leave with only a vague offer of help. She had even steered her away from a written complaint. The other car was quickly forgotten as her brain shifted into overdrive, trying to solve the puzzle.

Chapter 19

Mac tried to ignore Pamela's attitude. Her impatience was gnawing at him, and in the tight confines of the boat there was no escaping it. He was anxious as well, but knew the only way to figure out what was going on and to rescue Trufante was to follow the string of test sites. The stop to check the next site would only take a few minutes. Using the GPS on her phone, he located the station and pulled toward the bank of the canal. The Everglades Conservatory's web page had pictures of each testing station, and he scanned the area looking for the short boardwalk allowing access to the sawgrass marsh. The site was labeled inactive, and he soon saw why when the dilapidated structure appeared on his left. He turned to the shore and nudged the bow until it lodged in the soft berm.

"Can you hold her here? I'll be right back," he said to Pamela, leaving the engine in forward.

She nodded and took the wheel. Moving to the bow, he jumped onto the six-foot slope, hoping it would hold him. His feet slipped, but he regained his balance and was able to crawl to the top. From there he could see what the berm had hidden. Stretched out to the horizon and beyond was an endless prairie of sawgrass. Cutting through a section was a short boardwalk. Taking a tentative step onto the first board, he felt something crack under his feet and retreated. Since the walkway was short, he figured whatever samples he could get at the end he could also get here and reached down, pulling a handful of cattails and grass from the marl.

Climbing back down the berm, he saw the boat had drifted into the center of the canal. "Hey! What are you doing?" he yelled across to Pamela.

She shrugged and he knew he had to calm down, knowing he was dealing with a child in a woman's body. He and Mel had speculated endlessly, trying to figure out this woman who had attached herself to Trufante. There was a stream of money coming in, and Mel went as far as to run a background check from her credit card. What should have revealed at least her real identity or where she came from came up blank. It was as if she didn't exist. The mystery remained unsolved.

He motioned her over, waiting impatiently while she worked the boat toward him. Finally, she slammed the bow into the earth and he jumped onboard. After stowing the samples in the fish box, he used the fresh water wash-down to clean up.

"What are we going to do about Tru? I can feel him. He's here."

"Whoever took him is at the end of this road somewhere. We just need to keep working north. Why don't you call Mel and see if she's found anything?" He pushed the throttle forward and steered around a bend.

"She scares me," Pamela said.

Mac couldn't dispute her there. His attention turned back to the waterway as they approached another barrier. Turning the boat parallel to get a better look, he saw a dam-like structure with two steel guillotine-style gates, controlled from above. One was closed, restricting the flow of water, the other gate hung ominously overhead, about eight feet above the water. Pushing the throttle forward, Mac squared up the bow and using just enough power to retain steerage he crept into the opening. A surprisingly fast current took the boat, slamming it into the concrete abutment. There was no need to panic, but he needed to act quickly before the hull struck the other wall. With the choice of dropping power and letting the current pull the boat back, or pushing forward, he decided he would have better control under power. Mac pushed the throttle down. Anticipating the fishtail from the propeller, he cut the wheel to starboard, barely missing the edge of the structure. Once clear of the floodgates, he steered out of the current and slowed to an idle. He looked up at the parking area and saw a crowd of fishermen watching the action and applauding.

He knew he had been lucky and looked down at the phone. More floodgates lay ahead, and he knew sooner or later there would be one he couldn't handle.

* * *

Trufante laid out a simple pincer maneuver in the dirt. Splitting the group into two teams, he led one and assigned the other to Max.

"We need a diversion to take them off guard so we can get in position," Trufante said, looking around the abandoned building. To his right he saw an old pipe hanging from the ceiling. "Y'all get on that. Pull it down. It should make enough racket to scare those boys off for a minute. As soon as it goes, we move out."

With a boost, one of the taller guys was able to reach the pipe. He dangled from it, swinging his body back and forth, trying to break it free of the remaining straps. Suddenly it moved, dropping him to the floor and sending a screeching sound echoing through the building as it hit the concrete floor. After checking that he was all right, both teams headed for the entry and split up.

Trufante took his squad to the right, while Max moved to the left with his. Covering each other, they ran to the large steel building fifty yards across the parking lot. As planned, each group took one side of the building. Now he needed to draw the other club inside.

"We gotta make some noise so they think we're inside," he said.

"Come on. I have an idea," one of the boys said.

Trufante signaled the rest of the team to wait, while he and the other guy slid inside. A big grin spread across his face as they reached a steel grate cut into the floor.

"What's in there?" he asked, peering into the darkness.

"A rocket," the guy said, taking a tactical flashlight off his belt and shining the beam into the void.

"What in the hell!"

"Largest solid-fuel rocket ever built."

"I'll be damned." Trufante turned toward the entrance. "So, what's your idea?"

He pulled a bundle of paracord from his cargo pocket. "Tie this on the grate and loop it over that beam."

Trufante saw where he was going, but was mesmerized by the rocket. Sunk into a concrete-lined culvert was the biggest engine he had ever seen. "You think that sucker'd still fire?"

The boy nodded his head. "Solid fuel. No reason why it shouldn't. Come on."

Together they rigged the cord. With one end tied to the grate, Trufante tossed the bundle over an overhead beam. The boy caught the extra line and they both took hold of the end, pulling until the grate creaked and rose a few inches. "All you got. Let's make some noise," Trufante said. "On three . . ."

They pulled the grate several feet above the opening. "Go," Trufante said, and they released the line, sending the grate down with a large crash. Running toward the side door, they looked back and saw the other team approaching. With their weapons ready, they marched single file into the trap. Trufante watched the last man enter and signaled Max. Both squads simultaneously entered the building from the side doors and surrounded the unsuspecting team. Without a shot, with their backs to the huge hole in the ground, they surrendered.

The two teams stood together around the silo, shaking hands and talking about the game when they suddenly went quiet as a vehicle approached. Scattering like flies, Trufante was left alone in the center of the room. He heard a door slam and thought about running when he saw Jane standing in the entry with a gun pointed at him.

Orange and blue splatters appeared around her as both teams shot. Real gunshots streamed blindly toward the shooters and into the dark interior. Trufante heard panic in the voices of the teams as they faced live fire for the first time. Another stream of bullets sent them scrambling out the back door, leaving Trufante alone.

There were three figures in the opening: two men and a woman. "Leave the paintball nerds and get the tall, dumb-looking one," Jane ordered her accomplices. The two men, both holding what looked like automatic rifles, moved cautiously toward him. To leave cover now would only expose him. Suddenly the soft splats of paintball rounds rang out and color appeared on each man's vest.

Trufante didn't wait. Staying low, he ran toward the back of the building, feeling the paintball rounds fly over his head. Just as he stood, he heard the automatic fire again and the paintball rifles fell silent. Another round sprayed, and bullets ricocheted around him. Sparks flew from where they hit steel. He jumped to the side as one hit the concrete by his right foot.

"Over here!"

He heard Max yell over the shots and looked toward the back door.

"Come on, we'll cover you!"

Trufante looked toward Max and then to the entry where the two gunmen stood, one on either side of Jane. All three were shooting real bullets at him. He knew there was no choice and yelled to the back that he was coming. The building erupted in paint splatters as both teams opened fire. What they lacked in real bullets, they made up for in volume, and when Trufante chanced a look back at the opening, he saw the three figures were gone. Sprinting, he took off toward the back door.

* * *

Mel left the office park and drove west. For lack of any other plan, she took I-595 and turned south on the Florida Turnpike. She needed to find Mac and let him know what they were up against. She set her phone on her leg and pressed his name in her contacts list. With the speaker on she listened to the shrill ring, composing a voicemail in her head. She didn't expect an answer, and left a message to call her back. Before she turned away she saw a small map with a pin in it below the phone number. Slowing, she pressed it, remembering she had configured Mac's phone to share his location. There were too many times where he disappeared. It was not for lack of trust—he was as dependable and ethical as any man she had ever met. It was more for insurance. Things always seemed to be going wrong around him.

A button that said *directions* appeared below the map and she pressed it. A dark blue line showed the route, taking her farther south and into the Everglades. She braked hard, almost causing a collision, and slid into the right lane, which exited on Highway 41. Glancing in her rearview mirror after changing lanes, she saw a dark blue sedan that looked familiar, but then discounted it as paranoia. Half the cars on the road looked like that. But she caught a flash in her side mirror as the car cut off a truck and swung in behind her.

She turned onto Highway 41 west, hoping it was a coincidence, but the car stayed with her. The neighborhood started to change after she passed Florida International University. At a red light, she looked back to see the car stopped at the previous light. She thought about making a quick turn, to either confirm she was being followed, or lose the car if she was, but the signs were all in Spanish now and the increasingly Cuban neighborhood made her uncomfortable. The best thing to do was to stay to the security of the main road and find Mac.

After the next few lights, the neighborhood thinned out and she found herself entering the Everglades. Billboards for airboat tours littered the sides of the road, and ahead she could see the Miccosukee Indian casino. As she drove she tried to figure out who was behind her, and the only solution she came up with was Big Sugar. The bad feeling she had gotten from Janet now started to make sense, and, remembering her and her husband's early retirement, she recalled the millions of dollars in political donations Big Sugar had passed along to political action groups and the legislature directly. Some of the PAC money must have found its way to Janet's pockets.

As she approached the turnoff to the casino, she thought about seeking refuge there, but quickly dismissed the idea. Big Sugar and the tribes could easily be connected. Instead she accelerated, heading toward the red dot.

Chapter 20

Trufante stood behind a deserted building with Max and the blue team, who it turned out was the Florida International University paintball club. Several structures separated them from Jane and the shooters, and Tru leaned against the hot steel siding, trying to catch his breath. The Miami University team they had been competing against had run the other way, and he could hear several vehicles pull out of an adjacent lot and head toward the main road.

"That was rad, man," Max said.

Trufante looked at him wondering if he knew those were real shots fired at him. "We gotta get out of here before the she-devil finds us."

"Our way out's in that building," Max said, pointing toward a concrete structure adjacent to the silo.

"Y'all saved my ass. Best that you disappear before they find you," Trufante said. "I'll figure out how to distract them."

"We can't leave you like this," Max said. The team looked at each other, then to their leader. "First Bayou Brigade, reporting for duty."

"What y'all talkin' about? I just made that up. Y'all know those are real bullets?"

They all nodded and stood like they were waiting for orders. "I think we need to recon and see what these cats are up to."

He split the group into three teams and instructed them to fan out to see what Jane and the two men were doing. "Careful, that woman's got the devil in her." He sent two of the groups out, instructing them to stay wide of the silo and slowly work their way in. The last thing he needed was casualties.

"One of you guys got a phone?"

* * *

Mac continued his search for the origin of the flow of brown water bringing the fish kill to the Keys. He wondered if other explorers had the same feeling on their quests—that what they sought didn't exist. The canal here was straight and wide with no floodgates nearby, and he turned the wheel over to Pamela. While she drove, he plotted the remaining test stations. Stations two and three were inside Everglades Park and outside the network of canals they were in. With every mile he was feeling more pessimistic and out of sorts. It felt pointless stopping at each site and collecting samples that he already knew were contaminated. He decided to go straight to the beginning and the first site.

At the chart plotter he traced a straight line between their current location and the site. The map was sketchy, showing the canals starting and stopping seemingly at random. That meant they would have to go cross-country through the Everglades, and although the cuddy cabin only drew a few feet of water it might be too much. This was airboat country. He was out of his element, and he considered turning around and calling for help.

The decision quickly became moot as Pamela's phone vibrated in his hands. She looked over and grabbed it.

"It's Tru!" she said.

The screen had a 305 area code. "How do you know?"

"It's him, I just know it."

Right before she pressed the accept button, he pulled her hand away. She threw a scorned look and pulled back. "Careful. It might be the people that have him," Mac warned. "Let's put it on speaker and both listen."

She nodded, pressed the green button, and they stared at the phone. Nothing but static came from the line.

"Tru," she pleaded.

They listened carefully, vaguely hearing something in the background that sounded like a man's voice.

"Can you make it out?" Mac asked.

She held the phone to her head. Mac was unsure whether she could hear better or if she thought the contact with the device would bring Trufante back, but it didn't matter. The Cajun's voice emerged through the static, but it was hard to understand.

"Something about a rocket," she said.

Mac looked at her and spoke into the speaker. "Come on, man, we need more than that."

Pamela listened intently, turning the volume all the way up.

They both heard the word "jet" and shrugged at each other.

"Listen, Tru," Mac started. "If that's all you got, we can try and find you. I'm going to disconnect the call so you can save the battery."

Pamela shook her head, took the phone and turned away from him, saying something he couldn't understand. With tears in her eyes, she handed the phone back to Mac. "Now what?"

He started panning the screen, looking for anything that might have to do with a rocket or a jet. Suddenly he saw Aerojet Road and zoomed in. "That's it!"

"What?" Pamela asked.

"Aerojet. It's gotta be where he is." Mac looked at the phone, trying to figure out a route. There was no direct path, but he did find a series of wider canals that he assumed would be deep enough for the boat. Taking the wheel, he pushed down on the throttle and got the boat up on plane. It was a strange feeling, moving so fast in the enclosed waterway, the high dirt berms on both sides making it impossible to see over the top from the water. The turn to the right was narrower than he expected and he passed it on the first try. They backtracked and entered the skinny canal. If it stayed this wide, they would be able to reach the Aerojet Canal, but cattails were already slamming the sides of the boat. The growth thickened, and soon they were plowing through the tall grass. Passing an intersection, he saw from the map that they were halfway through. The depth finder was consistently showing three feet of water under them—just enough to run through—and all he could do was hope it lasted.

Finally he saw a clearing ahead and cut the wheel hard to port to make the left back into the Aerojet Canal. This canal was wider and showed eighteen feet of depth, just as it had when they entered it at Barnes Sound. He slowed slightly to survey what lay ahead. Unless it was a ruse, Trufante had escaped, but he had no idea if his captors were close. Several buildings came into view, and he looked for any sign of life. As he approached he could see they were in bad repair and abandoned. Slowly they approached the facility, scanning the banks for an entry point, when the first bullet hit the cabin.

* * *

Philip Dusharde looked at the bottle in his hand and put it back on the shelf. Things were becoming complicated, and he needed all his wits to see this through. The rocket had been the answer to all of it. After decades and millions of dollars fighting against environmental groups and do-good politicians, he had a plan to take care of it all. If they wanted the Everglades to flow freely again, he would accommodate them, but there would be no environmental impact studies showing some endangered strain of spotted-tail alligators. No more water samples and Army Corp of Engineers projects. They didn't like the dredged canals, then fine. He would let it all go back to nature and drain a million acres for agriculture in the process.

When ignited, the thrust from the two-hundred-and-sixty-inch diameter rocket would change the landscape of the entire Everglades, or at least that's what his geologists had told him. The shock waves from the rocket would open several shallow faults in the aquifer, creating a channel from Lake Okeechobee to Florida Bay.

He picked up his phone and pressed the button to connect to Jane. "Status?" he asked when she picked up.

The connection was full of static and he thought he heard gunfire in the background. "What the hell is going on there?"

"We've got some trouble, but we're mounting the charges now."

"Get it done and get out of there," he said, hanging up. If the explosives were in place he could blow the rocket now, but his plan involved another twist and would have to wait one more day. And it would have to be a sober day if the gunshots he heard were any indication of how close the plan was to unravelling. Whether bribing or blackmailing politicians or some of the dirtier work he needed done, he had always been able to count on Jane, and he hoped this assignment was not too much for her.

Planting the charges was fairly simple, requiring someone to drop into the silo and place the explosives on the outside casing in several strategic areas. The original rocket was meant to be ignited from within by a thirty-inch diameter charge launched directly into the nozzle. The solid fuel would then combust and send over five million pounds of thrust through the nozzle. His engineers had assured him that solid fuel would still be stable after fifty years and that placing explosives on the outside would turn the engine into a bomb. With the depth of the silo over two hundred feet into the ground, the blast would fracture the aquifer and change the entire drainage of the Everglades.

In many ways, the end result of the plan matched the environmentalists' Plan Six Flowway, but that would take almost a billion dollars and a decade to put in place. His plan was less than a thousand dollars in explosives and when triggered would take effect immediately. Once they got over the shock of it, they would thank him.

* * *

Mel was able to drive faster after the traffic thinned past the casino turnoff. She passed cars parked to the side of the road where people lined the banks, cane-pole fishing the canal to the north of the highway. There were several pull-offs, with airboat trailers along the way. Traffic was light and she saw more gators lining the highway than cars and trucks. This made her situation more tenuous as she drove the two-lane road. There was no place to go. She checked Mac's position on her phone again. He was moving, and she was thankful that their positions were converging. But there was only green between them. The last road that connected them was miles behind her.

Checking her rearview mirror, she saw the car closing and knew she had to make a decision. The gas gauge on the rental car was already down to half, and after trying to accelerate, she knew it was doubtful she could outrun whoever was following her. A billboard on her left made her decision for her. She had a mile to figure out how to buy some time. Without the speed to lose the car behind her, she did the opposite and slowed, allowing her pursuer to close the gap. She was down to forty mph now, and the car was within a hundred yards.

She willed it closer, not wanting to drop any more speed or he might figure out her plan. The parking lot appeared in the distance, less than a quarter mile away. Maintaining speed, she approached the turn and braked hard when she reached it. The car fishtailed into the gravel parking lot, barely missing several parked cars before she was able to pull it out of the skid.

Jumping out of the running car, she saw a sign for airboat rides and ran to the ticket hut, pushing past a waiting family. A quick glance behind told her the other driver had missed the turn, buying her a few desperate minutes. Pushing her credit card forward, she asked for a private tour, insisting it needed to leave immediately. The girl behind the counter didn't get her urgency, and she waited impatiently for the charge to go through, quickly signing the receipt and shoving it back to her. Just as she pushed through the turnstile, the blue sedan pulled into the lot.

She found herself on a roped boardwalk with alligators on both sides. A sign said these were nuisance alligators taken from Miami area residents' swimming pools and that they would find their way back if released. Passing several empty tour boats capable of holding twenty or more people, she took off at a run toward one of the smaller boats at the end of the line. Looking around for the driver, she saw several men drinking sodas under a palm frond structure and ran toward it.

With her receipt held in front of her, she must have looked like nothing they had ever seen before, but one of the men rose and greeted her.

"What's the rush, ma'am? Them gators ain't goin' nowhere."

"It's not like that." She held out her phone for the man. "I need to get there."

"Heck, ma'am. That's quite the ride," he said, looking at her receipt. "Guess you paid for half a day. Ought to cover it."

She followed him to one of the smaller boats. Looking back, she saw a man push through the ticket booth and look around. "We've got to hurry. It's a matter of life and death," she said.

The driver had only one speed and she hoped it was fast enough. Another look back confirmed the man had seen her and was running toward them. Finally the driver hopped onto one of the boats and offered her a hand. She took it, quickly sitting in front of the raised driver's seat, and prayed the man following her didn't have a gun. The engine cranked and started. Gripping the handrests firmly, she held on as the driver moved the boat forward into the narrow channel, gradually increasing speed as it opened up. They passed a clump of trees and she forgot for a second the danger she was in as she looked out at the miles of sawgrass spread out in front of them.

Handing her phone back to the driver, she looked back and, just before he accelerated, thought she saw another boat leave the channel.

Chapter 21

Mac did a double take when he saw the splatter of paint he had mistaken for a bullet and looked around for the source. Another shot hit, forcing him to duck back into the small cabin for cover.

"Call that number back," he told Pamela. "Tru's got his hands in this."

While she waited for an answer, he scanned the abandoned industrial facility. Whatever this had been, it was long gone. From the look of the buildings, they had been scavenged of anything valuable. Ductwork and conduits hung from ceilings and walls and graffiti marked the exteriors. It reminded him of something the Soviets might have built in the sixties.

She had the phone to her ear. "Hey. Tru there?" Pamela asked.

Mac took the phone. "We are in the boat. Hold your fire." He paused for a minute to see if he could see any signal relayed. "Who am I speaking with?"

"Max. First Bayou Brigade."

Mac muttered the name to himself and almost smiled. Trufante was here and apparently had recruited a paintball army. He had no idea the numbers involved, so he decided to play it safe. "Send your leader out." He thought he heard the unmistakable accent in the background.

"State your name," the youngish voice said.

"Tell that lame-brained Cajun it's Mac. Mac Travis."

Three figures became visible, moving from behind the cover of one of the buildings.

"It's Tru," Pamela said, and tried to jump from the boat.

Mac pulled her down. "It is, and he looks okay, but you gotta be patient. We don't know who else is here."

She moved behind him. Trufante motioned to the two fatigue-clad men, one either side of him, to wait and ran toward the canal. Pamela grabbed Mac's arm as a stream of bullets erupted around Trufante's feet. Within seconds he was back behind the building.

"They didn't hit him, did they?" Pamela asked.

"He looks all right. Boy's got more lives than a three-legged gator," Mac said, looking for where the gunfire had come from.

"Can you get him back on the phone?"

Pamela dialed and spoke to Max. Mac knew the second that Trufante was on and took the phone. She crossed her arms over her chest and glared at Mac, oblivious to the danger around them.

"What the hell's going on here?" Mac yelled into the phone.

"It's a little complicated." Trufante's voice came through the static.

Even though they were less than a hundred yards apart, they were at the limits of cell reception. There were no towers this far into no-man's-land. Mac took the phone and noticed only one bar on the screen. The battery icon was also in the red. It was always complicated with Trufante, and the story would be better told over a beer. "Who's shooting?" He cut the conversation short.

"She-devil and two of her boy toys."

Mac stared at the building in frustration. "Care to clarify?"

"Her name's Jane. Don't know much else besides she likes guns and fast cars."

The identity of the shooters could wait, and he was already getting frustrated with Trufante. "What are they doing?"

"I got a squad out doing some recon. Should know something soon."

Mac was trying to figure out what was going on when the phone died. He set it on a small table and looked around the cabin for a weapon.

"What happened?" Pamela asked, getting right in his face.

"Battery died," Mac said. He was done with her too. He needed to take the offensive and looked around the small cabin.

TJ used the boat for six-person charters, and commercial boats were required to carry additional safety gear not required on pleasure boats. He searched for the orange safety kit and removed the flare gun, whose twelve-gauge shells would also work in the shotgun. With only four shots left, he inserted one of the flares in the chamber of each weapon. He stuffed the rest in his pockets. He would save the shotgun shells.

"Can you use any of this?" he asked.

"I know how to shoot. My daddy taught me," she said.

He handed her the shotgun and immediately noticed that she knew firearms safety. Her trigger finger was outside the guard, and the barrel was pointed at the ground. That gave him a little comfort. If they were all playing with paintball guns he would have been well armed, but knowing there were automatic weapons as well did not leave a good feeling in his gut. They were sitting ducks if they stayed with the boat. He jammed the flare gun into his pants. It was time to move.

Just as he thought it, another flurry of shots fired. "We need to get off the boat," he told Pamela, leaning out of the cabin to see if he could figure out where the shots came from. There was a muzzle flash from a large steel building to the left, and he scanned the abandoned facility for a safe escape route. It didn't matter which way they went; they would be exposed for a least twenty yards. They needed to create a diversion.

"Look here," he said, making room for Pamela to peer around the corner of the cabin. "That building over there. Take your best shot."

He lowered himself and crawled out on the deck, making sure to stay below the gunwales. With a hand motion, he called her to his side and looked her in the eye. Underwater construction and salvage was a dangerous game, and in his career working with Wood he had been in some bad spots with a variety of men. Without the ability to read people and see panic before it could manifest itself, he would probably be dead. When he looked someone in the eye, he knew how they would react; wide eyes and dilated pupils were sure signs of impending doom. There was something odd about her look, but that was her normal; absent were the warning signs he was looking for. He nodded. "Ready."

She confirmed the signal and rose to one knee. Using the gunwale for support, she adjusted her position to a solid firing stance and braced herself. He watched her as she closed her left eye and sighted the weapon. With a bang and a whoosh, the flare left the barrel. The orange phosphorus trail showed the path of the projectile as it headed directly at the gunmen. They must have seen it too, because they left cover and ran back toward the building. Mac didn't wait. He grabbed her hand and together they jumped into the water.

After swimming the five feet to the earthen berm, he climbed on hands and knees to the pavement. Looking back to confirm Pamela was behind him, he sprang to a crouch. Bullets struck the dirt by his head. It had taken too long. They would have to use another round. Pulling the flare gun from his waist, he aimed and fired. Although not as accurate as the shotgun, the shot was good enough. He grabbed Pamela and ran toward the building where he had seen Trufante.

* * *

State Representative Vernon Wade sat in his office staring at his service weapon. The Colt 1911 usually resided in a display with his military citations prominently displayed behind him, but today he had it out on his desk. Several sheets of newspaper protected the oak surface from the rags, brushes, and oil he was using to clean the pistol. The question now was who he would use it on—himself or Philip Dusharde. The sugar magnate had him over a barrel, and the only way out was violence. He knew he was not the only legislator Dusharde had bought, but after the call he had taken a half hour ago, he was regretting his association with both the man and the industry.

It was common knowledge that Big Sugar bought political influence. It was rumored they had reached as far as the president, forcing Bill Clinton to push Florida's environmental disaster management back into the state's control in the late nineties, where it would be much cheaper and easier to buy what they needed. The cleanup costs and land deals proposed then paled in comparison to what was happening now. Times had changed and he was faced with an angry electorate, one that had been turned upside down demographically over the thirty years of his service; from farmers and fishermen to retirees and tree huggers. As a result, he was backtracking as fast as he could away from the sugar industry. His opponent in the upcoming primary wasn't squeaky clean, but following the current trend of non-politician politicians, she spoke freely, not worried about polls, and no one seemed to care.

His county was awash in polluted water and dead fish. The environmentalists blamed the dark brown flow routed to the Gulf via the Caloosahatchee River from Lake Okeechobee and the sugar fields below it. Back in the day, Big Sugar had paid off scientists to push the blame for the red tides and fish kills elsewhere, but it was so bad now a child could figure it out. He knew legislators on the East Coast were facing similar problems, and, with the rise of social media, there was nowhere to hide.

He'd told Dusharde he needed to back away or risk losing his seat—and more. Dusharde had laughed and told him he was expendable. But without the magnate's patronage he knew he would soon have a mailing address in a federal correctional institute. That might not be the worst of it once his trophy wife left him and his ex found out. Both would not hesitate to flay him publicly, and probably together.

It was a hot issue now, and every reporter and blogger in the state was interested. The probes were getting close. Several well-placed informants had told him a reporter from the *News-Press* had been asking questions in the county records office about real estate he owned. One of those deals that Dusharde had told him "would never see the light of day" was about to. His problem was not just taking the money, it was his greed. He had doubled down and used the "campaign contributions" and his inside knowledge to buy some of the real estate involved in the state's purchase plan.

The voters had approved the purchase of large tracts of agricultural land, which would have made him a quick buck if the sugar companies hadn't double-crossed him and stalled the transactions. The sugar magnates had used their influence and the land had never been sold. Now he was sitting on a pile of dirt that was worth pennies on the dollar and could put him in jail.

With the gun tucked into his belt, he put on his suit jacket and adjusted it to conceal the bulge. It was time to pay Dusharde a visit and settle this. Then he could move on to the campaign appearances he had scheduled for the weekend, all carefully fabricated to slide his position toward the environmentalists. You didn't get elected five consecutive terms without being able to take the temperature of the electorate—and it was running green now. To make the shift, he had to deal with Dusharde and, unfortunately because of the Colt, he would have to drive.

It was his habit to listen to National Public Radio, not that he agreed with their views, usually his were a hundred and eighty degrees from the liberal agenda, but he needed a source of motivation, and NPR provided a good one. He started to yell at the radio as he drove. A piece started about the Plan Six Flowway and he focused on the story.

The plan was to open drainage channels into the Everglades, in effect, restoring the original flow. That would entail buying tens of thousands of acres of public land—but the land purchases were to the east of his property, leaving it worthless. The project would also contribute jobs and money to his district. That was the good part. Promoting the environmental plan would likely get him reelected. But he was conflicted about the proposal to alleviate the flow of fertilizer-saturated water pouring into the Caloosahatchee and St. Lucie Rivers.

Though the plan looked good on paper, with big blue arrows showing the unrestricted flow of water to Florida Bay, buying the land and creating the drainage was problematic. The bridges to breach sections of Alligator Alley and Highway 41, the two roads that crossed the state connecting the east and west coasts, were necessary to the plan. From what he knew during his time with the Army Corp of Engineers in Vietnam, bridges brought unforeseen complications. The organic mush of the Everglades was all-too-similar to the swamps of Vietnam. These were not hard-bottom or sandy riverbeds they were planning to span. The bridges' piers would create channels that would form dams as silt and muck accumulated. In the end, he feared all those millions of dollars would be spent in vain. The plan would result in an ongoing multi-million-dollar dredging project to keep the water flowing.

Thinking about the inadequacy of the proposed project only fueled his anger. Whether the plan would work or not, he knew he needed to back it. It would mean jobs in his district and pacified environmental groups—both good things. But first he needed to salvage his investment, and, after the phone call, he knew Philip Dusharde had other plans. His resolve hardened the more he thought about it.

Chapter 22

Mel was pinned against the back of the seat by the forty-mph wind generated from the forward movement of the airboat. The 383 Chevy small-block engine put out 475 horsepower, and she was feeling all of it as the driver made a run for it. He must have seen the other boat come out of the channel and accelerate after them.

The low square bow sliced the tops of the cattails, sending them flying at Mel, who held up a hand to protect her face from the stinging spikes found on the top of the plants. Facing backward was more comfortable than forward, and she was able to watch the boat behind. It looked like they were maintaining the gap, although judging distance with only cattails and sawgrass between them was difficult. They had moved far enough from the highway that her entire field of view was now the same. Soon she started noticing subtle differences as they moved farther south. The Southern Glades, reaching from Highway 41 to Florida Bay, was the most pristine of what was left of the original River of Grass. Once spreading over much of South Florida, the Glades had been drained, filled, and rerouted so less than half of the natural area remained.

White Ibises scattered in front of them, joining other birds flying higher above. Every so often she saw a splash and a wake as a gator slid out of their way. Wondering if this was kind of a wetlands safari, she stared in awe at the natural landscape, mostly because she was powerless now, her life in the hands of the driver following the small red dot on the phone.

The boat behind them was keeping pace, and she wished she could communicate with the driver, but the exposed engine driving the airplane propeller was too loud to talk over. A minute later he reached down and handed back the phone. She looked at the screen and noticed the dot was gone. Frantically she pinched, panned, and zoomed the display, trying to find her link to Mac, but it was no use.

She looked up at the driver, who understood her concern and pointed straight ahead. Apparently he had an idea where they were going. He began to veer slightly to the east, and she saw the landscape to their left change. What had been all wetlands now showed signs of man. There were straight lines and agricultural fields in the distance. They entered a wide area of water that looked like a road running through the grass, heading straight for what looked like land.

Another glance back and she relaxed slightly. The other boat had been reduced to a spec on the horizon. It was still there and following, but showed no sign of being able to catch them. Turning forward, she focused on their surroundings, which had made the not-so-subtle change to a man-made canal. She had a feeling they were getting closer, but the waterway had narrowed, forcing the driver to slow. The other boat was closing the gap.

* * *

Out of breath, Mac and Pamela made it to the corner of the building. Trufante grabbed the woman in a bear hug and the couple exchanged a brief moment before Mac ordered the group to fall back. The distraction of the flare wouldn't last much longer, and now that they were together they needed to put some space between the group and whoever was shooting at them. "Scouts are out," Trufante said, still holding Pamela,

Mac saw the smile on his face and knew he was enjoying this. That was Trufante. "Where are they?"

"Went to see what the she-devil was doing. That woman's evil as a snake-bit gator."

Mac was about to respond when two boys and a girl who looked about college age called for cover and dove toward them. Again he wondered if this was still just a paintball game to them. "What'd you find out?"

They looked at Trufante for approval before talking. He nodded.

The girl started. "They're around the rocket. The woman is down in the silo. We couldn't get close enough to see what she was doing."

"Rocket?" Mac asked.

"Dude, it's the old Aerojet rocket factory. They left one down in the silo when they bailed in the late sixties," one of the boys said.

Mac didn't know what to believe. He needed to see this for himself. Scanning the area, he saw the building the scouts had come from and wondered how to get across the fifty yards of exposed asphalt to reach it without getting shot.

"I need to have a look," Mac said. This was spinning out of control.

"Max, take two men and Mac here over to the silo. We'll cover you," Trufante said.

"Cover me with what? You have paintball guns, they have the real thing," Mac said.

"Quantity over quality is what I always say. Just keep your head down. We'll keep them off you."

Mac looked at Max, who had picked two other boys from the group. They nodded to each other and, bent over in low crouches, took off at a run. Mac heard a continuous stream of splats as the rest of the group fired over their heads toward the building where the live fire had come from earlier. Something was missing, he realized, as they turned the corner inside of the silo shed and caught their breath. No shots had been fired back. That could only mean the shooters were either gone or had moved. He suspected the later.

With no threat from the rear, he looked forward. Max had already ordered the two other men to fan out to scout the perimeter. "It's over here," one of the boys whispered.

Mac followed him to a section of the concrete floor covered with a rusted and broken steel grate. The sun disappeared, casting the building into an eerie twilight. He looked back outside and saw storm clouds were building. Light streamed into the building the large openings where he suspected roll up garage doors had once hung. The roof had several large gaps where the sections came together.

Designed in a way to slide open when the rocket was fired, it was now only partially closed. Just as he approached the edge of the silo the sun came out, throwing beams of light into the building. Trufante was right. There was a rocket down there. It's metal finish was dulled by years of exposure, but he could still see the NASA markings. He moved toward a section of the grate on the far side that had been removed. There were fresh scrapes on the concrete where the steel cover had been dragged, and it looked like it had been moved recently.

"You have a flashlight?" he asked Max.

He handed him his rifle with a tactical LED light mounted next to the telescopic sight. Taking the offered butt from Max, he placed it against his shoulder and brought the barrel to his eye. He found the switch, and brilliant light illuminated a narrow area of the silo. Panning the rifle from side to side, he scanned the rocket and surrounding silo. It was much larger than he expected, spanning over twenty feet in diameter. Shooting the light into the void, it diffused before he could see the bottom. Not sure what he was really looking for, he lowered the weapon as he swept it back and forth. About halfway down the fuselage he saw a blinking red dot.

"Look at that," he said to Max as he pulled the gun away.

"What the heck," Max said.

A loud boom caused them both to jump, then they realized it was thunder. Standing above the opening, staring into the hole, they heard a gun cock behind them—a real gun.

Before Mac turned, he noticed two other dots attached to the rocket, and he realized what they were.

"Back away," a woman called.

She was backlit by the doorway and Mac could only see her silhouette. Looking like an Old West gunslinger, she stood there with pistols in each hand. On first glance as she approached it looked like she had bandoleers crisscrossed over her shoulders. A flash of lightning was accompanied by a thunder clap, and he could see it was the nylon webbing of a climbing harness.

She motioned Max away and approached Mac. Instinctively he stepped back, putting his weight on his left foot to catch himself and was surprised when there was nothing there. Falling backward into the silo, his body clipped something hard and he reached out desperately. A hard blow to his side turned him and he was able to see the rocket in front of him. He grabbed for a guide wire, hoping it would slow his fall.

The rusted wire immediately tore his hands, but he held on. Like a fighter taking body shots, he flinched as he bounced back and forth between the solid steel rocket and the concrete walls. Finally the momentum slowed and he hung in space. Grasping the fifty-year-old wire, he took several breaths and fought for a better grip before he looked up to see how far he had fallen. He was deep in the silo. The circle above him was small, and he thought he saw several heads sticking over the opening. He heard voices echoing down into the chamber. They knew he was down there.

A few shots fired blindly into the void, but a women's sharp voice ordered a stop to them. He was trapped and she knew it. After spending the last twenty-five years around demolitions, he knew what she had placed on the rocket and was probably worried a ricochet might ignite one of the charges. Feeling safer from the threat above, he had to face the unknown below as his sweaty palms and cramping muscles threatened his grip on the wire. Slowly he was losing the battle.

His eyes had become acclimated to the dark and he looked down, thinking he saw the hard bottom of the chamber. It was too far to jump, and he looked back around him at the rocket and casing. The rocket was smooth, the only rigging points were the ones the guide wires were attached to above him. The old cable was frayed and rusty, but he had no choice. Wrapping it around his hands, he placed his feet against the face of the rocket and started to climb.

* * *

Mel looked at the anvil-shaped cloud ahead. Thunder had already started to roll, a precursor of what was to come. But she thought she heard a different sound over the engine noise. After an hour of the constant whine of the engine, propeller, and cattails snapping as the bow crashed through them, the pop—pop—pop sound of a gun and the whiz of bullets flying by grabbed her attention. She expected them to be coming from the man in the boat behind them. Risking a look back, she could see him clearly, but there was no gun. She turned, willing the boat to go faster, when she saw the first building appear on her left. Several more came into view, and she almost forgot about the pursuit as she stared at the abandoned industrial complex and wondered what it was doing out here in the middle of the Everglades.

The roar of the boat behind her brought her back to the present and she turned. The airboat was right on their tail now, the gap only a dozen feet. Instinctively, she grabbed for the handrests when she saw the steel hull about to ram them. The first hit was just a tap, and she looked up at the driver, who accelerated. Just as he did, the canal took a forty-five-degree turn, and the starboard side of the airboat slid against the berm, causing the boat to spin. He immediately cut the engine speed to regain control.

Feeling like she was in a car skidding on an icy road, Mel fought the dizziness and gripped tighter as the g-forces built. Finally the boat slowed enough for the driver to straighten it out, but they were dead in the water. Turning back, she saw a gun in the hand of the pursuer. A shot fired and she jumped over the side. Clawing at the lukewarm, slimy water, she tried to reach the bank, ignoring the bullets slamming the water around her. A blast of air caught her by surprise and she panicked for a second. Her driver had the boat moving, using its position to screen her from the other boat. Besides the protection of the steel hull, the thrust from the propeller pushed her toward shore.

With the shooter distracted, she climbed the berm and lay on the rough gravel surface, surveying her position. The pursuing airboat had been forced to turn by the melee, and she could see the driver standing in the bow looking for her. The top of the berm concealed her from his vantage point. As long as she stayed low, she could move away from him, and she was about to make a run for the closest building when she felt the barrel of a rifle press into her back.

Chapter 23

Mel collapsed on the gravel lot, not caring about the fat rain drops that had just started falling. Thunder boomed again, this time shaking the ground, and lightning flashed in the distance. She berated herself for acting impulsively, but then realized that there had been no choice. With the man in the airboat shooting at her, there was nowhere to go but forward. She could have easily blamed her situation on Mac and Trufante, but she knew they were only pawns in a bigger game. Big Sugar was involved, and that steeled her for whatever was to come.

A hand grabbed the back of her shirt, pulling her to her feet, and she found herself face-to-face with her captor. Mel blinked the water away from her eyes and followed her directions, moving slowly, so she could evaluate her surroundings. A loud crack of thunder seemed to open the heavens and the rain intensified. Despite the reduced visibility, she had the feeling there were other people around, which was confirmed when she heard something crash by the side of the building behind them. The noise distracted the woman for a brief second, and if she had been prepared, she might have been able to catch her off guard and escape, but the moment passed.

It did alter their path. The woman pushed her to the right, toward an alley between two concrete buildings. As they approached she saw a shadow toward the end and noticed the woman tense. She heard a strange sound and felt something sting her thigh. Looking down, she saw a blue splat on her leg. Within seconds, several more appeared, and she looked around for the source.

Before she could figure out what was happening, the woman dragged her against the wall of the building. Their backs were covered now, but the paint splatter surrounded them. They were pinned down, with shots raining in on them from both directions. The woman was covered in paint from head to toe, the rain blending the individual spots into a mass of blue upon contact. She tried to return fire, but the incoming barrage was coming so quickly she fell back. At the same time that Mel felt the stings increase in intensity, she noticed their frequency had decreased. She wiped her face with her shirt. Instead of clearing her vision, it was now blurred from the rain and the paint smeared in her eyes. Squinting, she could see the vague outline of two groups approaching. A steady stream of fire coming from what looked like rifles was directed at the other woman. She was pinned down, taking all the shots now, and Mel saw her chance. She ran toward the tall figure leading the group approaching from her side, and even through her paint-clouded vision, she saw the two rows of teeth and knew it was Trufante.

This was not the time for questions, and she slid behind him. He signaled the two groups to continue fire as they backed away. Seconds later, she was around the corner of the building, staring up at the tall Cajun.

"What the hell?"

"You're welcome. First Bayou Battalion reporting," he said, flashing his thousand-dollar grin.

"I'm not even going to ask. But thanks." She looked around, surrounded by a group of camo-clad, paint-covered figures, surprised that Pamela was one of them. They lowered their goggles and looked to Trufante for direction. "Where's Mac?"

"Went to scout out the rocket. Heard some trouble over there, though. We was gonna check it out when I saw you climb out of the water."

"Let's go," she said.

"There's more bogies out there," he said, motioning to three of the group. Putting two fingers to his eyes, he sent them in the direction of a large steel building.

"Would you knock off the army shit? We need to find Mac." Her gratitude for the rescue was already forgotten. Trufante, even in the best of times, pushed every button she had. Avoiding his grasp, she left the cover of the concrete building and started toward the steel structure. The group he sent was moving there as well, using an Army-type maneuver that she didn't see the need for until several shots hit the dirt around her. She turned and ran back to Trufante.

She saw the "I told you so" look written on his face. Before he could say anything, three more figures emerged from the back of the building. They ran up to them, standing with their hands on their knees, catching their breath.

Mel moved closer, sensing something was wrong, and noticed

Pamela standing beside her.

"First Bayou Recon Squad reporting," the boy said.

Mel was about to smack him, but he quickly continued.

"Mac is in the hole. Not sure of his condition. The two bogies were firing on us, so we took the long way back," he said, still breathing hard.

"What hole? What's he talking about?" Mel got in Trufante's face.

Even though she only reached his chin, he backed away and rubbed his forehead. "We gotta get him."

"We're low on ammunition," the leader said. "I'm not sure how much we can help."

Mel saw several shadows grow larger as the two gunmen emerged from cover. With their weapons held at waist level, ready to shoot, one yelled over the rain. "Let's all drop our toys."

The paintball rifles dropped to the ground.

"Let the kids go," a woman's voice said.

Mel looked to the shadows and saw her standing behind the two men. Covered in blue, she had tried to wipe her face, but blue lines ran down from her cheeks, streaking her face like bad mascara. "Who is she?" Mel whispered to Trufante.

"Goddamn woman's the she-devil. Almost cut my other finger off." He must have seen her look and added, "Jane's her name. Don't know much more."

She ignored the comment. The paintball team was walking away backward. Once they reached a safe distance, Mel saw the leader give Trufante a thumbs-up.

"First Bayou Brigade dismissed," Trufante said proudly, watching as the group took off at a run.

Mel looked at the two automatic weapons pointing at them. The woman stepped forward. Trufante flinched as she walked toward him and backhanded him across the face. Under other circumstances, Mel might have applauded her. She turned to Mel. "You look like the only one with any brains here. Where is the other man?"

It took her a minute to realize she was talking about Mac. Her answer might determine his fate. "I think I saw him down behind that building."

"Did you hit him?" she asked one of the men.

"Might have. With all that paint flying around, it was hard to see."

"Check it out," she ordered him.

The man took off at a lope toward the building. With her gun drawn, she pointed toward a dark SUV in the distance. "Let's go. And no trouble from you or she gets it." She pointed the gun toward Mel.

The other man joined them at the car. "There's no sign of him," he said. "I did see some blood by the silo."

She looked toward the building. "Never mind him."

Opening the back door, she pushed the women into the back seat. Mel could see the look on her face and a chill, not related to the rainwater dripping down her spine, took hold as the woman spun and smacked Trufante with the butt of the pistol. He crumpled to the ground. With a smirk, she raised the gun and shot him.

Pamela tried to crawl over Mel, but the woman was already in the car, pointing the gun at her.

* * *

Vernon Wade pulled up to the stately entrance of Philip Dusharde's house. He was uninvited and expected to see guns pointed at him any second. After a minute, he relaxed and ran his hands over the Colt. Setting it under the seat, he decided that he would try and solve this civilly first. The eight-hour drive had taken some of the fire outta him. He got out, smoothed his clothes, and ran his hands through his thinning hair. Clearing his throat, he rehearsed what he planned to say and headed toward the large, arched double-entry doors.

Still surprised he hadn't been greeted, he pressed the doorbell and waited. Several minutes later, he was still wondering where Dusharde's woman was. It was seldom in the last few years that he had been seen without her. He was about to press the bell again when the door opened.

"Well, Vernon, if this isn't a surprise," Dusharde said, reaching out to shake his hand.

The grip was firm, and Vernon tried to squeeze back with equal force, but feared his sweaty palms would give him away. He clenched his gut to steel himself for the confrontation. The sugar magnate already had the upper hand.

"Come on in. Always a pleasure to have a member of the

legislature drop by, even if it is unexpected."

Vernon swallowed the barb, wishing he had brought the gun with him. The man was insolent, and he envisioned the red spot on Dusharde's chest after he put a bullet in him. "Thank you."

Dusharde led him through the living room and down a hallway to his study. He swept his hand, indicating an expensive leather chair, and moved to the bar. "Drink? Cigar?"

Vernon sat in the offered chair. Even before he spoke, he knew he had lost his resolve. Maybe a drink would help. "Sure. Scotch neat would be great."

He watched the man remove the top from a crystal decanter and pour a good three fingers into two glasses. Moving toward him, Vernon almost flinched as Dusharde handed him a glass and sat in a matching chair directly across from him. Even the setting of the room, with no table or barrier between the men, was making him uncomfortable. Knowing it was the wrong thing to do, he raised the glass and drained half of it.

"That's a thirty-year-old. I have it custom blended."

Vernon knew it was a reprimand for gulping the drink. He nodded, even though he hadn't tasted it.

"Well, Congressman, what can I do for you?" Dusharde asked, taking a sip of his drink.

Vernon froze. This was not how he had planned the confrontation. "It's about the Flowway project."

"Not going to work out for you the way you planned, is it?" Dusharde said, ending the question as a statement.

He felt the man's eyes bore through him. "Yes. But . . ."

"Oh, I know it's a conflict of interest. I told you to put it in an offshore corporation." He paused. "But you didn't take my advice, did you?"

In a few simple sentences, Dusharde had turned the conversation to his advantage, and he felt like a schoolboy in front of the principal. "I'm a member of the Florida Legislature," he said, trying to sound like his position carried authority.

"And a corrupt one who wasn't very smart."

Wade had already resigned himself to taking a loss on the investment. He wanted out of here, but he couldn't leave under these terms. "You can buy it."

Dusharde Sugar held over fifty thousand acres that abutted his property. The land was arable, where his own was not, and he regretted the decision to buy the cheaper acreage. "I have stockholders counting on me to make a profit," he said.

Wade was about to counter that they had made enough already. He couldn't even comprehend the numbers. Desperation set in. "I'll give you my vote if you buy me out." If he had the gun, he would have shot him. Instead he drained the glass.

"And why would I do that?" He sipped his drink and gave Wade a cold stare over the glass. "Face it. You're damaged goods. Back in the day, your constituency empathized with you. Y'all were one and the same. They had your back. Now, with all those big-city types moved in, things have changed. The old-timers might have overlooked some of your obvious flaws. They made their fortunes selling cow pastures to the yuppies, now they're done with you too. Maybe it's time to step down."

Wade knew his life would be over if he lost his seat. No one needed another washed-up career politician with no marketable skills. His only hope was as a lobbyist, and he needed Dusharde to help him. He stared at his empty glass and took his last stab. "Would you give me a job if I did?"

Dusharde's silence was a prelude to the answer he knew was coming and, for the second time, he wished he had brought the gun in with him. Before Dusharde could answer, he heard activity outside the door. Both men turned to look, and he thought he saw a ghost covered in blue paint enter.

"Ms. Woodson?"

Chapter 24

Mac knew the only way out was to first descend to the bottom of the silo. Squinting up into the dripping water, he couldn't see any way to climb out. His grip was already failing, and he could feel his muscles start to cramp. After being exposed to the weather for fifty years and weakened by the inevitable rust, the frayed cable tore his hands. Releasing one hand, he pulled his T-shirt over his head, then switched hands and pulled the shirt off. Wrapping each hand in a section of the material, he placed the cable around his waist and started to belay himself down the rocket.

With his feet against the rocket casing, he lowered himself one hand at a time, being careful to arrest any slide before it happened. The farther he descended, the cooler the air became, but the humidity increased in the damp, enclosed space, and sweat soon coated the wire, making it harder to grip. His forearms were tense and his hands were failing fast. Suddenly he stopped, seized by another cramp. There was no way he could continue, and he looked down into the dark hole, seeing nothing to indicate the descent was over.

A sharp staccato thunderclap echoed in the chamber and the rocket vibrated. Lightning illuminated the chamber, and water started cascading around him as the storm increased. The added moisture only made his situation worse and he felt his right hand slip. But just as it did, another flash of lightning illuminated the bottom of the silo, revealing water below, and it was closer than he thought. He would have to trust his instincts. The rain blinded him when he looked up, and the dark hole refused to yield its secrets when he looked down. Closing his eyes, he released his grip on the wire enough to allow himself to slide freely. There was no way to stop the descent now, and he bent his knees and braced himself for the impact he knew was coming.

His feet hit the water first, followed by the rest of his body. He dropped below the surface, knowing that the storm had saved his life. A second later, his feet found purchase on the hard bottom, and he used his legs to spring back to the stale air. It took several seconds before his head reached the surface, and from his diving experience he was able to estimate the water was about twenty feet deep.

Treading water, he gasped for air and closed his eyes, trying to acclimate them to the darkness. The bottom of the silo was pitch-dark. His only recollection of his surroundings was the outline of the concrete walls and rocket, briefly illuminated during the lightning strikes. Water still poured in around him, but the thunder was rolling now, and the lightning strikes were becoming less frequent.

Just as he thought the storm was fading, a loud crack of thunder boomed and lightning illuminated the chamber, though not as brightly as before. Taking the opportunity to survey his predicament, he studied his surroundings, finding nothing but the rocket and about five feet of water surrounding it. He swam around the circumference, feeling for anything that might aid him, but the metal casing was smooth. Another boom, briefer and quieter than before, shook the rocket and the sky flashed. The light briefly reached the bottom of the silo, giving him another chance to look around.

Something floated on the surface, undulating like a snake, and he reversed his path. Another flash of light showed it for what it was—near the concrete wall was a section of yellow nylon rope. The silo fell into darkness again, and he swam toward where he thought he had seen it. His hand touched the cold, wet concrete, but there was nothing there. He shivered and knew his situation was worsening. Not only was he tired, but he was getting cold. The sky brightened again and he saw the line just out of his reach. This time, his hand found it and he pulled.

The flow of water decreased to a tolerable drip now that the storm had moved on, allowing him to look up again. Using his feet to tread water, he coiled the line around his forearm, counting three feet for every full turn. For what he intended, he had to do some quick math. Knowing the rocket was about twenty feet in diameter, he multiplied it by three, not able to do the full pi calculation in his head. The circumference should be around seventy feet, to which he added in a generous allowance for error. He estimated he would need almost a hundred feet to reach around it. He was up to thirty turns, just short, when the line pulled taut. Yanking, hoping for a few more valuable feet, he felt a hard tug and knew he had reached the end.

Before trying to retrieve it, he swam the line around the rocket, tying a quick overhand dropper knot when he reached the beginning. Relieved there was enough line to circle the rocket, he still needed to free the end. Breathing in for a count of eight, he held the breath for two counts and released it under pressure, purging his lungs of carbon dioxide and enriching them with oxygen in the process. Half a dozen times, he followed the breath pattern he used for free diving and, after inhaling the last breath, he used the line to pull himself below the surface of the water.

Hand over hand, he descended, clearing the pressure from his ears several times, until he reached the end of the line. Feeling around, unable to see in the ink-black water, he worked the knot. His lungs started to burn and, unable to free the line, he surfaced. Rather than one extended dive that would tax his already drained resources, he decided to do several shorter ones. As soon as his head broke through, he repeated the breathing pattern. It took four efforts to untangle the knot, and when he finally did, he brought the end to the surface.

Able to use the line tied around the rocket to support himself, he rested. It would be a long way up. The rain had stopped, but the rocket was wet and slippery. He slid his hands under the loop and placed his feet against the metal casing. Using his hips, like a lineman climbing a telephone pole, he thrust the line upward, gaining a few inches, and started walking up the rocket. It was hard working with that much line, but the combination of the nylon material and the smooth casing offered little resistance, and he was able to slide the rig up several feet at a time. He was out of the water now, and he started to gain traction. With every few baby steps upward, he had to stop and shimmy the line higher on the cylinder, but it was working. The position was not uncomfortable, and he was able to rest along the way.

It became brighter as he rose and he became more optimistic. He continued and soon reached the climbing rope used to set the explosives. Tying it onto the nylon line, he started walking sideways around the rocket. The first charge was only a few feet away, and he looked at it, wondering what to do. It was one thing to reach it, another to disable it. As he got closer, he saw it was not the simple C4 explosive and remote detonator he expected. From his years of underwater salvage and construction, he had a thorough knowledge of demolitions, and what he was looking at was not something you saw every day. The tamper-proof charge was mounted to the steel casing with a powerful magnet. Simple enough, but he knew he would be unable to remove it without tools.

With the rope secured to the nylon line wrapped around the rocket, he had the additional security of being connected to the surface, allowing him to take his time and study the casing, detonation, and trigger mechanism. He tried to dislodge it, but soon realized that there was simply no way to remove or disable the charge without blowing the rocket.

Defeated, he continued his climb and focused on what he needed to do next. He knew the trail led to Clewiston, which he guessed was several hours away by car. With the boat it would take him twice that, if he could even find a route through the tangle of canals and channels of the Everglades. The northern area was more agricultural and much drier than the protected Southern Glades, and he suspected he would have to abandon the boat.

He was close to the surface now. Squinting in the sunlight streaming in through the open ceiling, he could see steam rising from the pavement above him and he started to miss the coolness of the silo. With one hand on the surface, he paused and pulled himself over the edge. He rose and took in his surroundings. The sun was low on the horizon, and he realized the climb, which he guessed had taken only an hour, had cost the entire afternoon.

Releasing the line, he ran through the puddles toward the canal, hoping the boat was still there. For the first time today, his luck was with him and he saw it about a hundred yards away, jammed into a small side channel. Taking one last look around the abandoned facility, he saw no other means of transportation. It would have to be the boat for now, and he jumped into the water and swam toward the dive ladder mounted on the transom. Climbing aboard, he saw the keys still in the ignition where he had left them. The engine started and he waited for the electronics to find his position. The screen showed him in a light green area, but, without his phone, he didn't trust the random blue lines on the GPS. The navigation chip was for the ocean and only vaguely showed the inland waterways.

He remembered the last uncharted trip through the waters of Florida Bay with Alicia and their encounter with the tweakers led by the wannabe golfer who went by Bugger Vance. It could easily happen again if he got stuck in a dead-end canal. He picked up the microphone for the VHF radio and called out for TJ on channel sixteen. It was late, but he knew the dive shop would hear him on their base station. The tall aerial antenna mounted to the building drastically increased their range. A minute later, his call was answered and the young voice asked him to go to channel seventy-two.

TJ was on the radio a minute later. "Can you give me your location from the GPS?"

Mac read the position from the screen. "I need to get to Clewiston."

"Roger. Easier by car," TJ said, "but give me a few minutes and I'll get to the war room. We'll get you there."

A few minutes later he heard TJ back on the radio. The signal was weaker. "What's with the signal?"

"I'm upstairs on a handheld. I'm pulling your position up now."

Mac envisioned TJ sitting in his captain's chair manipulating the images on the large-screen HD monitors mounted on the far wall in a rectangular array. It allowed him to configure the units to display separate images on each screen, use the dozen screens as one, or a variety of combinations. Alicia had a space to the side that, although it was less ostentatious, had all the firepower the ex-CIA agent needed. "Alicia there?"

"She went out to the store. For now, it's you and me, buddy."

Mac could tell by TJ's voice that he was excited. The gamer relished these real-life challenges. "It's getting dark."

"Just about have the course plotted out now. Start heading north on the large canal to your right. I'm looking for a way through Highway 41."

"How far is that?" Mac asked. "At some point we're going to lose reception." He knew the VHF radio worked on line of sight, and he could already tell from the difference in signal between the base unit in the dive shop and the handheld that TJ was now using that the signal would not reach much further. "Let's just get there for now."

The canals were straight and, besides the occasional fishermen and the few gators sunning themselves in the fading light, he was alone. He stared at the GPS, trying to connect the dots.

Chapter 25

Dusharde looked at Wade. "You know that woman?"

"What the hell is she doing here? I've been fighting her kind for decades. Damned save the earth do-gooders," Wade said.

Sipping his drink, Dusharde studied the woman. "Go on. Tell me what you know," he said to Wade while watching the new woman's face for any reaction.

"Her name is Melanie Woodson," he spat. "Worked for Davies and Associates in D.C. They were the firm trying to block the Feds from passing the land purchase deal back to the state. I don't remember her being a part of that, but she's been in and around the progressive camp for quite a while, first with the ACLU, then with Davies. Woman's nothing but trouble."

Dusharde could see it was true from the look on her face. Jane stared at her as well, obviously not knowing her background. This was troubling, and there was only one surefire way to deal with problems like this, and he didn't hesitate. "Have another drink, Vernon," he said, rising and moving back to the bar. He took the decanter, poured a generous dose into Wade's glass, and added just enough to his for show.

"What do you want me to do with her?" Jane asked.

"Not sure why you brought them here. And who is the other one?" Phillip said, looking at the tall woman standing behind them. She was more his type and he could see from the look on her face that she would be a handful in bed. Instead of waiting for her to answer, he got up and went toward her.

"What would your name be, sweetheart?" he asked.

"Pamela," she replied, with a fierce look on her face.

These two were getting him excited. It was like being in the lion cage at the circus, with Jane as the ringmaster, controlling the beasts with a gun instead of a whip. "Well, Pamela, can I get you a drink?"

He could see the fury build in her eyes and he became aroused.

"She shot my boyfriend. Tru's dead because of all your greed," she said, looking at Jane.

The Woodson woman moved in between them, sensing something was about to happen. She whispered something to Pamela.

"I hope you cleaned up your mess," he said to Jane.

She shot him a look. Dismissing her attitude, but not her actions over the past few days, he asked for a rundown of what had happened.

"With them here?" Jane asked, looking at the two women.

Dusharde thought for a second. "Yes." He wanted to use the women as a barometer to see if she was telling the truth. And the tall one had him intrigued. He turned to Wade. "Don't know if you want to hear all this. Plausible deniability and all."

The representative brought his glass to his mouth. "Wouldn't miss this for the world. I'm thinking anything said here is never going past those doors."

"Nixon thought the same, but suit yourself," Dusharde said, looking at Jane to begin.

* * *

Trufante squeezed one eye open. He was not dead. Immediately, pain signals flooded his brain, and it took him several seconds to see the gunshot wound dripping blood from his thigh. Not sure how long he had been unconscious, he looked around. He was in the back of an SUV and moving. The squad must have heard the shots and investigated. The first Bayou Brigade had probably saved his life. Looking back at his leg, he could see the dressing was saturated, but the bleeding had stopped. He screamed in pain when the truck hit another bump. The roads were wide and straight, but the weather cycles fluctuating between rain and drought here were hard on the asphalt surface.

"Hang in there, commander," Max said, turning from the front seat.

"Where y'all takin' me?"

"We have to get you to a hospital. I think you lost a lot of blood back there."

Trufante was good with that. He was done playing commander. All he wanted was a shot of morphine and Pamela. The thought stopped him. It surprised him how high on his priority list she was.

Even after six months together he was interested, which was unique for him. He had always been a friends-with-benefits kind of guy, and the longevity and intensity of the relationship with Pamela was a mystery to him. He still hadn't figured her out. Since finding her wandering the backstreets of Key West, dragging a suitcase behind her, he had discovered little more about her background than there was always a pile of money on the first, that usually lasted for a week or two, then she used a credit card until the last week of the month, when it disappeared and times got tough.

The SUV swerved, throwing him against the side of the truck and bringing him back to the present. He leaned back, trying to get comfortable, and saw the reason: a twelve-foot-long gator sunning itself on the road. Gradually, the natural landscape changed and they entered an agricultural area. Large fields were planted with laser-straight rows of small palm trees and other landscape bushes. Then the inevitable track homes became visible, first as small isolated areas between the fields and finally encompassing the entire landscape. Strip malls and traffic lights now made their appearance, finishing the transformation from pristine nature to the concrete jungle.

"Y'all just gotta drop me off. They ask questions about gunshots," Trufante said as the SUV slowed and, with one last bump, pulled under the overhang in front of the Homestead Hospital. "Not here. Pull 'round to the side. I'll get help."

"You can't walk," Max said. "We'll help you. The First Bayou Brigade doesn't leave its own behind."

Trufante looked at him sternly. "Look here. This is a bad bit of business, and y'all don't need to be associated with it."

Max started to say something, but Trufante cut him off. "And that's an order."

They left him by an abandoned wheelchair near the back of the parking lot.

"Y'all been good soldiers," he said, dismissing them. He hobbled to the chair and sat. A few minutes later, with blood dripping from the saturated T-shirt that bound the wound, he wheeled himself into the entrance and was immediately surrounded. With experience in these matters, he feigned unconsciousness to avoid the prodding questions and paperwork, and was careful not to show his grin when the IV was inserted in his forearm.

* * *

Mac ran the boat hard. He worked to the north, staying to the less-vegetated channels whenever possible. The GPS display was highly detailed, showing contour lines and other information for the ocean, but here the boat was displayed as a small icon in a field of nondescript green. With the GPS only useful for showing his proximity to the larger landmarks, he knew he needed help. He was coming up on Highway 41, and tried to raise TJ, but as he suspected, there was no answer. Having driven the route to the west coast, otherwise known as the Tamiami Trail, several times, he recalled all the airboat rides and small alligator venues along the way. There were few waterways underneath the highway, and he could only hope the course he was taking would lead him to one. Otherwise he could be delayed hours trying to find a path to the other side.

Night had already closed in on him, making it easy to see the headlights from the road and the security lights of the businesses ahead. He steered toward a large area with a halo of light around it and slowed the boat as he entered a small canal. The distinctive groan of gators surrounded him as he idled into the docking area for the airboat tour venue. Bugs swarmed around the security lights that reflected dozens of pairs of prehistoric eyes, all looking at him.

He tried to ignore the beasts and eased the boat into an open slip where he tied it off with a slipknot in case he needed a quick escape. He walked toward the venue. The docks and boardwalks were all lit by yellow-tinted lights, probably some measure of security that was also supposed to discourage mosquitos. They were partly effective at the former and worthless at the second. He swatted the bugs around his head and followed the signs toward the exit and saw a building ahead with a thatched hut for a roof. Just before he reached it, he encountered a locked gate. Probably there to keep outsiders away from the boats and gators, it was instead holding him hostage in the Everglades. He looked around, but the boardwalk was the only path. There was another section that looked like it served as an entrance, with a ticket hut blocking its path, but another yellow lights showed it had a gate as well.

Just behind him was a small display with a large-scale map of the Everglades that might guide him, and he turned back to the boat. He stopped when something moved in front of him on the boardwalk.

A gator blocked the way, its eyes glaring at him from the shadows. Its tail slapped against the wooden decking as it inched toward him. There was no way around it, and with his back to the locked gate, he riffled through his pockets for anything that could help.

He came up with a few shotgun shells and flare cartridges, but without the gun they were useless. Desperate, he looked around thinking it might be safer to hop the rail and swim to the boat. That option was quickly discarded when he saw four more sets of eyes pop out of the water. He was surrounded.

Thinking he could stand on the wood railing to get above the reach of the gator, he grabbed for the top board, only to have it break away when the end grain of the post released the nail. The thick humidity in the brush could corrode even a galvanized fastener in months. With the five-foot piece of wood for a weapon, he waved it in the direction of the gator, who backed slightly to evaluate the new development. The rusted nail caught his eye and, just as the gator inched forward, deciding that the weapon or the man wielding it were no threat, he had an idea.

The gator took another few tentative steps, his primitive brain trying to decide what his dinner was doing and moved forward again. Mac waited. His best chance for success was to get the gator as close as possible. When it was ten feet away, he wound up, figuring if it didn't work, he would still have time to hop on the rail. Swinging the board with as much force as he could garner in the awkward position, he ran forward and smashed the nail into its head. At first he thought nothing had happened and was about to leap for the rail, but then he heard a groan and the gator dropped to the dock. With a tight grip on the board, he tiptoed past the remains.

Glancing back every few feet to see if he was being followed, he made his way to the small kiosk where he had seen the map. It was dark and he ran his hands against the rough-sawn cedar poles in search of a light switch. Finding one, he flicked it on and a minute later he could hear the ballasts of the fluorescent lights buzzing, and finally he was bathed in cool white light. If the yellow lights were made to deter bugs, the fluorescents were like honey. Between the light and the sweat covering him, within seconds he was attacked by every manner of flying insect.

With black flies and mosquitos swarming around him, he swatted aimlessly and stared at the detailed map. The scale map of the Everglades had the mandatory "You are Here" symbol marking his location, but as he studied it, he saw the blue lines he was looking for and started tracing a path, following a series of canals all the way to Clewiston.

He would have taken it if he could, but the map was laminated onto the wood below it to prevent the moisture from rotting it. Instead, he studied the route. Moving backward from the bottom of Lake Okeechobee, he decided on the well-marked canal running parallel to Highway 27.

He reached the boat without incident and climbed back aboard. Releasing the slipknot, he let the current move the boat away from the dock, started the engine, and reversed away from the massacre. In the channel he found the bridge he had seen on the map and steered into the darkness below the highway. Emerging on the other side, he saw a sign for the ValuJet Memorial and the L-67 canal. He steered into the wide canal and followed it north. A half hour later, he saw lights ahead.

The headlights from Highway 27 became visible ahead of him and he turned left into the canal running parallel to the road and settled in for the seventy-mile ride. At thirty mph, it would take him just over two hours, and he glanced down at the fuel gauge, thankful that TJ had filled the tank. It would be close, but he should have enough gas to get there and back if needed.

Chapter 26

Mel watched the faces of the two men, looking for any opening she could get. Not expecting any help from Pamela, she knew it was on her to get them out of this. Dusharde was obviously under Pamela's spell, and she tried to think how she could use that to her advantage. The other man she knew by acquaintance, and her previous opinion of him was only reinforced by his presence here. He was lucky she dealt mainly at the federal level, or she would have relished taking him down.

Jane started to describe the day's events in the Everglades, but Wade interrupted her.

"What are you into, Dusharde?" he asked. "I think I'm going to take your advice. This is way over my pay grade. You're right—I need some plausible deniability here. I never saw any of you." Red-faced, he got up.

"That's a good idea, Vernon. If I may be frank, there's nothing I can do for you either. Perhaps the best thing is to vacate your office and keep your head down," Dusharde said.

This was unfolding faster than Mel's brain could process. The representative had hate in his eyes as he walked out of the room. She had seen that same look in the faces of opponents she had beaten in court, and it was not something to be ignored. Dusharde had a reputation for buying political influence, but she couldn't figure out what Wade could do for him. Just by his voting party lines, Dusharde would get what he wanted from the representative. From what she knew of Big Sugar, they were too smart to make individual donations, channeling most of their influence through PACs. In theory, the political action committees were independent of their individual donors, but, in fact, they executed their agendas behind a legal shield.

There had to be another answer. Turning the question upside down, she asked herself what Dusharde could do for the representative. Often politicians came begging to large donors or influential patrons for favors, offering votes in return. With no way to run a background check from her current circumstances, Mel relied on her experience and decided that this was the likely scenario and it had failed.

Her thoughts were interrupted by Jane and Dusharde going back and forth, bickering like old lovers. She renewed her focus on the argument, realizing their fates were being discussed in plain language. Her lawyer brain was churning, searching for anything she could say to keep them alive, and was surprised when it was Pamela that did it.

"I thought you wanted to spend some time with me," she said coyly. Dusharde's ears raised like a dog and color flooded to his face.

"One has to separate business from pleasure, but you are a

unique specimen, maybe worth keeping alive," he said.

Mel was disgusted at the way he referred to her as an object and bit her tongue. Whatever was happening was to their advantage, and she would take her revenge later.

"Let's make a decision in the morning." He thought for a minute. "Put them in the wine cellar."

Jane marched them out the door and down the hallway. Mel memorized each room as they went. Passing a bathroom and bedroom suite, they turned and headed down a wide stairway. She could tell from the coolness that they were moving underground, and that made sense for a wine cellar. A large room with a well-outfitted gym was at the bottom of the stairs. Jane opened a closed door and pushed them into a concrete-lined hallway done in the style of some of the wineries she had seen on a trip to Napa. The concrete floor was stained a dark brown, coated with a glossy finish, and the ceiling was made to look like a mine shaft with rough-sawn exposed beams. The faux finish on the plaster made it appear the walls were sweating. Which after touching them, she realized they were. Basements in Florida were rare and expensive. The unstable and moist soil making subterranean construction difficult.

She sensed they were getting close and looked around for anything she could use for a weapon, but there was nothing. Approaching the end of the hallway, she saw a glow coming from behind an etched-glass door with a decorative steel grate over it. Jane reached into her pocket, removed a key, and with a click the heavy door swung open. Despite their circumstances, Mel couldn't help but look around in awe at the collection. There had to be a thousand bottles, all in identical racks. Catching them off guard, Jane pushed them in and slammed the door. Mel heard a key turn, latching the dead bolt and locking them in.

"Now what?" Pamela asked, running her hands over the locked cases.

Mel was looking past the wine for a way out. They might break the glass set in the door, but the steel grate, although decorative, looked substantial and would stop any escape. She searched the room for any other openings to the outside. There was no other way out, not even an air vent. "We have to be ready when they come," she said.

"Be nice to get one of these bottles. I'm thirsty," Pamela said.

Mel was about to ignore the comment when she looked at the locked cases. If they could get to a few bottles, they could use them as weapons. "Right. Let's see what we can do about that."

She went to the first case, admiring Dusharde's taste. Built into each of the two dozen racks were eight sections built at forty-five degree angles to each other to hold the bottles. In front were doors with scaled-down steel grates that matched the style of the door. Again, they provided security as well as decoration. The grid was so close together, she could barely get a finger through one of the openings, not enough to provide enough leverage to break the lock on the front. Turning her attention to the hinged side, she studied the decorative hasps. Looking past the etchings in the handworked black metal, she saw they were basic barrel hinges welded to the face of the frame. If she could dislodge the pin, they could remove the doors.

Together they searched the room for anything thin and durable enough, but the cellar was bare.

"All this good vino staring at you sure makes you want some," Pamela said. "What do you think they're going to do with us?"

Mel didn't want to speculate. They just needed to get out. "Your belt. Give it to me." Mel took the offered belt and turned the post ninety degrees to the buckle. Hoping it would fit, she inserted it in the open end of the barrel and, with the buckle against her palm, she pushed as hard as she could. The metal pin popped out of the hinge and hit the floor. She moved to the top hinge, which was out of her reach, and gave the buckle to Pamela, who easily released the pin. Together they lifted the door and set it on the floor. Pamela grabbed a bottle, stared at the cork, and without hesitating, slammed the post of the buckle into the opening, sending the unsuspecting cork into the bottle. She took a long drink and handed it to Mel, who took a small sip. Both women smiled at each other, but were distracted by a gunshot. They hit the floor thinking someone was shooting at them, but the house was quiet. It was a lone shot.

* * *

Mac stared at the end of the canal. He was out of water. The GPS, of little use other than providing his general progress and speed since he had left Florida Bay, showed Lake Okeechobee dead ahead. It also told him it was one thirty in the morning. With four hours until sunrise, he needed to decide what to do. He didn't want to waste the precious hours or the cover of darkness that might save Mel and Pamela's lives.

The smaller canal that he had been following for the last three hours had dead-ended into a larger waterway flowing east and west. The map he had studied earlier, still etched in his memory, told him that Clewiston was to the west, so he turned left. With the dark waters of the lake hidden behind brush to the right and a twenty-foot-high berm concealing the agricultural fields on the left, he sped toward Clewiston.

"What the hell're ya doin'?" a voice yelled.

He had just rounded a slight bend and hadn't seen the boat until it was too late. Although he was already well past the small bass boat, he could see it rocking in the large wake trailing behind him. Dropping speed, he said a silent apology to the anglers, thanking them at the same time for waking him up. He was back in civilization now, and as sparse as it looked, there would be people here. Watching the banks of the canal ahead of him as he drove, he looked for any sign of life. On his left he saw several lights and slowed further. A floodgate appeared, several times larger than the ones he had passed down south. Fortunately, this one ran parallel to the waterway.

The lights he had seen moved, and he recognized a truck pulling away from what looked like a boat ramp cut into the dyke. Dropping to an idle, he coasted toward the small boat thinking if the fishermen were friendly he could borrow a cell phone and call TJ. He had been hailing him on the VHF with no luck, even trying a radio check as a last resort. It had gone ignored, and his hopes of relaying a message to Key Largo disappeared.

"Hey, guys," he called out as he approached the ramp. The aluminum boat painted in a dark green camouflage was pulled up to the bank, waiting for the driver of the truck to park.

Instead of an answer he was greeted with the barrel of a rifle. "Hurry up, Glen. We got a live one." He turned to Mac. "Let's see them hands."

Mac complied, wondering what was going on. The boats slid closer, and he could see the black grease on the man's face and the dirty clothes he wore. Another few seconds and he could see the man's nicotine-stained teeth.

The man spat over the side. "You ain't Fish and Game, are ya?" he asked. The second man, he had called Glen, joined him and hopped into the bow.

"No. No," Mac said, keeping his hands over his head. This time of night, dressed as they were and armed, he didn't need the confirmation of the bloodstains on the outside of the boat to know they were poachers. "I'm just needing some help is all."

"We got no time for help," Glen said. "Unless you've got cash for it."

Mac rummaged through his pockets and pulled out a wad of wet money. "Here. It's all I've got." He reached out and handed it to the other man.

"Ain't gonna buy you much," the other man said, grabbing the bills and counting them. "Bit wet, but it'll spend. We accept credit cards too." Both men broke out laughing.

"Not my style, guys. Listen, I just need to make one phone call and I'll leave you be," Mac pleaded, scanning the water for an escape route. If the answer was no, he was going.

"He looks like he's pretty desperate and maybe in some trouble too," Glen said, eying the boat. "Sorry, mister. It's gonna cost you the boat for a call. You good with that, Len?"

Mac hated the redneck habit of using good manners when they were stealing from you. He thought about his options, hoping TJ had insurance. "Your boat and a phone and you've got a deal." He paused for a second. "And I'll take that shotgun too."

"Damned city boy's got some big'uns," Glen said.

Mac looked around the boat to see if there was anything he could take. This had gone easier than he thought. He heard Len moving something in the skiff and turned, but it was too late. The barrel of a rifle slammed against his head, knocking him to the deck. He was stunned, but not out, and just as he tried to regain his footing, both men vaulted the gunwales and were on him. In seconds they had him trussed like a poached gator and pushed him into the corner.

The boat started and he looked at the helm. Len backed off the embankment and quickly spun the wheel, trying to make the hundred-and-eighty-degree turn in one move, but was not used to a boat this size. Misjudging the angle and momentum, he hit the other bank before straightening out and accelerating. Sliding his body against the gunwale, Mac was able to sit tall enough to see the skiff following behind them. They must have had a prearranged spot, because the smaller boat was soon out of sight.

After passing the floodgates, Len cut the wheel to the left and entered a series of small canals. He steered through this maze for about fifteen minutes and turned again. The further from the main canal they moved, the narrower and more overgrown the canals became. Soon any kind of definition disappeared. Mac tried to remember any features besides big and small, but between the lack of light and the monotonous landscape of the lake, there was nothing he could do except judge time and direction.

Another fifteen minutes passed, with enough turns to cause Mac to lose his bearings entirely. Just as he became totally disoriented, the boat slowed and coasted to a small patch of dry land. He could see it clearly in the moonlight. Too small to be an island and probably submerged during the rainy season, the small hump held nothing but a clump of cypress trees.

Shoving the throttle forward, Len accelerated and Mac felt a jolt as the boat hit land and plowed up the sandy shore. It came to a stop with the bow poking past the other bank. Mac slumped down, feigning unconsciousness. Len ignored him and vaulted the gunwale. Mac heard the top of a can crack and a small motor in the distance. Len came back with a beer and rested against the gunwale, waiting for his partner.

Chapter 27

Wade knew he had to get his rage under control. His exit had been too late. Intrigued by Melanie Woodson's appearance, he had stayed to see if there was something he could use to his advantage. Scolding himself for his curiosity, he knew he should have left immediately. Now, he had heard too much, and his only way to leverage Dusharde into helping him was to find out more.

Moving quickly through the house, he reached the front door and went outside to his car. Cursing himself for not bringing the gun in the first place and with a new resolve, he grabbed it from underneath the seat, stuck it in his waistband, and went around the back of the house. He crept carefully around the estate until he reached Dusharde's study window, which overlooked the pool. Hiding behind a large plant, he suffered the mosquitos, trying to hear what was said inside. Struggling to get closer to the glass, he realized the well-made windows were not going to reveal any secrets. He could only watch when Jane took Mel and the other woman out of the room at gunpoint.

Scenarios played out in his mind. He could rescue Woodson and use her against Dusharde, but he had dealt with her kind before.

The memory of saving her life would be all too short. He could see it in her eyes that she was after Dusharde, and he would almost certainly be collateral damage. The answer lay with the man sitting behind the desk. He either needed to force Dusharde to protect him or eliminate him. After his service in Vietnam, he knew how to turn on the right part of his brain to do what was needed. When he was sure Dusharde was alone, he went around to the front door. Slowly he opened it, peering inside to make sure there was no one watching. With no sign of the women, he slid inside, eased the door closed and walked back down the hall to Dusharde's office.

"I need to wash my hands of this mess, and you need to help me," he said, surprising Dusharde when he entered the room.

"Why, Vernon, you're as much a party to this as I am."

"I've done your dirty work all these years, and the least I should expect is an easy retirement."

"Let's not forget our places," Dusharde said as he reached back to the sideboard.

Wade reacted quickly—too quickly—and drew the gun. Dusharde turned around with a sheaf of papers in his hand.

"There's no need for that," he said. "I have a proposition for you."

Wade put his arm down, holding the gun at his side. "Go on."

"I'll buy that property from you."

"That's the least you can do."

"You're not going to like the price." He sat back in his chair. "You see, to wash your hands of this mess, you're going to get what you paid for it. That way, if it ever comes out, and it will, you can tell your constituents a good story about the loss you took for the benefit of the environment and all that. Weave it however you want. Do we have a deal?"

Wade stood there stunned. Getting his money back was actually a huge loss. After having to pay his ex-wife half the appraised value of the land when they divorced, the loss was into six figures. "That's your offer?"

"I'd think about how I left this room, if I were you. It might not be the way you think." Dusharde reached his hand under the desk.

Wade jumped and raised the gun, but it was too late. The bullet from Dusharde's gun was already on its way. It took him in the chest and he fell to the floor.

* * *

Mel glared at Pamela and rubbed her eyes. She had finally fallen asleep, and now the woman was pacing the wine cellar. "I told you not to drink that much."

"I'm not drunk. I just need a bathroom. If I could do it in this," she said, extending the empty bottle, "believe me, I would."

Mel rolled her eyes.

"You said we needed two empties. I got 'em. Two dead soldiers, right here," she slurred.

She had mentioned just pouring them out, but Pamela had not gone for that. She was on her third bottle now. It was just a matter of time before someone came to check on them—she hoped.

Surprisingly, in the middle of Florida, she was cold. Sitting on the hard concrete floor had sucked the heat from her. All she could do was wait, and she stared at the door, waiting for the light in the hallway to come on. That would be the signal.

It happened sooner than she thought. Popping to her feet, she grabbed the empty bottle and signaled to Pamela. They had already agreed on a plan and took their positions. A shape could be seen through the etched-glass door. Footsteps were audible now. She hoped it was Jane.

"Ready?" Mel asked Pamela.

"Yupper," she said, taking the last swig from the bottle and stepping behind the hinge side of the door.

Mel hoped she was sober enough to execute her part. She didn't doubt the wine would supply enough courage to strike a man over the head with an empty bottle. But motor skills might be an issue. They had replaced the cabinet door, and she doubted a casual inspection would reveal the broken lock. Everything was in place, and she moved to the wall to take her position. For their plan to work, whoever opened the doors would need to face her, allowing Pamela to strike them from behind. With the wine bottle behind her, within easy reach, she settled back in the corner, pretending to be asleep. Taking one quick look around the room to make sure they were ready, she breathed deeply and closed her eyes.

Every noise was accentuated by the concrete, and Mel could hear the key slide into the lock and the bolt click. She readied herself when she heard the knob turn. It happened faster than she could have anticipated. The man turned toward her, as she had guessed, and Pamela sprung from her position behind the door, slamming him on the head with both bottles.

He dropped onto the hard concrete floor, unconscious.

"Hurry. We have to tie him up," Mel called to Pamela, who stood over the man. She looked like she was about to freak out, and Mel gave her a hard look that seemed to bring her back. "He's not dead," she said to reassure her. In fact, she wasn't sure and didn't want to risk finding out before the man was bound and gagged.

Taking Pamela's belt, she pushed the end through the buckle and cinched down hard around the man's wrists. After winding the rest of the material around, she tucked the end under a few loops and tied a knot. She then tore a piece of the man's shirt and stuffed it into his mouth. Trying to stop her hands from trembling, she reached for the man's neck to feel for a pulse.

"He's alive," she said, looking at the wound. There was a large bump on his head, but he would live. She looked at his face. It was no one they had seen, and, from his brownish skin and dress, she assumed he was a worker. A pang of guilt rang through her, thinking maybe they could have talked him into letting them go, rather than assaulting him, but it passed. There had been no option.

Pamela was already out the door, both bottles still in her hands.

"Where are you going?"

"Bathroom," she said, turning into a doorway.

Mel thought about locking her in and leaving her to sleep off the wine, but she emerged before she could act. With that much alcohol in her, Mel would have to watch her closely. "Let's go upstairs and scout things out. Maybe we can take a car and get out of here." There was no telling what was going on upstairs, and she remembered the gunshot from last night. Without windows, she didn't even know what time it was.

"What about the man?" Pamela looked back to the wine cellar. "Maybe he has keys or something we can use."

Mel cursed herself for not thinking about it. "Go look. I'm going to the top of the stairs to see if anyone's there."

She moved toward the staircase and climbed to the main floor, stopping a few treads before the landing. The huge windows in the living room adjacent to the stairs showed a predawn sky with faint tendrils shooting colors over the horizon. She took another step and peered around the corner. Illuminated by the glow of the laptop in front of him, Philip sat alone at a table by the kitchen. He had a cup of coffee in front of him and was already dressed. They would need to wait until he moved before they could do anything.

Mel turned around and crashed into Pamela, who started to fall backward, her balance affected by the wine. Mel reached for her, but it was too late. Pulling back to recover, she felt a hand reach out and grab her. Both women found themselves tangled at the bottom of the step. She looked up and saw the barrel of a rifle pointing at them.

* * *

Mac remained in the same position, squinting to make it look like he was asleep, while Len stood there drinking just a few feet away. The man drained the beer and tossed the can to the ground. Mac heard another top pop and then the faint sound of the skiff's small outboard in the distance.

A few minutes later, Mac watched as Glen pulled up in the skiff, executing the same maneuver to ground the boat. He got out and came toward the other boat. Rough hands grabbed him, hauling him over the gunwale. Mac found himself on the ground in the only small patch of land not taken beside the two boats and the cluster of trees.

"What we gonna do with him?" Len asked.

Glen ignored the question. "You drink all the beer?"

"Nah. There's still a few up in the stand."

Mac looked up and saw the poorly built but well camouflaged hide. Constructed like a treehouse between the trunks of the cypress trees, the roughhewn platform extended over the water. Although crude, it was functional; probably used to lure gators right below it before they killed them. He heard another beer crack.

"Let's tie him up to a cypress and use'm for bait," Glen said. He went to the skiff and pulled a bucket out and dumped the contents on the ground around Mac. "Ground chicken gizzards and blood. Maybe that and our friend here'll bring out that big sucker we keep missing."

Mac didn't want another gator encounter tonight. He squirmed, trying to get a feel for the knot that bound his wrists together. Working with his hands tied behind his back was difficult, and he pried his fingers into the rough rope, trying to work it free, but was surprised to find a well-tied knot. There was nothing to be done about his feet if he couldn't free his hands. Although they weren't much use independently, he was able to use his hands together and pulled on the line that was tied around the base of the tree. If he was at least able to free that, he could make a run for the boat.

He discovered about a foot of slack in the rope, enough to allow him room to manipulate the line to where he could reach the knot securing him to the tree trunk. What he found was a feeble attempt at a bowline, and within seconds he was free. It occurred to him that only one of them could tie a knot, but that knowledge was useless. Now he had to decide what his next move was. He could hear the two men talking in the tree stand built above him, and discarded the idea of running. They would have the perfect vantage point to shoot him, without even moving—and he didn't doubt they would. Then, with his blood running in the water, they would surely get that big gator.

Instead he rolled on his back and slid his butt, then his legs and feet through his bound hands. He waited a few minutes to see if Glen and Len suspected anything, but all he heard was their idle chatter and the tops of two more beer cans pop. Working quietly, he untied his feet. Several gators grunted, and Mac looked out into the dark water, sensing that they had smelt the chicken. He was out of time. His hands would have to wait. He needed a diversion to get the men out of the stand or at least vulnerable to an attack.

Channeling his inner redneck, he thought about what Trufante would do. This was the Cajun's element, and he tried to remember the stories of his days back on the bayou that he only half listened to when they were fishing. A gator grunted, interrupting his thoughts, and he looked around the small hump of sand and found what he needed. On the other side of the tree stand was a small fire pit and, to the side of it, a pile of cypress logs stacked against a trunk.

Slowly he crawled to the wood, waiting for the sounds of the gators grunting to disguise his movement and knowing at the same time they were getting closer. When he had five sections sitting beside him, he started with the smallest diameter log. The rope they had used to tie him to the tree was about ten feet long, and he roughly measured halfway up the length and tied a loop around the log. Leaving six inches of rope between them, he tied in the next largest log. Continuing with the fattest log, he started reducing the size until another small log was tied to the end.

The men above must have sensed the gators were getting close and were quiet, waiting for their chance. Grunts surrounded the small island, and Mac knew it was time. Hoping the gators were still out of reach, he slid away from the tree and quietly waded a few feet out into the murky water, Dragging the chain of logs behind him, he pulled it in front and jerked it back toward him without letting the logs leave the water. It was like fishing a jig, and within a few casts he had the decoy working as he intended. Moving closer to the stand, he whipped the logs into deeper water.

"That's him. That's the goddamned lunker," Glen whispered.

Mac felt movement above him as the men positioned themselves for the shot. He wiggled the line and heard the almost silent sound of their safeties release. Once more he jerked the line, and the water erupted with pellets. Mac jumped as several gators, closer than he expected, were spooked and fled. The water was chaos, and when the men fired again, he pulled the log chain from the water, stood, and swung it up at the stand.

He felt contact, and a man screamed then dropped into the water. Mac shuffled toward him and grabbed his shotgun before he could move. Len squirmed in the water.

"Toss it down," Mac called up to Glen. A gator grunted and was answered by a chorus of amens.

Len was spooked. "Do what he says, damn it. Ain't no time to be playin'," he called up to Glen.

Mac heard the splash as the gun was thrown into the water. He motioned the barrel of the shotgun at Len. "Get out of the water and climb back up. I'm going to take my boat and go."

"That's just fine, mister. Just let me get out of here," Len said.

Mac held the gun awkwardly in his bound hands. With the barrel still aimed at Len, he watched the man run from the water and climb the rough steps nailed to the tree and into the stand. "No trouble and I won't tell the sheriff," Mac called up as he moved to TJ's boat. Still encumbered by the logs, he went around to the skiff, where he found a knife, which he used to cut the bindings.

Free now, he cast one eye at the stand and checked the small boat for anything that might be useful. He kept the knife and found a box of shells for the shotgun. Then he saw what he really needed sitting on the seat and picked up the cell phone. Before leaving the skiff, he released the shroud covering the motor, pulled one of the spark plug wires, and tossed it into the water. The water churned where he had thrown the wire, and he found himself staring into the moonlit eyes of a ten-foot gator. They were back, and he wasted no time stuffing the shells and phone in his cargo pants before jumping into the cockpit of the cuddy cabin.

After starting the engine, he pulled back on the throttle, hoping the propeller was deep enough to pull the boat off the sand. It struggled at first, but he was soon free and drifted back into the weeds. A few minutes later, he was cruising back out through the narrow channel. Now he just had to find his way back to Clewiston.

Chapter 28

Mel yanked the still-sleeping Pamela upright. It had been several hours since their escape had been foiled, and Dusharde had them tied back to back in two patio chairs. After this morning's attempt to escape, he was taking no chances; the ties were tight, and they were secured within sight on the lanai. He was right inside, working at the same table where Mel had seen him earlier, and she caught his eye whenever he looked up. Sleep eluded her, especially with Pamela jerking her every time her head nodded forward. Looking around, there was nothing she could think of to force their escape. She would have to be patient and take whatever opportunity presented itself—not her strong point.

The patio door opened and Dusharde came outside. He stretched his back and walked over to her. "You and your friend seem to have good taste in wine. Those were some of my more expensive bottles. If I were a vindictive man, I would make you pay. Or should I just send her the bill?" He walked over to where Pamela was still sleeping. "As much as she appealed to me last night, drinking and women don't do much for me."

That was something they could agree on. Mel was furious at

Pamela for the bungled escape. "What are you going to do with us?"

He walked back around to face her. "It turns out that your being a minor celebrity in the progressive world may suit me."

"How's that?"

"Why, you're going to be the face of my plan," he said.

The patio door opened again and Jane walked out. She approached the group and checked their bonds. "Nice work," she said to Dusharde.

"Unfortunately, Manny is not in good shape. He could use a doctor. And then there's the mess in the study from last night."

"No doctors. I'll go have a look at him," she said, walking back inside with Dusharde following behind.

Mel tried to put the pieces of the puzzle together and figure out what they intended. But more importantly, she needed to buy some time. They were not going to escape this time. Rescue would be their only way out, and she wondered what had happened to Mac and Trufante. Even that group of kids he was hanging out with, that Bayou Brigade or whatever they called themselves, would be a welcome sight right now.

* * *

Mac was lost. There seemed to be no pattern to the waterways of South Bay, which was probably why it had been a poacher's haven since the regulation of alligator hunting in the 1920s. The propeller had already nudged the bottom a few times, even though he had it tilted up as much as the water intake would allow. He constantly checked behind him for the telltale stream that told him the engine was getting enough water to cool it. Blowing the motor here would be bad business.

He had idled back and forth in the dark night, aimlessly looking for any opening he could find, and finally gave up. With limited gas, he at least needed sunlight to help him unravel the maze. Pulling into a small cove, he shut off the engine and let the boat coast into a clump of brush. Mosquitos immediately found him, and he ran for the cover of the small cabin, quickly closing the doors to keep the beasts at bay.

Lying on the single berth, he tried to unwind, but found that impossible. Every so often he swatted at the lone mosquito that had gained entrance, never seeming to get the last one. The cabin was hot, cooled only by the single hatch. Fortunately, it had a pullback screen that still worked, but it provided little airflow. He turned the cell phone back and forth in his hands, reluctant to use it on the chance the poachers had gotten free and had a way to track him. He got over his paranoia and turned the power on.

The screen lit up and he smiled. Despite being lost, civilization was close—three bars showed on the top left of the screen. He scrolled through the apps, finding mostly games. There was no email setup, and the few text messages were one or two words each. Maybe when he was done with it he would turn it over to Fish and Game and see if they could get any information and track the owner. Wiping his brow, he pressed the button for the dial pad and entered Alicia's number. The ex-CIA agent had forced him to memorize it rather than rely on the contacts list in his cell phone, and now he was glad for it.

"Hello," a sleepy voice answered.

Mac looked at the screen and saw it was four thirty. "Sorry it's so early, but I'm in a bit of a jamb."

"Mac?"

He could tell she was awake now. "Yeah. Not my phone's why you don't know the number."

"Are you okay? TJ wants to know if the boat is in one piece."

"Tell him it's all good," he said, thinking the poacher story would be better told under better circumstances. "I'm good right now, but Mel and Pamela are in trouble, and I have no idea where Trufante is." He gave her the CliffsNotes version of the story.

"Why didn't you let me know sooner?"

He ignored the question. "Can you pinpoint this phone and get me out of here? I'm stuck in South Bay at the bottom of Lake Okeechobee."

"Give me a minute and I'll call you back," she said.

He didn't want to break contact, but figured she was right and it was better to conserve the battery. He heard noise outside and looked at the window. The first sign of pink was on the horizon. That gave him some hope, and he opened up the cabin, only to be immediately assaulted by mosquitos when he stepped onto the deck. Ignoring them as best he could, he riffled through the holds. Finding some insect repellent, he liberally coated himself and waited for her to call back.

As the sky lightened, he realized that daylight alone was not going to get him out of here. Back at the GPS, he looked at his position on the screen and saw nothing that looked like where he was. Finally, the phone rang.

"I've got you located," she said, wasting no time. "I'm going to hand you over to TJ to get you out of there. I'm working on Mel and Pamela."

Mac was glad to hear that she was on top of things and wondered if Trufante was okay. TJ came on the line and started guiding him through the channels. "How are you doing this?" Mac asked.

"Google Earth, bro. It's like I'm right there with you."

Mac steered, following TJ's directions until he was back in the wide canal with the tall embankment. "I'm back where I started. Now what?"

Alicia interrupted. "I've traced every link I could find and came up with nothing."

Mac's heart dropped.

"But you said you followed the trail of the monitoring stations, right?"

"Yeah." He had no idea where she was going with this.

"Okay, so there was a report I picked up about two guys rescued out in the Gulf, claiming someone blew up their engine. It was right by the station at Sprigger Bank."

Mac almost laughed. Thinking about the trouble with Hector and Edgar seemed insignificant compared to what he had dealt with since. "That was me."

"I thought so. I know your MO. Apparently there were enough warrants out on those two that they sang like birds trying to cop a plea deal. They might have exaggerated to get on the good side of the DA, but they started talking about some terrorist plot to blow up the Everglades and how Big Sugar was implicated. Pretty farfetched, huh?"

Mac didn't answer right away. He had left the rocket and explosives out of the story. With her relationship as a contractor with the CIA, she might have been conflicted and reported it. Somehow he knew he was going to need to leverage that information to get Mel and Pamela back. If the Feds showed up at the site, there would be no reason to keep them alive. "I'm right in the middle of Big Sugar country."

It was her turn to ignore him. "Stay in the main canal and head west toward Clewiston. I'll have something by the time you get there."

* * *

Alicia spun in her chair and looked at TJ scrolling through the overnight scores on his latest online game. Frustrated, she said, "I don't know where to go from here."

"Turn it on its head, babe," he said. "That's what you always tell me."

She thought for a few minutes. One of her training classes at Langley had been about lateral thinking, a technique used to change the problem to find different solutions. It only took a second to figure out the missing link. "Trufante."

"Bingo. That boy's in the middle of everything." He got up and kissed her forehead. "Gotta go. Have to do double time on the charters since Mac's got the six-pack boat."

She whispered Trufante's name out loud and smiled thinking about him. There was a place in her heart for the Cajun. As much of a shit magnet as he was, he had helped her through her first field operation. She had gained more experience from being around him for twenty-four hours than she had learned in a year of classroom lectures. Hoping he was okay, she turned her attention to the computer and started with the low-hanging fruit—the police. With easy access to the Florida Law Enforcement database, she scanned the last few days of activity and smiled. At least he wasn't in jail. That would have required her to go up the ladder at the agency to help him. Next was the morgue, and after a quick search she found no one with his name or any John Doe's that fit his description.

Hospitals were the last place she could hope to find him. She started in Key West and moved toward the mainland. As there was no interconnected database between them, she had to check each hospital individually. Finally she found him, under his own name, in Homestead. Picking up her phone, she quickly jumped to the hospital's website and found the number. She dialed and waited, pressing zero for every question the automated phone tree asked. A woman picked up after a few minutes and she asked for his room. After a lecture about how she could have got that information from the automated system, she said she would connect the call.

"Hellooo."

It was good to hear his voice, although from the slur, she could tell he was drugged—not that he minded. "Tru! It's Alicia. Are you okay?"

"Righty oh."

She sensed she might have trouble getting any information out of him. "I need your help."

"And I need your credit card or I'm gonna have to pull the great escape out of here."

There was no way he had insurance. But that was a problem she would deal with later. "I'll handle that. Listen, Mel and Pamela are in trouble."

"Pajamabama?"

"Yes, and I need your help."

"Roger that."

At least she thought she had his attention now. "I need everything you can remember—anything with a sugar connection."

The line was silent for a minute, and she thought she heard him humming in the background. Patience didn't come easily for her. From her San Francisco childhood under her mother's constant pressure to be the best, through Stanford and on to MIT, where she had to admit she had run across the country to escape her tiger mom. After graduating, she had moved back to the Bay Area and done well working for several start-up tech firms that had gone public, only to become frustrated when the companies were sold or their products became obsolete before they hit the market. A friend who had gone the government service route, and seemed happier than she was, told her about an opening at the CIA and she jumped on it. The money wasn't as good, but before the budget cuts, she had worked all the time anyway. Since meeting TJ and moving to Key Largo, she realized everything her mother had preached about getting ahead was wrong.

"Sugar, huh?"

Her patience was thin. "Come on, give me something."

"Well, there's that she-devil—name's Jane. Drive's a bitchin' fast car. Don't know much more than that."

She kept him on the line while her fingers flew across the keyboard. There were only a handful of sugar companies left operating out of the Clewiston area, and she went into the database of the Social Security office and scanned their payrolls. She found a Jane with a six-figure income at one and checked her W-4 information. "How old was she?"

"Evil don't wear age," he said.

"Thirty-eight sound right?" she asked.

"That'd be about right. So, can you help me out of here?"

"I'll see what I can do."

"Just make sure I get a doggie bag."

Chapter 29

Mac heard the phone and dropped to an idle before answering.

"Tru's all right. He's in the hospital in Homestead," Alicia said.

That was the first good news he had heard in days. "Good work. I'm sure he's enjoying the hospitality."

"That's our boy. He was actually helpful and gave me a name who I connected to Philip Dusharde."

"The sugar guy?" Mac paused. "And Clewiston. Sounds like we're on the right track."

"I've got an address where he lives. I looked on Google Earth, and it's a large compound. The rear property line is a canal. You can drive right to his back door."

She gave him directions; he disconnected and accelerated. The route was straightforward. Used for irrigation water as well as drainage, the canals were better maintained here than farther south. They were wide and free of obstructions and weeds. Now that he had a destination and a clear route, he pushed the speed to twenty knots.

At this speed he had an hour run ahead of him and he settled in, watching the landscape as he sped through the canals. Cruising through the acres of planted fields he caught several strange looks from workers and equipment operators surprised to see this large a boat here. Doubting they would raise an alarm, he waved back and kept on going.

It was afternoon when he arrived. The trip had taken several calls to Alicia and a few changes in route, but he was sure he was in the right place. With the shotgun in one hand, he waded to the berm with a dock line in the other and climbed the five-foot berm to level ground. After tying the boat to a small tree, he studied the property. The landscape was very different from what he had seen all day. Dusharde had spared no expense in making it appear to have been transported from Palm Beach. Man-made contours gave the native terrain an undulating appearance like a well-crafted golf course.

Moving forward carefully, using the landscape to conceal himself, he walked toward the roofline of the house just visible over the rise ahead. As he moved, the flora gradually changed from native trees and brush to carefully installed plantings, many in rock outcroppings. He appraised the house, now in full view. It looked like the clubhouse for a country club, with the main floor stretching for what looked like a football field and a second story about half the size. Red clay tiles capped the steep angular pitches of the roof. Even from this distance it looked like money.

He slowed down when he heard dogs barking and realized they were coming toward him. Hopefully they weren't trained guard dogs and barked at anything that moved. Otherwise he was in trouble. Backing up, he used the cover of a cluster of scrubby-looking oaks and climbed a few feet into the largest. From this vantage point, he could see a low fence running around the property, carefully disguised to blend in with the landscape. The dogs were running along it on the other side. They looked like they were playing.

They still created a problem, even if they were friendly. He waited several minutes to make sure they had not attracted any attention and climbed down. Moving to the fence, he kicked at the brush and held his hands out, waiting for them to find him. It only took a few minutes for them to come running, barking and nipping at each other. He crouched down and extended his hands through the fence, hoping his instincts were right.

The lead dog bounded up and barked viciously, but he knew better than to flinch. Slowly, he saw the hair on its back fold back down and the tail start to wag as it moved toward him. The other dog was by its side now and together they approached the fence. With one dog licking each hand, he relaxed and let them get used to him. Sensing they were becoming bored, he scaled the low fence and with his new companions headed toward the house.

The sun was still high when he reached the low stone wall separating the groomed backyard from the back forty. On his belly, he crawled toward the barrier and raised his head just enough to see over it. A large pond was in front of him, and it took a few minutes for him to realize it was actually a pool. Off to the side was a detached garage, built to look like a smaller version of the house and connected with a covered walkway. He turned back to the house and saw a large covered patio, and, underneath it, he froze when he saw

Mel and Pamela tied up back to back in two chairs.

Relief spread over him, knowing they were still alive. After that passed, his first reaction was to jump the wall and rescue them, but he held himself in check, knowing that would be foolhardy. Even if no one was watching, the dogs would be alerted by the activity and cause a commotion. His thoughts were interrupted by a burning on his chest.

The pain was indescribable, and he knew immediately he was lying on a nest of fire ants. The brutal insects, common throughout the South, were biting him repeatedly, causing his chest to feel like he was on fire. He rolled over and brushed himself off, only confirming what he already knew. On the ground below him the ants swarmed out of two concealed dens. Tearing the T-shirt off, he flung the ants from his chest. The stinging faded, but he knew he was in worse trouble than the pain when he felt his throat start to swell.

He needed to get back to the boat and took off running through the brush, not caring if he was seen. When he reached the fence, he collapsed and fell to the ground.

* * *

Mac felt something wet and rough scratch his face and opened his swollen eyes to see the two dogs hovering tentatively over him. He took a minute to get his bearings, rolled onto his back and sat up. The burning on his stomach was intense, and he almost lay back down in the dew-covered grass to soothe the pain, but thinking about Mel and Pamela and the hours that he had lost got him to his feet.

The high clouds diffused the light from the three-quarters full waning moon, throwing a medieval cast over the landscape. He had been out for hours.

Climbing over the fence, he accidentally rubbed against the exposed wire on top of the chain-link and growled in pain as it scraped across the bites. He felt a liquid oozing down his stomach, but there was no point stopping until he reached the boat. Fighting off the nausea and lightheadedness that came from his reaction to the fire ants, he struggled across the last hundred yards. Reaching the berm, he slid down into the water and waded to the boat.

Once aboard, he found the first aid kit and silently thanked TJ for keeping it stocked. Being a dive boat, it had antihistamines and sting ointments for treating the myriad of underwater maladies that assaulted the unprotected skin of divers. He took several Benadryl and stood on the dive platform, where he used the wash-down hose and some baby shampoo, which the divers used as an inexpensive anti-fog, to clean the swollen bites.

Slowly the burning dissipated, and he climbed back aboard. Fortunately there was a supply of dive-shop shirts in the cabin. He grabbed another and dressed. Another look in the first aid kit revealed some antibacterial ointment. He took it and used the entire sample-sized tube to cover the bites. Feeling better, he took several large gulps from a gallon-sized jug of water he had found and started assembling anything that might prove useful to rescue Mel and Pamela.

* * *

When the sun went down, Dusharde and Jane moved the women into the living room. First the killing of Wade and now Jane's plan to dispose of the women's bodies had made him anxious. Neglecting his ritual, he had taken the whiskey straight, and he was finally starting to calm down. Now he stood with a glass in his hand looking at Jane over the kitchen counter, wondering how she could be cooking a meal when the walls of his empire were crumbling around him.

Even the dogs had seemed out of sorts, running along the fence all day, barking at some unknown danger that was probably just a raccoon. He had sent Manny to have a look, but he had reported nothing unusual.

"Can't we do this tonight?" Philip asked Jane.

She continued to slice the frozen chicken breasts into cubes. "You could use some real food around here. Everything is frozen and processed."

He walked over and grasped the hand that held the knife. At first she didn't struggle, but he increased the pressure and she fought back. For a brief second she panicked and then gave into his superior strength.

A look of fear crossed her face and he released her. He had already killed once, and he would do it again. The emotions were unique, and he realized he needed to step back and take the ten-thousand foot view instead of becoming emotionally involved. He had people for that. "Why not now?" he asked again.

She didn't hesitate this time. "If an environmental group were going to blow up the rocket to open the flow of water, would they do it at night, or make it a media spectacle and blow it during the day?"

Her answer made sense and he relaxed. It would be a long night, but better to spend it here than sitting in an abandoned warehouse being eaten alive by whatever critters cruised the Everglades at night. With his back to the two women, he sat at a barstool and watched her finish dinner. Surprised by his appetite, he finished the plate she set in front of him.

Turning to the two women, he wondered if he ought to feed them or at least get them water, but decided to leave it to Jane. He would make sure she left in the morning, and he'd monitor things from his boat off Palm Beach. There was no need to get his hands dirtier than they were.

"I'm going to need your help tomorrow," she said.

It was like she could read his mind. "What about Manny?"

"I sent him home and told him to get his wife to take him to the hospital. He almost passed out getting your congressman in the car."

Philip had wondered who had cleaned up the mess in the study. "Don't you have anyone else?"

"Not that I can count on like you."

He sat back and gulped the remainder of the whiskey. Now that the plan was almost complete, he wondered if he would have the stomach to see it through on a personal level. Watching the news from the salon on his eighty-foot convertible would have been more comfortable.

"You shot a man last night. Blowing things up is child's play compared to that."

Chapter 30

Mac looked at the horizon and noticed the sky was just starting to lighten, and he knew he needed to move. Losing the cover of darkness would be a mistake. Slowly he crouched and took one last look before he slid away from the bushes and found the narrow path he had used yesterday. This far from the house he was more alert for the gators, deer, and pigs that lived in the backwoods than for man. Carefully he moved toward the house with the shotgun in one hand and the fillet knife in the other.

He reached the fence separating the natural environment and the landscaped yard. It was still a good distance from the house, and he remembered how skillfully the two worlds had been blended together. He stopped every few feet to watch and listen, but there was no sign of activity. The dogs must be in for the night. The path turned from dirt to mulch, then to gravel, and finally flagstone as he approached the back of the pool.

Skirting the boulder-strewn perimeter, he thought he heard movement around the front and stopped. A car door slammed, then another. He had to move fast now; the time for stealth had passed. He ran across the yard and reached the back of the house. With his back against the building he caught his breath and slid across the rough, stuccoed exterior toward a window several feet from the corner. A table lamp illuminated the room. He could see it was an office and looked in, his eyes scanning the room's built-in bookshelves and rich furniture before settling on the pool of blood on the hardwood floor. Even through the double-pane glass, he could see it was still wet.

Thinking the worst, and not worried about being seen or heard, he moved to the side of the house as fast as he could. He reached the corner and slowly poked his head around. Mixed emotions flooded through him. He was at once relieved and enraged.

Jane shoved a bound and gagged Mel into the back of a Mercedes sedan. Faster than Mac could have done anything to stop her, she reached around her back, pulled the pistol from her waistband, and smacked Mel on the temple. Mac fought the urge to go after her and waited. He cradled the shotgun in his arms, but the women were too close together to use it. The shells contained buckshot. From what he estimated to be twenty-five yards away, they could still pack a punch, but the spread could easily hit Mel. He might as well have been unarmed.

Jane moved away from the car, and he thought he might have an opening. He had to move back when she crossed the walk in front of him and went to the door. The second she was out of sight, he started to make a move toward the car but froze when he saw Jane pulling another figure from the house back toward the car. There was a pillowcase over her head, but he could immediately tell it was Pamela. Dusharde followed the pair and went around to the passenger seat. Fortunately for Mac, she was fighting back, giving him just enough time to retreat before being seen.

Back behind the house, with the knowledge that both women were alive, he could do nothing but watch from a distance as Jane shoved the taller woman into the back next to Mel, knocking her unconscious as well. It was apparent she was leaving. He looked across the covered walkway to the garage, where a sports car sat in the driveway. But before he could reach it, he heard the engine start and saw the running lights of the Mercedes recede into the darkness.

He ran to the Audi. It was locked. From where he stood he could see the sedan reach the end of the long driveway and turn right onto the road. At least he knew what direction she was headed, but his hopes sank as she accelerated and, even from this distance, he could hear the turbo booster kick in and the car sped away.

Head down, he went into the main house and after a quick search found the keys on the kitchen counter. He fumbled with the electronic lock, wasting valuable seconds trying to unlock the door. Finally allowed access, he tossed the shotgun in the passenger seat and squeezed into the luxurious cockpit. He found the starter button. Within seconds, he was following the Mercedes. He accelerated and watched the needle move north of eighty mph. Traveling mostly by boat, he couldn't remember the last time he had gone this fast, but the luxurious car made him feel like he was going twenty.

In the distance he saw the taillights of the other car. Jane was moving much slower, probably staying to the speed limit, not wanting to risk being pulled over with Mel and Pamela in the back.

He followed suit, careful to match her speed. She had no idea he was there, and he intended to keep it that way. There was nothing he could do except follow and formulate a plan for when they got there. It didn't take a rocket scientist to figure out where they were going.

Mac felt out of place driving the Audi. He looked at the buttons, reluctant to touch them in case there was a mechanism built into the fancy electronics for the car to eject him through the smoked sunroof. Even after his cleanup attempt, the layer of grime between his skin and the soft leather felt abrasive. On the brighter side, it had appeared the medicine was working, reducing the pain and swelling from the bites to a manageable level.

It was no surprise when they turned off Highway 27 and took the Florida Turnpike south. The closer they got to the Aerojet plant, the tighter the knot in his stomach became. Breathing deeply, he dropped back when they turned onto US 1 and then turned right at the sign for Everglades National Park. The traffic thinned to almost nothing, and he was forced to drop back further to stay out of sight. The road appeared flat but had slight elevation changes. Even the slightest uphill or downhill grade showed the road for miles ahead or behind them. He pulled onto the shoulder after turning left onto Aerojet Road. He wanted to give them some time to park and do whatever they had planned before he took action. With only the fillet knife, shotgun, and a handful of shells, he was underarmed and needed to plan accordingly.

Chapter 31

Mac waited about five minutes before pulling back onto the road and entering the abandoned facility. When the plant came into sight, he stashed the Audi behind the first building he saw and took off on foot, almost stepping on a copperhead when he exited the car. Hoping the snake wasn't a bad omen, he ran from building to building, with the shotgun in hand, using the decaying structures for cover.

He reached the building where they had parked and, using the concrete wall to shield himself, he peered around the corner and saw the silo. There was no one in sight, and he ran across the open asphalt lot. Unseen, he reached the steel building that housed the rocket and moved to an opening on the side, away from the front, where he expected them to be. He waited a long minute for his eyes to adjust to the dim light inside.

Dusharde and Jane stood looking over the lip of the silo, and at first he thought he was too late. They were in a heated discussion, and he used the creaking of the metal building's panels that were expanding as they warmed in the sun to cover his movements. There was nothing to conceal him inside the building, so he stayed to the exterior and ran to the front, again using the door opening as cover.

"They'll find no traces of any of them?" Dusharde asked Jane.

"Not once that rocket blows."

"All right. Let's get it done." Dusharde rubbed his hands on his expensive slacks. "Then I'm heading to the Bahamas until the dust settles. I've got the boat ready to go in Miami, and the log will show it left last night with both of us aboard."

Mac breathed a sigh of relief when he heard they hadn't ditched the bodies. He watched as they went back to the Mercedes and opened the trunk. Struggling with a tarp that looked like it held a body, they let it drop to the asphalt and dragged it to the opening. Without a word, they rolled it over the side, and seconds later, he heard a splash as the body hit the water below.

Jane went back to the Mercedes and removed a half dozen signs. With Dusharde's help, they set them alongside the silo. Mac read them aloud: "The real Flowway," "This is the way God intended it," "A simpler solution." Each sign had the name of an environmental activist group.

"Get your phone ready. We'll get the Woodson woman first and set her in front of the signs." Jane grabbed Mel and pushed her in front of the staged signs.

Mac got the implications. They intended on making Mel a martyr and push the eyes of the media away from the sugar companies and onto the environmental groups.

Together they went back to the Mercedes, each opening one of the passenger doors. Pamela fought Jane, but gagged and restrained there was nothing she could do. Jane landed another blow to her head and she fell to the pavement. Led by Dusharde, Mel staggered from the car.

Jane joined him and together they brought her to where they had set the signs. "Be a good girl now and hold this." Jane handed her one of the signs, then ran back to Dusharde.

"I'm not very good with this thing," Dusharde said, fumbling with the phone.

"Just point and shoot."

Before Mel even realized what was happening, he had taken several pictures from different angles. They went back and grabbed Pamela from the pavement and brought her to the edge of the silo next to Mel.

Mac could tell Mel was regaining her bearings, and, as they were about to push Pamela over the edge of the silo, she swung back with both bound fists, landing a hard blow to Dusharde's head. He staggered backward.

Mac had to do something. The group was clustered together, making a shot impossible. Suddenly a hissing sound took him by surprise, and he saw a large copperhead slithering alongside the building, using the weeds growing at its base for cover. It had been an omen, but a good one. After years in the Keys, handling snakes didn't bother Mac, but the copperhead's venomous fangs had to be respected. Using the barrel of the shotgun, he set the barrel to the ground and allowed the three-foot long snake to curl around the warm metal. Once it had secured itself, he stepped into the door opening and flung it at the group. He was less concerned about his aim than creating a diversion, knowing the bite, although poisonous, was not lethal.

The snake landed with a thud in the middle of the group and they jumped and separated. Mac took the only chance he might get and sprung from behind the building and walked toward Dusharde with the shotgun pointed directly at his chest. Dusharde lifted his arms over his head and Mac watched as something flew from one of his hands. He ignored it needing one eye on each of them. Jane was more dangerous, but Dusharde was the decision maker.

"Let them go."

Pamela turned and saw him. She and Mel and moved several feet away, but Jane's hand went behind her back faster than Mac could react and pulled a pistol from her pants. Mac leveled the shotgun at her, giving the women an extra few seconds to escape. He thought the Mexican standoff would work until he heard a scream. They both turned and saw Pamela clutching her leg. She fell to the ground writhing in pain while the snake slithered away.

The split second of concern gave Jane the opening she needed. "Get in the car," she yelled at Dusharde. With the blinding speed of a marital artist, she executed a jumping front kick, easily covering the half dozen feet between her and Mel. She struck Mel in the jaw with her foot.

Mac raised the shotgun, having no concerns about collateral damage with both Mel and Pamela on the ground. But Jane fired first, causing him to duck. Before he could recover, they were both in the car. On one knee, he aimed the shotgun and fired, but it was too late. The Mercedes was out of range.

Allowing them to escape was acceptable, for now. The first priority was to diffuse the charges on the rocket. He figured he had at least a half hour before Dusharde and Jane were out of the blast range and still close enough to activate the explosives.

He went to Mel, giving her a hug. "I have to go into the silo and try and deactivate the charges. Pamela got bit by a snake."

Mel went right to Pamela and bent over her. "I got her. Do what you have to."

He nodded to her and took off at a run to the Audi. Retrieving the car, he pulled up at the silo and opened the hatchback. He opened the bottom access panel that hid the spare tire compartment and removed the tire iron. Mel was still hovering over Pamela and gave him a thumbs-up before he grabbed the climbing rope, wrapped it twice around his waist, and started to rappel into the void.

Immediately he felt the cool air hit him as he descended. He grabbed the nylon line, still wrapped around the rocket, and worked it down with him—he would need it to climb out. One foot at a time, he released line, allowing him to drop down into the silo. He glanced at his wrist and realized time was running out. He had only ten minutes left. Finally, with only feet of rope remaining, he reached the lowest charge. He stared at the explosive, hoping he could gain enough leverage with the tire iron to remove the charge.

Pulling the nylon line into place to support him, he swung from the exterior of the silo to the rocket casing and grabbed for the yellow line. He transferred his weight to the rocket and tied the end of the climbing rope to the line, then, with both feet planted firmly against the rocket, he leaned back and set the chisel end of the tire iron in the small gap behind the detonator and the rocket. With a deep inhale, he tried to pry the charge loose. It didn't move. Cursing, he changed position and tried again. This time he was able to slide it along the casing. He took one more attempt and realized this wasn't going to work.

Leaning back, he felt the seconds ticking away. Staring at the problem, he saw what looked like a row of smooth-head rivets a foot below the charge. Hoping that if he could slide the detonator to the rivets, they would protrude enough to catch the edge and prevent it from sliding, allowing him to pop off the magnet. Knowing it was his last chance, he started to move the device lower and toward the first rivet. It stopped on contact, and he took a deep breath before setting the bar firmly. He popped the bar and flinched, expecting some kind of sound or the trigger to fire, but the charge popped off the rocket and he caught it before it dropped.

Moving quickly, he climbed to the other two charges and repeated the procedure. With all three charges bulging from his cargo pockets, he slid the tire iron into a belt loop and started to climb. Despite the coolness, he was sweating. His hands slipped and his feet cramped as he worked his way out of the silo. Several times he had to stop to release the tension accumulated in his muscles before he could continue. He didn't dare look at his watch—he knew by now he was on borrowed time. Finally he reached the edge and tried to haul himself to the surface.

His exhaustion and injuries overcame him and he fell backward. Hitting his head against the rocket, he dangled in the void between the wall of the silo and the casing of the rocket. The rope still wrapped around his waist was the only thing saving him from dropping to the bottom.

He screamed for Mel and tried to catch his breath, alternately tensing and releasing his muscles to relieve the cramping. Finally he saw a shadow fall over the opening.

"Mel!"

"Here. Where are you?"

"Just a few feet down over here." She came into view. "Can you pull on the line?"

She grabbed the rope, and he heard a grunt, but there was no perceptible change. "I can't get anything on it."

He hung in space, only feet from the rocket, knowing if the charges were detonated now, they would probably still trigger the explosion. "Hold on, maybe I can help."

There were voids in the concrete casing, from either the original formwork or from fifty years of water dripping into the silo. After checking the knot holding the line to his waist, he kept one hand on the rope and tentatively used his other hand to remove the tire iron from his belt loop.

Wiggling his hips, he was able to start swinging, at first only a few inches at a time. Inertia worked its magic and he was soon touching the outer wall with each swing. He pushed off with his feet and, when he hit the rocket, he kicked hard. The force propelled him back into the concrete wall. Just before he started to swing back to the rocket, he found the largest void he could reach and jammed the end of the tire iron into it.

"When I yell, pull!" he yelled up to Mel and hauled himself up on the iron like a mountain climber using a pick. He felt the rope move. Releasing the tire iron, he found another void a few feet higher. With each swing, he was able to pull himself further to the edge, and when he finally reached it, he grabbed her arms and with her help gained the surface.

He pulled the charges from his pocket.

"We have to get rid of the them," she said, looking around for a safe place to ditch them, not knowing how far away they needed to be.

Picking up one, he turned it in his hands. He was able to see it clearly in the light and thought he knew how to diffuse it. "It's similar to some of the underwater charges we used to use on the old bridges. Just a different fuse." He pulled the small receiver out of the clay-like substance and showed Mel the two pins that activated by cell signal would ignite the C4 explosive. "Harmless now." He separated the detonators from the charges and stuck them back in his pockets.

"Great. Now you're a walking time bomb. We need to get to Dusharde before he leaves the country," Mel said.

Mac looked at her. "Evidence. Where is Dusharde going?"

"I heard him say something about the Bahamas," she said.

Chapter 32

Mac cursed the traffic as he drove east. He had spent enough time in Miami, picking up parts and materials over the years, that he knew the area, especially the commercial port. But first he had to make a detour and rid himself of Pamela. She and Mel were crammed together in the passenger seat, and neither was happy about it. To make matters worse, Pamela was wailing. Mac wasn't sure if it was about the snake bite, which had clearly proven not to be fatal, or Trufante, who he had told her was all right.

"The hospital's not far out. Let's just drop her there. She can get treated and find lover boy," Mel said.

"Just drop me there. I need to see him and get back to Cheqea. She can cure me," Pamela said.

"You should see a doctor," Mel said.

Mac had enough of the two women and accelerated, trying to block their bickering from his mind. The delay to drop off Pamela was the right move, but he still had to get to Dusharde before they left port—and the sugar magnate had a half-hour head start. They needed to stop him and buy some time for the authorities to follow their onerous procedures that would be complicated by a man of

Dusharde's wealth and power--and the team of lawyers on retainer sitting by their phones. This was also personal now, and he intended to see it to its conclusion. He wanted Dusharde and the woman to stand trial and suffer the public scrutiny of their failed plan.

Mel had located the Homestead Hospital on the navigation system built into the car. Mac followed the route, pushing through yellow lights and dodging slow traffic. The hospital came into sight and he followed the signs, pulling up to the emergency room entrance. "Take care of him," Mac said as Pamela opened the door and climbed over Mel to get out.

"Rock on, Mac Travis. *In another time, in another place,*" she said, and walked toward the entrance.

He stared after her for a second, making sure she was really gone before putting the car into drive and taking off. "Hope she's all right."

"No worries about that one. She's the Cajun's alter ego. Where to?"

"Can you get me on the 836? The boat will be somewhere between here and Palm Beach."

Mel worked the screen built into the dashboard. "That's a lot of area."

"What else can that thing do?" Mac asked, looking at the screen built into the dashboard. "We need Alicia."

Mel started pushing buttons on the *embrace* system. A woman's voice came through the speakers, asking what she could assist with.

Mac asked the lady with the sexy British accent to make a call, and when she responded that she would be delighted to, he recited the phone number from memory.

"I'll bet it's registered to Dusharde Sugar and he is writing it off," Mel said, waiting for an answer. After a half dozen rings, she left a message and disconnected.

"What now?" Mac asked, tapping the wheel with his palm.

She didn't answer. Engrossed in the screen, she was pushing buttons, panning and scrolling like it was a computer, which he realized it was. "Got it." She pushed another button on the screen.

"What?"

"Dusharde Sugar took third place in the Miami boat parade of lights last Christmas," she said, quoting an article. "The eighty-foot convertible is docked at the Miami Beach Marina."

With only the voice of the navigation system telling him what to do, they drove in silence as he cruised up the Florida Turnpike and turned onto the 836. A few miles after they passed the airport, at the intersection of I-95, the road turned into I-395, and they saw the downtown skyline. Crossing the McArthur Causeway, he looked to the right at the new baseball stadium and then saw the cruise ships ahead.

Knowing they were close, Mac accelerated. They drove past the cruise ships and entered South Beach, where he made a quick right onto Alton. He stopped in a loading zone in front of a large condo on the right. "Come on." He grabbed the shotgun and ran toward the marina. Standing on the seawall, he stopped, looking at a billion dollars in boats docked in front of him and wondering which was Dusharde's.

"Any one could be his," Mel said as she caught up to him.

Spread over a dozen piers, spanning almost a half mile of seawall, were close to five hundred luxury vessels, a mix of sailboats and powerboats. The largest were docked at the end of the piers, which each jutted a hundred yards into the Intracoastal Waterway.

"We can't check each one," Mel said.

Mac scanned the marina, looking for any sign of activity. There were a few empty slips, probably from boats that had already left for the day. Most of the rest of the yachts were deserted. Toward the end of a pier to the right he saw some activity, but it looked like a wedding party boarding one of the larger boats. The internal clock in Mac's head was ticking, and he knew this was taking too long, but he also knew there were always last-minute things that came up, and there was still a good chance Dusharde's boat was still here. You didn't just drop a few lines and take out a boat that size—especially if they were leaving the country.

"Keep an eye out. I'll be right back," he said and ran toward a large three-story building with a turquoise-colored metal roof. He entered the building and looked for the maintenance desk. The marina had an office, but no facilities here. For fuel or any other kind of services, the boats needed to cross the Intracoastal to the more industrial Dodge Island.

He slowed and approached the desk. "Hey, I'm just down from Port Everglades and have a part for Dusharde."

"Do you have the vessel name?" The man across the counter didn't give him a second look.

"Darn." He made a show of rummaging through his pockets. "The invoice is on my phone and I must have left it in the truck."

The man looked sympathetic. "What did you say the name was?"

"Dusharde. Sugar guy, I think. Big eighty-footer."

"Right. We just fueled and changed some filters on the *Plantation*. They might have left already."

"This is kind of important. If you don't mind, I'll take a run out there and see."

The man gave him the slip number and the code to the gate. "Better hurry, the captain looked like he was in a rush."

Mac thanked him and ran back outside, looking around for the pier. Just when he reached the gate, he saw the name on the transom of a large convertible pulling out of its slip.

"Hurry, we may have one more chance," Mac said to Mel. They took off down the sidewalk, catching looks from the tourists walking along the path, and he realized he still held the shotgun. Several put phones to their ears and were talking frantically, others were taking videos of him, and a general panic soon spread. That only helped them in the short term as the baby strollers and families on the congested sidewalk scattered, opening a large space for them to run through.

He could see the *Plantation* idling toward Government Cut, but it would be restricted to five knots until it cleared the first buoy.

Hoping they could keep pace, they followed the pedestrian trail and ran along the waterfront. The marina ended and they turned a corner. His stomach was cramping, and his breath was ragged, but the end was in sight. They ran past a large restaurant and entered South Pointe Park. Expecting to be tackled by the police any second, he ran harder and they reached the end of the paved trail. There was nothing between them and the Bahamas except for a long rock jetty and a pier running next to it. It was narrow and he had to slow down to push through the fishermen clustered against the rail.

Reaching the end, he tried to catch his breath, knowing he would only have one shot. With a quick glance he saw the boat had less than a hundred yards to cover before reaching open water, and he pulled the last flare shell from his pocket. With trembling hands, he loaded it in the gun and chambered the round. The boat was approaching now. The captain had started to accelerate, and he could see the white water from its wake as it picked up speed. He grabbed the C4 from his other pocket and, with the shotgun under his arm, rolled it into a ball. He could only hope the gunpowder charge in the flare shell would take a few seconds to burn through before it ignited the flare which would trigger the explosive. It was only a matter of a second, but he knew as he placed the ball of explosives on the tip of the barrel that if it went off too quickly he was dead.

Putting the thought from his mind, he braced himself against the rail and took aim at the *Plantation*. It was still farther away than he would have liked. He needed a few more seconds, but out of the corner of his eye he saw a commotion at the end of the pier. The police were here, and two officers were running down the boardwalk. With no time to spare, he sighted the boat and pulled the trigger.

The shell left the barrel, taking the explosive with it. The C4 slowed the projectile, but the target was close enough. Just before it hit the bow of the boat, the gunpowder burned through and ignited the flare. A loud explosion filled the air. The boat stopped and in slow motion wallowed in the water. Flames were visible now and he saw the crew come on deck. Just as he saw two figures dive into the water, he felt the cold steel of handcuffs about to close on his wrists. Mel was behind him, screaming at the police to listen to her, and it bought him just enough time to vault the pier. He dove into the channel and stroked after the two figures. They had a hundred-yard lead, and he hoped he was the stronger swimmer.

The incoming tide carried them back inside the channel. He paused his stroke to get his bearings and saw the tip of Dodge Island emerge across the Intracoastal. The pair were headed directly toward it, but they weren't reading the water and he saw his chance to close the gap. Changing his course to the right and farther into the channel, he swam at an angle to use the current to his advantage. They were swimming straight toward the island and would have to fight against the tide that was pulling them farther away from their goal with each stroke. His tactic was working, and he closed to within twenty yards, hoping the choppy waves hid him. Taking advantage of the moving water, he conserved energy, pacing the swimmers in front of him. He worked his stroke and breath together, regaining energy with each revolution as they approached the island.

The tide had pulled Dusharde and Jane past the point, and the current was no longer a factor. Mac wanted to get on land before them and focused on the row of huge black bumpers secured to the seawall to protect freighters when they docked. Picking the closest, he looked back at the water, cursing the small ferry running between them. Deciding it would be better to be on land, even if Dusharde continued in the water, he stroked hard for the bumper and grabbed the thick rope securing it to the dock. Once he had a firm grasp, he pulled his legs onto the hard plastic and used it as a step to reach the seawall.

Once he gained his feet, he looked back at the water. They were gone. He scanned the water again, not believing they could have escaped, when he saw two figures huddled near the transom of a tender running toward downtown Miami.

Chapter 33

Mac stared into the dark hole, watching the headlights of the Dade County recovery team flash back and forth as they rappelled into the silo. What had taken him hours took them only minutes, and he heard the call over the radio to send down a body bag. Minutes later, Vernon Wade was unceremoniously dragged back to daylight. The group stood around the bag while the coroner opened the zipper and inspected the body, allowing Mac and Mel to move away unobserved.

"Wait," he said.

Mel looked at him as he moved inland. "I remember something flew from Dusharde's hand when I tossed the snake."

"His phone!" Mel said. "He had just taken a picture of me with the signs."

They quickly separated and started a search of the parking lot. Mac stood by the posters and closed his eyes, trying to remember the scene. He moved to where he recalled Dusharde had stood, mimicked the movement, then walked in the direction his hand had gone. A glint of glass caught his eye, larger than the other specks scattered on the ground from broken bottles and windows. He moved to a clump of weeds where he found the phone. The screen was shattered and black. With a hand signal, he let Mel know he had recovered it, and they moved quietly away from the silo in the direction of the canal.

They were quiet as he drove to Key Largo, allowing him time to reflect on what had happened. The adrenaline had faded, and he felt the accumulated fatigue of the past few days. Looking over at Mel, he saw the same worn look on her face. As with all life-and-death situations, it was hard to return to the real world. He was not even sure this was over. Jane and Dusharde were still at large, and he would probably have to make at least one court appearance in Miami.

After losing Dusharde and Jane, Mac and Mel had spent the rest of the morning with the Miami police. Word of the incident had gotten out, and a confusing fight about jurisdiction ensued between the alphabet agencies. Finally, after much pleading from Mel and a few calls to some well-placed, and not sugar-related, political contacts, they were released. The Dade County coroner's office agreed to let them have another look at the abandoned Aerojet facility.

"Damn." Mel was getting frustrated trying to power up Dusharde's phone. She glanced over at Mac with a look that could have been defeat, exhaustion, or probably both.

"Maybe better get Alicia to look at that," he said. "We should be there in another hour. Why don't you try and reach them on the car's system."

* * *

"Where's my boat!" TJ exclaimed when they pulled up in the driveway.

"That story'll have to wait. She'll clean up okay," Mac said.

"Never mind the boat. Let's get upstairs and see what you have," Alicia scolded him.

Before they entered the house, Alicia gave Mac a look that told him to wait where he was. She came back with a towel and directed him to the outside shower down by the shop. He complied, and after several rounds of wash, rinse, and repeat, he couldn't smell himself anymore. The bites on his stomach had subsided to small pricks, and although they still stung, there was no sign of infection. Otherwise, he felt beat-up, but they had made it.

With another new T-shirt and a pair of TJ's shorts, he dressed and went back upstairs. "How'd you get the indoor facilities?" he kidded Mel, who was drying her hair with a towel in the guest bedroom.

Together they entered the war room and watched the couple busy at work. Alicia had Dusharde's phone apart and TJ was working lines of code that Mac couldn't understand.

"He's got a pro wiping this thing regularly. I'm not going to be able to get much. But I did get this," she said, clicking on a small image on her desktop monitor. The staged picture of Mel with the protest signs taken at the silo showed on one of the big screens.

"I'm glad that won't see the light of day," Mel said. "Can we destroy it?"

"Not so fast. This could be our way to get him," Alicia said.

Mac moved closer. "Aren't we done? We sunk his boat and stopped the explosion."

Alicia and Mel both turned to him. Then looked at each other. It was Mel who spoke. "If only it were so easy. I'd be fine with walking away too, but do you really think he'll leave us alone? We're eyewitnesses."

"We didn't see the murder," Mac said.

"I don't think that matters to him. His MO is to bulldoze everything in his path. And that woman's with him. I wouldn't be surprised if she's on her way down here to find us."

Mac thought about what she said and had to agree. Dusharde was not a forgive-and-forget kind of guy, and looking at Mel, he could see she was not that kind of girl either. Her sights were set on him, and she wouldn't rest until he had paid for what he had done.

"I suppose you have a plan?" he asked.

The room fell silent.

"What kind of phone is that?" TJ asked.

"iPhone 6s. Why?" Alicia turned the phone in her hand.

"Live photo. I've seen some of the customers on the dive boat use them. It records a few seconds on either end of the picture, like a video. Shoot that file over here," TJ said.

They watched the big screen as he went to work. First he took the picture file and saved it as a video, then opened a player and they stood mesmerized, eyes glued to the screen, as the five-second clip played over and over. It clearly showed a headshot of Dusharde, then he must have flipped the screen to show Jane moving Mel in position, then the actual picture he intended. Finally Jane was back in the frame, pulling Mel away. It was only five seconds, but it was enough.

"He said he wasn't good with that thing. But it looks like he was good enough for our purposes," she said.

* * *

Jane pulled the Mercedes out of her driveway. The tires squealed and she accelerated to correct the fishtail, cursing the cumbersome vehicle. She quickly hit ninety as she flew down the highway. The project had gone off the rails and the loose ends needed to be handled—and now. Dusharde did not seem to be concerned. With a slew of lawyers, he would suffer no repercussions from the failed plan, and he was already working on another. But his ignorance was her problem. It was her job to protect him.

He had done surprisingly well yesterday, and she silently thanked his personal trainer. After throwing him overboard, he had held his own during their swim and had actually signaled the launch driver to pull them from the water and with a wet billfold had paid for a ride to the marina and the Mercedes.

Now he was back in his office and she was on her own—with her black duffel in the back seat—the way she liked it. She drank coffee and focused on the road. The miles flew by, but her fury remained and she reached Key Largo just before noon. Forced to slow by the local traffic, she tried to remain patient. There were a half dozen people on her list, and she knew it might take a few days to erase them. Just before she reached Islamorada, she got an idea.

Hitting a number in her contacts, she waited for the call to be answered. "Call that redneck and get him and that crazy woman over to the bait place. I'll be there in an hour."

The two Cubans were on top of her list, and if she could use them to help knock off the Cajun and his girlfriend without having to search them out, so much the better.

* * *

Trufante looked sideways at the phone. "There's no way I'm going near that bait chum grinding place."

"I'm telling you, Hector said he'd pay for the net. Something about some deal with the Feds or something. I heard those two cried pretty loud when they got picked up after your buddy toasted their engine," Jeff laughed.

"Shit. I'm laid up hurt. You go get it, and I'll split it with you."

"No dice, dude. I beat up and finally got my boat. Can't believe I walked away from that jet ski. I'm on the straight and narrow now."

He pushed himself up on the couch and took another sip of beer. The way things were going, he would need the money.

Pamela walked into the living room. "You need to get some exercise instead of lying on your butt all day drinking beer and popping pills. I heard the doctor."

"Ain't a thing, babe. I'll start tomorrow."

"You'll start right now." She pulled his feet off the couch.

Her mood had been severe since they had gotten back yesterday. After putting the hospital bill and taxi ride back to Marathon on her credit card, his crude calculations showed she was probably well into next month's funds. And that made him broke too. If those jokers at the bait place were serious, it was worth a shot. If not, nothing ventured. He turned to Pamela. *"There must be some way outta here, said the joker to the thief."* It was his turn to quote lyrics. Swinging his feet to the floor, he tested his balance and stood. The world swayed, but in a good way, and he went for the door.

Riding his motorcycle was out of the question and he decided to walk. He had heard the doctor too, and although he liked to be contrary, he wanted to be back on the water. With a slight limp and wobble, he set off for Monster Bait. By the time he reached the gravel road, the handful of pills he had taken, aided by the exercise, were coursing through his bloodstream. He was feeling good until he saw the Mercedes parked by the bait shed. Even in his current state, he knew he had been set up.

He turned, but it was too late. Hector had seen him.

"Yo, Tru. Where's your wheels, man?"

"Just give me the money and I'll be gone," Trufante said.

"Sure thing, man, but it's the lady that's gonna pay you."

Trufante hesitated, knowing this was not going to end well. He was about to turn to leave when he saw Jane step out of the shack with a rifle pointed at him.

"That's right. The lady's going to pay you," she said,

approaching slowly.

He'd spent a lifetime studying women, and he noticed something different about her, but with the cloud of drugs swirling around his system he couldn't put his finger on it. "Ain't no need. I'll just be going."

"No, I don't think so. You remember the chum grinder, don't you?"

Looking around for anything he could use against her, he reached for an old trapline, but lost his balance and fell.

"Drag him over here," she called to Hector.

The Cuban came toward him flashing a knife and a grin. Trufante grabbed the barnacle covered line, and pulled, trying to regain his feet. Just as he stood, Hector grabbed his arm and twisted it behind his back. He frog-marched him toward the bait shack. Jane entered behind them and he stared at the teeth of the grinder. The same teeth that had already taken the tip of his finger. Edgar smiled from behind the machine. He was getting tired of this scene replaying over and over and swore he would make the machine a reef if he walked out of this.

"It would be easier if he was dead," Hector said.

"Maybe after I hear him scream. For all the trouble he's caused, I need to see some pain," she said.

Edgar came toward him and took his free arm. Sweat rolled down Trufante's face and the adrenaline overcame the drugs. He saw clearly where this was going as his good hand moved closer to the whirling blades. They were only inches away when he saw the gaff leaning against the far wall. Yanking his arm away, he tried to reach it, but the two men were on him and his hand resumed its descent.

"Wait. I want to do it," Jane hissed over the sound of the motor.

She moved in front of Edgar and grabbed Trufante's arm. In the split second that Edgar looked over at her, Trufante tensed his neck and brought his head back before slamming his forehead into the bridge of the big man's nose. The impact stunned him and he fell, pinning Jane below him and feeding her arm to the waiting teeth. Three hundred pounds of unconscious man held her in place. As she fought to move the man, gore flew from the opening as the teeth pulled the woman's arm deeper.

Trufante turned, grabbed the gaff, and faced Hector. They both stared at each other as Jane fell to the floor. Blood streamed from what was left of her arm, but neither man moved. Another minute passed and the blood stopped. She was dead.

Trufante looked at her and then back at Hector. "We got what you might call a common bond now. Ain't no reason we have to like each other, but we can coexist and share this secret," Trufante said. Using the gaff as a cane, he walked out of the shack.

Chapter 34

Mac was deep in thought. He and Mel had were headed up Highway 27 to Clewiston, the hum of the Audi's engine the only noise. The plan had been laid out last night with Alicia and TJ; now it only had to be executed. Dusharde would not be expecting them, and the surprise of seeing them would hopefully be the first step in unsettling the sugar magnate. Mac knew his role, and he expected Mel was rehearsing her lines or whatever lawyers do before they go into court. His job was to get them in the room; she would take it from there.

Jane was out of the picture, which he hoped would make this easier. Alicia had found Trufante last night and had come away with a story about Jane feeding the crabs in the canal by Monster Bait. She couldn't pry any kind of a coherent story out of him besides him saying that he had taken care of that problem.

The shotgun lay under the back seat, just in case, but they had agreed it was a last resort. Dusharde was worth more alive than dead. They turned into the long serpentine driveway and parked.

"That car's still here. I wonder if it's Wade's," Mel said.

Mac looked around the front of the property. There was no sign of anyone.

"Ready?"

He nodded and reached into the back for the shotgun. "One thing first." He walked toward the sedan parked in front of the house. Bending over, he noted the parking pass for the state capitol. "You're right. It's the congressman's car. We ought to take a picture with the house in the background."

"Good idea." Mel pulled out the phone that Alicia had lent them and took several pictures, showing the license plate and the parking pass. She moved toward the entry. "Remember, the gun's a last resort. Let me do the talking," she said.

Mac followed her, standing back and ready as she pressed the handle. It was locked. He was about to press the intercom button.

"Wait. A place like this'll have surveillance cameras," Mel said.

Mac pulled her away, hoping they hadn't been noticed and hid the shotgun behind his back. "We need to surprise him." Remembering the office windows, he led her around the garage to the back of the house. With their bodies pressed against the stucco exterior, they slid along the walls, ducked underneath the large window behind his desk, and stood next to the double glass doors leading to the patio.

"I'm going to see if he's in there," Mac said, creeping back to the window. He rose slightly and looked inside. Dusharde was there. Back at the patio doors, he tried the handle. It was locked and he gave Mel a questioning look. Before she could answer, he heard barking and the dogs were quickly on them. Thinking this could be what they needed to get Dusharde away from his desk, and the gun he expected was there, he got on his knees and started to play with them. "Take over, and lead them away from the doors," he said to Mel. Once she had their attention, he slid to the side and readied the gun.

The dogs continued to bark and he saw movement inside. Without hesitating, Dusharde opened the door and called to the dogs. Mac moved quickly before Dusharde could see what was happening and stepped behind him, pressing the barrel of the shotgun to the back of his head.

"No one needs to get hurt. We just want to talk," Mac said.

"Then put the gun down," Dusharde said.

The dogs must have heard his voice and came bounding around the corner. Mel followed behind them.

"You?"

"Let's sit down and have a little chat," Mel said, leading him to the chair she had been tied to. "For what I'm sure you paid for them, these are pretty uncomfortable." She placed them face-to-face and sat in one, indicating for him to take the other.

Mac stood behind her, keeping the shotgun aimed in his direction. Dusharde appeared helpless, but Mac had seen too much over the last few days and remained vigilant.

Mel started. "We have an offer that you might want to consider." He raised his head and looked at her, and she nodded to Mac.

He lowered the gun at the prearranged signal. Dusharde was already showing signs of stress, and she wanted him more relaxed.

"Maybe you should have a look at these before we continue. Kind of lay out the playing field, so we know where we stand." She handed him the series of pictures they had printed from his phone.

He took them, slowly going through the dozen sequential shots that TJ had extracted. They clearly showed his face and then Jane pushing Mel toward the signs.

"That's all you have?"

"I know. Staging a protest is no big deal, but here's the part that maybe you should pay attention to. It places you at the scene where Wade's body was dumped. That and the pictures of his car in your driveway would give a judge, even if he was in your pocket, enough probable cause to sign a search warrant for your house. I'm guessing you still have the gun, and we all know the ballistics will match."

Mac knew from the look on both their faces that she had him.

"What do you want from me?"

She paused as if considering her options. "To do the right thing."

"And pray tell what might that be?"

Mac could only watch the exchange.

"Build the flowway, and donate the land the state needs for the holding reservoirs."

"My dear girl, that's millions of dollars. Surely the state will get it done eventually."

"You of all people know how the private sector can get something done. Tallahassee will muddle this up and take ten years to build it, if it ever gets done."

He nodded in agreement. "The planning is a mess. Even Wade saw better than the engineers how the bridges will become dams," he said.

"It is, and you have access to the right engineers. I don't get why you and your buddies are so reluctant to clean up your mess?"

He was silent for a moment. "And if I do this?"

"Business almost as usual. Grow and sell your sugar, stop the pollution, and you're free to move on."

"The murder business?"

"There were dozens of people that wanted old Vernon out of office. Let him take the fall for some of this. Maybe that'll scare some of his buddies straight," she said.

"I see. And you will of course be overseeing this?"

"I will be your new best friend." She paused. "You know, there's no harm in any of this."

"I know—all the goodwill. The public will eat it up." He paused. "I wasn't born yesterday, Ms. Woodson. Sometimes the game is more fun than the score. It's easy to get carried away."

She reached out, took the pictures back, and walked away.

Mac followed, glancing back at Dusharde every few steps, but he just sat there, staring out at the landscape.

"You're not worried about him coming after us?"

"He understands. What he said about playing the game. It's the same with all of them. You play until you win, lose, or the rules change. We just changed the rules."

They were back at the Audi now and exchanged a quick smile of relief as they got in and headed back to Key Largo.

Epilogue

Mac pulled the laptop closer so he could see the screen. The *Miami Herald's* web page was open, showing an image of a new section of bridge being built alongside Alligator Alley. The pilings were being set, and the headline praised the progress and the benefits. This two-mile stretch of bridge alone would allow millions of gallons of water to resume their natural course to Florida Bay. Mel had shown him the reaction from the other papers, from Tampa, on the west coast, to St. Lucie, on the east, all rallying behind the project that would alleviate their own water issues.

It had been three months since the meeting with Dusharde. So far, he had been cooperative and had used his influence with the government and the other sugar companies to build a coalition and show the power of the private sector. The project had been taken over by Big Sugar in its entirety. This had been his one condition, and Mel, acting in her new role as liaison between his coalition and the state, had backed him.

The sugar companies had donated or bought the land needed, hired the engineers, and commissioned the environmental reviews. The efficiency of private enterprise was on full display. The costs were confidential, but from what she had seen, they were well under the state's projections. The big factor was time. The project, void of government bureaucracy, was already years ahead of schedule. The irony of it was that the cost would probably not exceed what Big Sugar had been paying to buy influence and stall it before. The sugar companies had lost little in the deal, in many cases allowing easements instead of giving up land, and had now ensured their future.

Mel had been consumed with the project. Mac was happy she had something to sink her teeth into that really meant something. She had that renewed vigor and purpose that had been missing before. The only cost was her traveling and the satellite internet connection she had added to the island.

Since that afternoon on Dusharde's patio, he had been restless. He'd done well through dolphin season and had his lobster traps soaking now, but there was something missing. A voice from below broke his train of thought and he went to the door.

Trufante stood at the base of the stairs, still leaning on an old gaff he now used as a cane. His recovery was complete, as far as Mac could see, but he suspected the Cajun liked walking around with a hook.

"Y'all want to go fishing?" he called up.

"I might go. What are you thinking?"

"Heard there was some broke up rafts from the last round of Cubans to come over. Coast Guard's been using them for target practice after off-loading the refugees. Southeast wind's stacking it up. Probably some big dolphin sitting under the flotsam," he said.

"I'd be good with that."

He went inside and told Mel where he was going, kissed her on the forehead, and turned for the door. "Better watch your back. There's always something when Trufante's around," she said.

Author's Note

I hope you enjoyed the latest adventure of Mac, Mel, and Trufante. When starting a new book, I usually have a general idea of where I want to go, the main characters, and locations. Then I let it go where it will. In this case it went deep into the Everglades, all the way to the shores of Lake Okeechobee.

I first became familiar with this area when writing the first book in the Tides of Fortune series: *Pirate*, where Nick and the gang are forced to flee into the Everglades. I used Marjorie Stoneman Douglas's book *River of Grass* as my primary resource to describe the ecosystem as it was before man had a hand in changing it.

I had planned on writing about Big Sugar, but had no idea the overall impact a few companies and their executives have on the State of Florida, both politically and environmentally. I generally research enough to try and make the stories believable and minimize the "suspension of disbelief" that an author must tread lightly with, but in this case it went much deeper.

Skimming the surface in the search for realism didn't work, and I was drawn in to the history of man and nature. Since the 1920s, farmers and developers have been tinkering with this delicate and important ecosystem that feeds Florida Bay. When I started reading, I found it hard to stop. I came in with the general impression that Big Sugar was evil and came out knowing it. The disregard for our health and environment, by these few companies and politicians willing to turn a blind eye, was appalling.

I hope I have given this information in small enough doses to allow the reader to enjoy the adventure, but at the same time to learn what is happening. I also got a little Ayn Randish in the end with my advocacy for private enterprise being more effective than big government. To quote her: *"The hardest thing to explain is the glaringly evident which everybody had decided not to see."* This is how I see the sugar industry. If they channeled their resources into fixing this, rather than fighting it, the cost would remain the same, yet the benefits would be indescribable. And I believe one of them would be their own companies' long-term success.

The discovery of the Aerojet plant in the middle of the Everglades was a side benefit of my research and provided a good backdrop for an important part of the story. The plant and canals built for it are real and in the condition described. The silo, still housing the rocket, was covered over with concrete sections a few years ago. The largest solid-fuel engine ever built is sitting in a 180-foot deep hole in the Everglades.

Thanks for reading, and please feel free to write me with any comments. I'll be posting from time to time on my blog and Facebook about this important issue.

Steve Becker

February 2017

Thanks For Reading

If you liked the book please leave a review:

https://www.amazon.com/dp/B06XMRJ89Q

For more information please check out my web page:
https://stevenbeckerauthor.com/

Or follow me on Facebook:
https://www.facebook.com/stevenbecker.books/

Also By Steven Becker

Mac Travis Adventures

Wood's Relic

Wood's Reef

Wood's Wall

Wood's Wreck

Wood's Harbor

Wood's Reach

Wood's Revenge

Tides of Fortune

Pirate

The Wreck of the Ten Sail

Haitian Gold

Will Service Adventure Thrillers

Bonefish Blues

Tuna Tango

Dorado Duet

Storm Series

Storm Rising

Storm Force (May 2017)